THE FRAT CHAT 2

Books by Edward Allen Karr

The Frat Chat (Adult drama, sexy & twisted romance)
The Frat Chat 2 (Adult drama, sexy & twisted romance)

* * * * *

SERIES: Risk and the Killers
(Action/adventure/adult urban fantasy)
Below the Bay – Book One
Dying To Be Widow – Book Two

* * * * *

SERIES: Thrills N Kills in the Hills
(Racy, Comical Horror in Beverly Hills)
Dayzee Dazzle and the Kildare Killers – Book One
Dayzee Dazzle and Her Manic Mansion – Book Two
Dayzee Dazzle and the On-Set Onslaught – Book Three
Dayzee Dazzle and the Cadaver Collectors – Book Four

* * * * *

SERIES: Socrates Lewis Stories
(Psychological/Religious Fiction)
Crosswinds – Book One
Crossovers – Book Two

* * * * *

SERIES: Fringes Of Infinity
(Contemporary Fantasy Fiction)
Lin Finity and Her Mayhem Rising – Book One
Lin Finity in Holding On – A Novella
Lin Finity and the Words Unspoken – Book Two
Lin Finity and the Islands of Time – Book Three
Lin Finity and the Flights to Forever – Book Four
Tayo Tersoo and the Hunter of Souls – Book Five

* * * * *

SERIES: A World So Close
(Middle-grade Fantasy Adventure & Coming of Age)
Jayden Blue and the Gift to Imagine – A Prequel
Jayden Blue and the Sword in His Shadow – Book One
Jayden Blue and the Call of the Wings – Book Two
Jayden Blue and the Lair of the Iron Lions – Book Three
Jayden Blue and the Journey to Val ka'Yoom – Book Four
Jayden Blue and the Forest of Night Fallen – Book Five
Jayden Blue and the Wait of the Sun – Book Six

* * * * *

THE FRAT CHAT 2

Edward Allen Karr

LAKESIDE
LETTERS, LLC

Lakeside Letters, LLC
30628 Detroit Road, #247
Westlake, OH 44145

First Edition, 2025
Lakeside Letters, LLC

Cover design by JD Smith Design

ISBN-13: 978-1-950886-75-3

From the bank of a river of molten bones and flesh, twisting upward with every tortured flame, the voice, smug and petulant, called out: "Can a woman dare face that hidden side of her nature, where lust reigns, then believe she can rebuke her hungers as if she had not seen and felt them? No. What might have been for her only a playful spark will fester and smolder. In time, that spark will explode like a fiery hurricane, attracting to her sinful forces that will surely burn her to ash. And still, she'll crave more."

– Another message found in another book.

Excerpt

From Chapter 6 – They're All Forcing Me

"Laura, I'm not saying it."

Laura laughed and said, "Oh yeah, you know what I mean. You should say it. You're being forced to . . . what?"

"Hmm. I have my mouth open because—"

"In just panties and heels, Lenore. Add that."

"Oh, Laura. I'm wearing only panties and heels, and I have my mouth open because they're forcing me to—"

Table of Contents

Excerpt vii
Chapter 1 – It's Making Me Insane 1
Chapter 2 – Even Wilder, Huh? 12
Chapter 3 – You Can't Stop 22
Chapter 4 – A Penchant for Drama 29
Chapter 5 – A Slut Like Me 38
Chapter 6 – They're All Forcing Me 44
Chapter 7 – Star of a Wild Sex Party 52
Chapter 8 – I'd Have to Say What I Am 57
Chapter 9 – Crave Something You Don't Have 63
Chapter 10 – No Divinity for You 69
Chapter 11 – A Pair of Red Shoes 75
Chapter 12 – I Want More 78
Chapter 13 – Like Someone Could Grab It 88
Chapter 14 – Oh God. Frat Chat 2. 92
Chapter 15 – What Laura Would Say 95
Chapter 16 – What You Really Are 99
Chapter 17 – Like It's Meant to Be 105
Chapter 18 – You Up for a Real Interview? 112
Chapter 19 – Just Play Along 116
Chapter 20 – So Pretty Kneeling There 123
Chapter 21 – Is That What You're Offering Us? 128
Chapter 22 – God, What an Experience 146
Chapter 23 – You Need More of It 154

Chapter 24 – Get Yourself Sexed Up 159
Chapter 25 – We Also Play for Keeps 164
Chapter 26 – Quite Good at Following Orders 171
Chapter 27 – You Need to Be Ready 176
Chapter 28 – In Very High Heels 179
Chapter 29 – It's Not Life or Death 186
Chapter 30 – My, Uh, My Urges? 189
Chapter 31 – Both Doing Fun Stuff Tonight 194
Chapter 32 – Any Tasty Drops 197
Chapter 33 – All Types of Talent 202
Chapter 34 – Just a Soft Little Thing 209
Chapter 35 – For Our Amusement 218
Chapter 36 – A Plaything Only for Fun 223
Chapter 37 – I Think I Want a Turn 228
Chapter 38 – Her Dirty Lips Found It 232
Chapter 39 – Quite a Helpless Thing Now 240
Chapter 40 – All Used-Up 246
Chapter 41 – God, She Feels So Good 256
Chapter 42 – You Wouldn't Believe Me 264

Chapter 1 – It's Making Me Insane

Amos kept his back straight and stiff and barely touching the couch cushion behind him. When he cocked his head to listen for any signs of life in the quiet house, he sensed only an abode suddenly devoid of sound from his muting of the TV.

Despite the thing's silence, it kept spraying its chaotic colors around the living room, strobing its invasive light onto every wall, furnishing, and the trimmed, graying beard of the silent, attentive man on the couch displaying his enviable posture.

Not respecting the timing of the TV's flashing, the clock on the wall tapped out its usual steady beat, dragging his existence along. So many seconds had clicked through the house since the previous Sunday morning, when Amos had staggered in from crashing on another couch, away from home after a Frat Chat night with Emilio and the whiskey bottle they'd shared and drained dry.

Already, a week had passed since Amos had found Lenore, his fiancé, the owner of the house and a respected local business owner, comfy on their couch, wrapped in a layer of thick flannel pajamas which was buried and largely unseen beneath an even thicker robe.

And every night since then, he'd honored his promise to leave that heated conversation—that talk burning with realizations and passion and lust—to cool some and let them get back to their comfortable, baseline relationship.

With his thumb still squeezing the remote, crushing it toward eternal silencing of the flat screen hanging on the wall, he muttered only for himself to hear, "It's been long enough."

Somewhere beyond the dim light of the living room, hidden in more complete darkness, a door closed with a soft, controlled thump.

He tossed the remote to the couch, focusing next on the bead of sweat tickling down his forehead, causing a harsh swipe, then a flicking away of the moisture.

"Yes, like that. Why did I wait a week to even think of this?"

He blanked off his grin and held his breath at the sound of slippers scuffing across the hardwood floor, approaching.

Then, her shapeless form, again cloaked by the same bulky robe tied neatly at her waist, appeared at the entrance. Her eyes, big and beautiful and boasting a fresh innocence, stayed focused on the quieted TV. And her hair, long and thick and blond, showed none of its length and waves from how she'd bound and constrained it all in a neat bunch that left not a strand to escape and hang free.

Still hearing the scraping of slippers, Amos glanced lower, then scoffed silently at the sight of the baggy pajama pants that bunched up around her worn footwear, hiding the loose white socks that he knew were wrapped up in there too.

Watching her tight blond knot mounded over a face without expression as she walked past him, around the coffee table, Amos said, "Lenore, it's been a week."

Without looking or even slowing, she said, "So?"

She continued around, then sat on her end of the couch, leaving an expansive flat fabric field between them, barren except for the remote, which she grasped, pointed, and began clicking.

"I've been, uh, patient. You know I have."

"Yeah, and you should be," she said, each word timed with a channel change.

He squinted, unseen by her, as he focused on the delicate beads of sweat on her temple, a light pattern on her smooth cheek, and a distinct wet shine beginning at the tip of her earlobe.

"It's just that, uh, you must remember what—"

Still pointing but not switching, she turned her head to face him.

"What I like more than anything?" she said, bouncing her head once with a patient smile. "You like hearing me say that, don't you?"

"Oh, God, yeah. And what I can't get over is how much I like that it's true."

"Amos," she said, her smile turning into a pained version of one, "sure, it's fun to say. Just because you heard me fantasizing in the bedroom that one time, it doesn't mean—"

"I, uh . . . I did what?"

"You heard me. A girl's allowed to have some fantasies. You shouldn't have been snooping around at the door."

"Oh," he said, still studying the tiny bits of sweat dotting her skin. "Oh! Oh, I get it. Yeah, I heard you talking about some fantasy through the door. Huh. I get it."

"Well, yeah, and I might even say it again sometime."

She was monitoring the changing scenes as she clicked, and he said, "Uh, how about now?"

Without looking, she said, "I don't know. Maybe."

"Yeah, now. Say it."

She turned to him, took a breath, and before she could speak, he said, "Maybe lose that robe, though, huh?"

"The robe? Last week, you were kind of thrilled by my modesty while I whispered that in your ear."

"Yeah. My God, that was something. The contrast. Hot and cold."

"Hmm. Hot and cold."

"Speaking of which, aren't you hot in all that?"

"Now that you mention it, yeah. Why's it so hot in here?"

"Beats me, Lenore, but you'd feel better if you got out of that robe."

"It is awfully hot in this house."

"The pajamas too. You'd be more comfortable when you're sitting on my lap, whispering to me that what you like most is—"

She snorted out a sharp laugh and said, "Oh, wait a second. Amos, you cranked up the furnace? That's your plan?"

"I, uh, might have mistakenly dialed it higher than—"

"It was no mistake. Amos, you're terrible. I'm not playing along with this."

"Fine," he said, on the verge of pouting. "Keep yourself all bundled up, but say it. Say it, Lenore, even from way over there."

"No. Stop it."

"Come on. You can't deny it—not to me. I know."

"You don't know anything. You can't hold me to some nonsense I was saying alone in the bedroom just for fun."

"Yeah. Sure. Alone? Huh."

"Amos, leave me alone. And don't mess with the furnace anymore."

"Forget the furnace. Tell me, Lenore. Say it."

"No."

"Tell me what you are. Tell me how all you really want to be is a—"

"Amos! Just stop!"

She clattered the remote onto the end table and stood, pulled her belt tighter, then hiked quickly around the table, saying, "It's just too hot. Don't play this furnace game anymore, alright?"

"Hey."

She stopped close to him, then turned to face him.

"Come on. Say it. Say it because we both know it's true."

"You'll quit pestering me if I do?"

Laughing, he said, "Lenore, you know I can't promise that. You're making me crazy. The hot and cold—it's making me insane."

"Fine," she said, then took a step closer, then another, then enough that she stood with her legs, still hidden away under endless layers of thick cloth, on each side of his as he sat without any slouching on the couch.

He stared up at her faint smile, then focused on her hands, the nails nice but not fabulous, as she untied her robe's belt, then pulled it open. With both hands, she bunched up the baggy cloth around her waist, showing how slim it was and seeming to magnify the size of her breasts, which were only large, round mounds locked away behind the plaid cloth.

"Mm," she said as she gave them both a slow squeeze.

"God . . ."

"Mm, I'm so soft and smooth everywhere under all of this flannel."

"You, uh . . . you . . ."

He looked up higher, away from her hands that couldn't hold entirely what she was fondling, to see her sliding her tongue across the top lip, then the bottom.

"And what I love most, Amos, is . . ."

"Yeah? Yeah?"

". . . is being a . . ."

His breaths were short and raspy, and his lips quivered but couldn't form any actual speech.

"Slut. Uh-uh. Yeah, Amos, you heard that. More than anything at all, I love being a total slut."

"Oh my God."

"See how I'm all wrapped up in pajamas and robes and things?"

"Yeah. Yeah."

"Hmm, under all that, I'm just a slut."

"Oh God. A slut for, um, for . . ."

"Mm. Anyone. No . . . everyone."

"Because . . ."

"Because being a slut is all I'm good for—nothing else. All I really am is a slut."

"Oh God . . ."

"That makes you crazy, Amos? Yeah, I look so modest, but I'm just . . ."

"A slut? You're really just a slut?"

"Mm. Mm-hmm."

She laughed while snapping shut her robe, then tied a quick knot.

"Happy now?"

"Uh, I mean, but you really—"

Scoffing as she walked out of the room, she said, "Where's that damn thermostat?"

* * *

Lenore leaned back into the closed bedroom door, smiling still, and listened to the quiet of a house without its furnace cooking her alive inside her flannel. She waved one hand around, feeling the air already cooling.

"How could that be?" she said softly as she began walking toward the bed and its weakly glowing lamps on each nightstand.

She threw aside the covers, reached for her robe's belt, then left it alone.

"You heard me one time, in here, alone, saying some crazy things just for fun. And that's enough to turn you into some kind of . . . oh, I don't even know what."

She'd sat on her side of the bed only a second before she sprang back up and strode over to switch off the lamps. The feeble nightlight took up the slack, distributing just enough light for a careful walk back to the bed.

Sitting again, she scoffed at the sound of the furnace launching into its campaign, directed by Amos, to coerce her to strip off at least the outer shell.

"Oh, come on, Amos. Stop with the heat."

She stayed seated, kicking enough to send her ratty slippers off toward the dresser, and listened to his footsteps drawing near. They stopped only when the doorknob gave a soft rattle, enabling the door to swing in.

Her eyes had adjusted to the low light level, and she saw his arm first as he reached in and flipped the switch, filling the room with lamplight.

"Amos. Not the lights. Come on. Not the furnace either. I'm going to roast."

With a silly grin, he stepped inside and shut the door, then waited with his hand poised to hit the switch again.

"I'll make a deal. We can do without those lamps, but the furnace is performing an essential function. You know what I mean."

"You're trying to burn me out of the robe?"

"Uh-huh. Keep going."

"Oh—the pajamas too."

"Yeah, all of it. Strip first, then I'll switch off the light. That's the deal."

"Amos, you're being ridiculous. Just because I said that—"

"We both know what you said, and we both know you mean it."

He left the lights on and walked to stand in front of her. She remained seated, bundled up, her hair fully under control.

"Amos."

"Stand up, lose the robe, get rid of those god-awful pajamas, and—"

"They're god-awful?"

"For a woman like you? Oh, yeah. Get rid of all of it. Stand here for me just in your panties and,"—he paused to glance toward the closet—"and some heels. Really high ones. A woman like you—"

"Amos, stop it! A woman like me, you said—just panties and heels for your amusement?"

"Well, yeah. It's been a week, Lenore. Strip. Let that hair down too."

"Even the hair, huh?"

"Yeah, let me see all that soft, smooth skin. You're good for sex, right?"

"Well, I, uh—"

"And nothing else?"

"Amos. You'd better—"

"That's all you're good for. You know why."

"Because I'm a—"

"Yeah, you sure are a—"

"Amos, stop. This isn't funny anymore."

"After you strip and show off how sexy you are, you can sit right back down. Do you know why?"

She watched one of his hands fumbling around by his zipper.

"Amos. Stop it. No."

He snapped both hands to his hips and said, "Oh, wait. I know what a woman like you wants."

Looking up at him, shaking her head slowly, she said, "And what is that, Amos?"

"Huh. You want a crowd. You want a lot of guys."

"I do?"

"Uh-huh. You want to strip, let your hair down, and sit right there as a line forms."

Laughing, she said, "A line now, Amos? Come on, you're being—"

Reaching for his zipper again, he said, "I wouldn't even have to be first. Would you like that better?"

"You're saying I'd rather—"

"Uh-huh. Exactly. You'd like to strip down, get all sexy, and start with a stranger."

She laughed again and said, "Start what, exactly?"

He held her chin for a second, then let it go to touch a fingertip to her lips.

"Get that mouth going."

"On a line of strangers? Because I'm—"

"Nothing but a slut. That's right. A slut that can pretend to be modest, too, which makes me crazy."

"Hmm. Like this?"

She leaned into his finger, parting her lips enough to take it in, and she bobbed her head and moaned, letting her wet lips rub all along it several times.

"Oh my God . . ."

"Mm, I don't even know you, do I? And still . . ."

She moaned and sucked it some more.

"God . . ."

She backed away enough to let it go, then said, "Amos, that's fun to joke about, but you have to stop. Just stop."

"You're a slut, Lenore."

"Really, stop."

"You're nothing but a slut. Oh sure, you act all—"

"Hey!"

She pushed him away with both hands, forcing him a few steps back, then she stood and cinched her belt tighter.

"Stop. Enough, Amos."

"Look, I know, Lenore, that you're really nothing but a—"

"You don't know anything! Get out, Amos."

"What?"

"You heard me. Go park your ass on the couch. Take your line of horny strangers with you."

"You're serious?"

"I'm serious. All of you. Out."

He hung his head, walked toward the door, then turned back to look at her, seated again, wrapped in flannel, and bathed in the gentle light from the lamps. She was pointing toward the door.

With a sigh that was more of a groan, he pulled in the door, exited quietly, and gave it a soft boom to close it.

* * *

Lenore listened for his footsteps, but no sounds of any came through the door. She turned enough to almost touch her ear to it and still heard nothing.

Her scoff didn't make a sound and when she said, smiling, "What would Laura do?" that wasn't loud enough for Amos to hear either.

She walked to the bed and let her fingers drag along the soft blanket as she kept going farther, to the closet. When she pulled open the bifold door, it was with enough force to make some noise for the insistent man locked outside of the room.

While reaching for a pair with high heels, she said, over her shoulder, "Yes, these high heels are what I need."

She set them on the bed long enough to wiggle out of her pajama bottoms, which she tossed up onto the dresser before putting on the heels. The robe got dumped and left where it fell.

Her walk was solid and caused the sharp points to strike the hardwood floor on her way back to the door.

Covering a grin with one hand and shaking her head, she rolled her eyes then coughed lightly.

"You like me in these heels?"

She'd said it to the room and when Amos said, "I, uh, I—" she hurried to say, "Not you. You just stay quiet."

"Uh, okay. You, uh—"

"Shh. Don't disturb us."

She nodded at the lack of any further response, then strutted back toward the bed.

"Oh, I sure will strip down for all of you. First, this pajama shirt. It's just one button after another, all the way down, then—oh, there we go. Now, there's nothing covering them. Let's just toss this shirt aside."

She glanced at the door, smirked quietly, then looked at her reflection in the mirror above the dresser. While gazing at herself, naked except for lacy panties and footwear that she couldn't see but that had elevated the rest of her, she reached up with both hands.

"Yes, the hair has to come down. I hope it doesn't get in the way when I'm so busy."

As she was removing pins and clips and letting it all cascade down her back, her smile dwindled, and she held a breast in each hand.

"There, just like that. I'm ready. Are all of you?"

No longer smiling, she gave the quiet door a quick look, then watched her hands gently squeezing her breasts in the mirror.

"Oh, you do look ready. Mm, so do you. All of you. You want me to sit? Okay."

She backed herself to the bed and sat, bouncing to rattle it, then looked down as her hands found her thighs instead.

"Mm-hmm. I'm smooth and soft all over. Only these tiny panties covering anything, and—oh, you want those off too? Mm, I'll sure be naked except for my heels, won't I?"

She shifted herself around, worked the thin fabric down across her thighs, then down to her ankles, then kicked the garment to one side.

"There we go. Nothing but skin for all of you to use however you want. As long as I'm sitting, at just the right height, who's first?"

She paused, gave the door a peek, then watched herself in the mirror. She didn't smile when she held her hair back with both hands and held her mouth open, her lips forming a neat circle.

"Oh, wow, that's nice. For me? Oh, but you want me to say what I am first?"

The door seemed to be bending into the room, as if some heavy hunger was pressing against it.

Looking at herself in the mirror again, her breasts bare and her thick blond mane held back, she said, "I'm not good for anything but sex."

She listened, but no noises came from the direction of the door.

"Yes, I'm a respected business owner, all very proper. And I'm engaged to be the wife of a university professor someday. And still, look at what I'm doing."

Almost laughing, she exaggerated some gagging sounds.

"Hey, I'm not done! You'll get your turn. I have to say first that I'm all those things, but more than anything, what I love being more than anything, for all of you, is a complete slut."

She gagged more, then added, "Mm, yeah, like that. That's all I'm good for. All I want to be is a slut."

While making more soft gagging noises toward the door, she tipped herself back onto the bed, then let go of her hair.

And both hands found someplace else that responded immediately to her urgent attention.

Chapter 2 – Even Wilder, Huh?

The gentle rapping on the bedroom door got Lenore to stir, but she stayed under the blankets long enough for a lazy, cozy stretch. A glance at the clock beside her brought out a groan, and she sat, fluffed her hair back, then rubbed her face a few times.

"Coming," she said toward the door.

She stood and caught sight in the mirror of her complete nakedness.

"Oh. Hmm. That was, uh, something. What could have been."

She scooped up her robe on her march toward the door, used it to cover everything that she could, then pulled her hair all back behind her, hiding it as much as possible.

The nearly useless locking mechanism got a quick click, then she turned the knob. Amos, awake and appearing nearly ready to rush off to the university, stared in at her.

"My clothes," he said.

"Oh, of course," she said, then took a few steps back.

She scoffed at him pausing to watch her steps.

"You're looking for high heels, Amos? Come on, I don't sleep like that."

He didn't attempt a smile as he held her gaze and reached around for his shirt and pants hanging on the door's hook.

"You do everything else with them, though?"

"Last night? Come on, that was just for fun. You deserved that."

"Huh. I deserve some of what they all got."

"They, who? Listen to yourself."

"You know what I mean," he said, his clothes folded over an arm as he scanned around the room, lingering on a pair of shoes, panties, pajamas . . . all scattered across the floor.

"I know you think you can call me whatever you want whenever you want."

"You didn't mind telling them, then you—"

"Amos, stop it. There was no 'them.'"

"But if there was, you'd tell them, so why not tell me whenever I need to hear it?"

"When you 'need' to hear it?"

He looked down and mumbled, "Like you can't imagine."

"Well, just keep using your imagination. I need to get ready for work."

"Yeah, it's late. I have to rush out. Come on, be a good sport. Before I go, just say—"

Her face locked into a snarl as she stared at him.

"Stop it, Amos. I'll say it when I want. You know what else? I'll be it when I want. You want to hear more about that?"

"You, uh, you—"

"That's right. Yeah. Hey, Amos, I'll be a total slut when I want to be."

"Fine by me. Maybe later, we can—"

Still frowning, shaking her head, too, she said, "No, I mean whenever. That doesn't mean you have to be anywhere around."

"But you mean—"

"How about that, huh? You want to push me? You think about this: your fiancé can decide to be a total slut, and I mean a 'total' slut, anytime she wants, and you don't even have to know about it."

"I know," he said, pointing and snarling too. "Just like when you . . ."

"When I what? Go on, finish, Amos. When I what?"

He wiped his face clean and grimaced at the floor.

"Um, like when you were, uh, pretending. Last night. That's all I meant."

"Yeah, like that. Good, we understand each other. God, you can be so goddamn pushy sometimes. You deserve to hear me say that I'll be a slut anytime I want. Go. You're going to be late."

He was trembling slightly as he took quick glances around the room, lingering on her high heels, then her panties, then—

"Just go!" she said and shoved him into the hallway before slamming the door.

"God," she said, then looked toward her nightstand when her silenced phone vibrated with a soft rattle.

* * *

"Laura, good morning."

"Hey, I didn't wake you up, did I?"

"No, Amos did that. I just shooed him back out of the room and off to work."

"Back out of the room? Uh-oh. Don't tell me."

"I'd rather not. It's just that he must have overheard me that day I was alone in the bedroom, fantasizing. Saying things out loud."

Laura laughed for a few seconds, then said, "Oh, that's funny. He heard you saying you love being a slut more than anything?"

"Uh-huh. Oh yeah. And it's making him crazy. It started last Sunday morning, and he was weird about me being modest and supposedly a slut at the same time."

"Yeah, I could see how that would be a turn-on for the old prude."

"It sure is. Now, he keeps calling me a slut, trying to get me to be a slut whenever he snaps his fingers. He's really pissing me off."

"And you're not a slut whenever he says. Not a slut on command?"

"No way. Last night, I actually told him I could be a slut whenever I wanted, and he wouldn't even know about it."

"Good for you. The nerve that man has."

"Yeah, I could tell you more. Later, maybe. So, what's going on?"

"Nothing special—just wanted to get your Monday off to a good start."

"Sounds good. How, exactly?"

"Who else am I going to tell, Lenore? And you like hearing the details, don't you?"

"Oh, you mean that Frat Chat last week? I suppose. Yeah, tell me more. How was it?"

"Mm, you should have taken the offer and gone instead of me. We look almost identical, and no one would have known the difference."

"Someone would have known. You mean, there was no one there that's seen you there before? No one would know we'd switched?"

Lenore had lined herself up for a view in the dresser mirror, and she tipped her head at the sight of the large mounds her breasts were making under the tight robe.

"Hey, we don't even use names there. This one guy, though, a talkative character, told me his name was Emilio, so that's one that—"

"Wait. Did you say Emilio?"

"Yeah, I think that's what he said. Lenore, think of all the non-stop sex I was having. I'm pretty sure that's his name."

"That's not a common name."

"I don't suppose so. Anyway, not the point. Not his name anyway. How he was acting, though? God, Lenore, that was a trip."

"How so?"

"I said he was talkative, right? He made some kind of fun drama out of the whole thing. Even when he had his camera out, he was—"

"He took photos of you, Laura?"

"Oh, he sure did. He said it was some kind of requirement, to prove that it was all consensual, which it was, of course. Lenore, I was on the bed, on my hands and knees, and my cheerleader skirt was way up out of the way, and—hey, you really want to hear all this?"

Lenore was loosening her belt, then let the long, thick robe open on its own. She got her free hand up to a breast before answering.

"Yeah, I mean, uh-huh. Details, Laura."

"Alright, so, I'd already done two of the guys, and Emilio, he was standing on the bed, and I was looking up at him."

"Wait. You were blindfolded, right? Isn't that what you told me?"

"Oh, I was. Yeah. Then, he's talking, and I can't because, well, you can just imagine, and he peels back my blindfold and points the camera down at me."

"You let them take your photo?"

"Well, hmm. Right then, I didn't care. Oh, that must be some wild photos, me looking up at him, my mouth full. Can you imagine?"

Lenore gave her breast a final squeeze then caressed her way lower, along her belly, then lower still.

"Mm-hmm. Yeah, I can."

"Are you okay? You sound kind of funny."

Lenore laughed and said, "No, I'm fine. What else?"

"Well, this guy liked to talk, especially when he shot a video. He—"

"Laura! You didn't have your blindfold hiding you at all, and you let him take a video of you?"

"Yeah, damn, I sure did. And shit, Lenore, the things I was saying. Kind of like the stuff you told me you were saying that time, remember?"

"I, uh, yeah. I remember. About being something just for sex?"

"Yeah, exactly. Lenore, it felt good to say it for the video. It was a weird kind of excitement. And don't forget how, um, busy my mouth was too."

"That's in the video too?"

"Oh God, yeah. And when I could talk, those few times, all I said was how I was nothing but a slut."

"Oh my God. Laura, you're incredible."

"That's an interesting word for it. You sound kind of jealous."

"What? Um, I was just—"

"You should have switched with me, Lenore. Try to imagine that: you're just about naked, your shirt is off and your breasts are just hanging there. You're on your hands and knees and servicing him, which is what he called it."

Lenore gasped softly as one hand held the phone and the other had found just the right place, the right touch, the right rhythm.

"Mm-hmm, I can imagine."

"So, Lenore, I'm telling the video how I want everyone to know what a total slut I really am, that it's all I'm good for, stuff like that."

"You meant all that?"

"Not at first. When it started, I was just playing along. But then, it just felt good to say all that. Like you when you were fantasizing. Didn't that feel good? Just to dare to say out loud that you're nothing but a slut?"

"Uh, yeah, it did. So, that guy filmed all of it?"

"No, just some. Then, some other guy that I didn't see took me from behind. Oh, I was sure ready for it by then. And Emilio, he was enjoying how I was 'servicing' him, and he liked my big eyes looking up at him."

"I'd bet he would."

"We're almost twins, Lenore. That could have been you."

"We do look alike. I would have had to say all that, too, Laura? Let them take a video of my face?"

"Just think about how all of that would have felt, Lenore. To just say the hell with it—who cares what anyone thinks."

Lenore picked up her pace, then lay back on the bed with her knees up.

"I, uh, am thinking about it. Yeah, maybe I should have switched with you."

"Seriously? You would?"

"Right now, at this moment,"—she paused for a few focused rubs—"I would definitely say yes. Yes, I'd be that total slut."

"Uh-huh. In a video too? You'd say all that for the camera? I mean, when you could actually talk."

Lenore laughed choppily, kept her hand busy, and said, "Hmm. Tell the camera that I'm nothing but a slut. Hey, any more Frat Chats scheduled?"

"No, they actually put those on hold for some reason. Someday. Oh, there's something else coming up, though. Something even wilder. Lenore, my gorgeous almost-twin girl, you have to switch with me for this one."

Still giving herself gentle touches, Lenore moaned softly and said, "Hmm, even wilder, huh? I don't know, Laura."

"Let me see if I can get some details for you, you sexy slut."

"I'm a sexy slut?"

"Mm-hmm. Lenore, I know you. You're a lot of things, all good things, but maybe what you love the most is . . . what?"

The timing couldn't have worked out better with Lenore's busy hand, and she said, fighting to not sound so breathless, "Being a slut. A total, total slut."

Laura laughed just once, then said, "You're not just saying that?"

After a pause, Lenore said, "Damn that Amos. No, I'm not just saying that. Laura, I want to be such a bad girl."

"How bad?"

"Mm. A total slut."

"That's my girl. Oh, I have to go."

Lenore looked at the clock and said, "Oh my God. Me too! Bye!"

* * *

"Emilio."

His phone had barely rung where it lay on the picnic table while he devoured a breakfast sandwich.

"Hey, it's Laura. I know it's early."

"Yeah, and I have class in a few minutes. But I always have time for you, you sexy thing. Love those big eyes."

"You're still thinking about that Frat Chat? I did give a good performance, didn't I?"

"The best. I'll admit, I got carried away, babbling like a fool with you all naked and sexy as hell."

"Well, thanks. I kind of just played along with all that you were saying. Even the photos and the video. Shit, I didn't expect that."

"Hell, I didn't even plan that. I never know what I'm going to do next."

"Right, Emilio, except for class."

"Which is about a minute away. Shit, I'm already late. What's going on?"

"After the Frat Chat, you got me to volunteer for something else, some other kind of party."

"Yeah, and it isn't a Frat Chat. Hey, let's call it that, though. That could be like our secret code."

"The Frat Chat 2?"

"Good enough, yeah. What about it? You're not backing out, are you? Because these people, Laura, they don't—"

"No! I'm not, uh, exactly backing out. I'm just thinking about what I've heard of Michael and Eva—mostly Eva. I mean, Michael is probably"—

"Shit, just get to the point, will you? I just choked down the last of a crappy muffin sandwich, and I'm already late."

"Sure. I want out of the deal, but—"

"What? No, forget that—it's this Friday. It's too late for you to bail."

"Oh, Friday? That soon. Look, I want to send a replacement, someone who—"

"Whoa, wait a second. You're hot, and I already know that. That's what these folks need. They're damn particular. You can't just throw anybody their way and assume they won't get pissed."

"No, listen a second. This woman could be my twin. I mean, like, an identical twin."

"Same hair? Figure? All of it?"

"Yeah, all of that. Same big eyes. And she's sexy as hell too."

"That whole bit you had going at the Frat Chat, with the sexy talking, is something these folks would love. This substitute can handle that?"

"I know for a fact that she's been practicing."

"Huh?"

"I mean, just by herself, you know, fantasizing. She's been telling me about all the wild, sexy stuff she likes saying."

"If she's only practicing, she's just an amateur."

"Uh, yeah, she's probably more on the innocent side. It might be kind of pushing her limits to do all that."

"Actually, that might be even more fun. You know me—I like the drama, and pushing someone innocent into all kinds of stuff could be a blast."

"I don't think any of you would have to do much pushing."

"Hey, work with her. See if you can get her more receptive to doing outlandish things. Just get her started, and everyone at the party will push her the rest of the way."

"What kind of outlandish things?"

"Oh, shit, I don't know. Does she like talking dirty? Maybe start there—make sure she's willing to say things that someone 'on the innocent side' wouldn't usually say."

"Alright. I can do that. So, we're good, then, for the switch?"

"I'll tell you what: let's do it, and if it doesn't work out, it's your ass on the line. Remember those photos and that video I have of you?"

Laura blew out a deep, agonized breath, then said, "Yeah, I remember. Nice, Emilio. Go straight to the blackmail, huh?"

He looked at his watch, then said, "It wasn't straight to it. We've been talking a few minutes. Look, think of what that video will do for your life. Ever hear of an obscure little thing called the Internet?"

"Dammit. Once or twice, yeah."

"Good. So, I have you under control, but I don't know about this other one, your replacement. Tell you what: you tell her that someone named Drake is going to contact her. I'll grab a burner phone and give this a go."

"Okay. That'll work."

"What's my name?"

"Drake."

"And I'm going to act like her name is Laura. That's the game, right? She's Laura?"

"Yeah. She'll have to be Laura."

"It's going to be a wild time, actual Laura. You should reconsider."

"Hey, I know enough about these folks to have a bad feeling about the whole deal."

"Oh, stop it. They're just, I don't know, theater people or something. They like to play games and crave drama even more than I do."

"Shit, is that even possible?"

"You got me there. Probably not. But they're probably harmless. Your new Laura will have the sexual adventures of her life."

"Okay, good. Then, you'll destroy those photos and that video?"

"Now, you're just being stupid. Think it through, actual Laura. Once you get leverage, you never, ever give it up."

Chapter 3 – You Can't Stop

Amos stood behind his lectern at the lowest point in one of the university's spacious lecture halls. Ascending rows curved around him with a wide aisle running up the middle toward a closed set of wide double doors.

After a glance up toward the left, at a specific seat in the back row that was still empty, he scoffed and looked around the room more. Up close, off to the right, a waving hand caught his attention.

Nodding to the attractive young woman, he mouthed the words, "Hi, Lindsey," which wouldn't have been heard unless he had shouted to overcome the chatter and laughter and an occasional yell.

Looking down again at the books and notes that he'd brought for the class, he scoffed and wiped at the wrinkled sleeves of the long-sleeved shirt that he'd hastily tossed on when rushing out of the house. His efforts didn't smooth out any of it, so he reached behind him to where he'd left his dark tweed jacket, then put that on, covering to some extent the clothing that he'd worn the last time he'd taught that class.

He gave that empty seat another quick look, then scanned around the room while saying, "Class. Class, let's get things moving. I have an important announcement to point us in a productive direction."

It took a few seconds to reel in some of the more sleepy eyes and faces showing their lack of interest.

"And that news is that we are not, like happens so often in this intro psychology class, leading off with a staggering detour into indecipherable, incomprehensible philosophical debates about—"

One of the double doors at the back of the room, behind all of the seats, swung open and banged into the wall, and Emilio took a few quick steps inside.

"About hot and cold!" he called out, causing the majority of students to snicker, laugh, and offer a few choice expletives.

"Emilio," said Amos. "Your timing is impeccable—not adequate for the class start time but quite appropriate for a perfectly timed interruption to the beginning of my monologue."

"Ah," he said while shuffling past other students toward the empty seat, "your monologue. Yeah. About that."

Amos gave Lindsey a look and grinned at her smirk and shoulders locked in a shrug.

Focusing again on Emilio, Amos said, "Hot or cold. Again, we're going to—"

"No. Oh, no, no, no, professor, sir. Hot *and* cold. A small detail, but a very important one."

"Right. Hot and cold at the same time."

While pointing at Emilio, jabbing a pen toward him and looking around the room, Amos said to the class, "I'm actually onboard with his hot and cold philosophy. Don't ask me for details, though."

He heard Emilio snort out a loud laugh, gave him a quick look, then continued.

"The principle has to do with divinity. To experience hot and cold, as an example—and there are many other pairs such as that—is to bring one's self closer to divinity, whatever that—wait, are we still not allowed to speak of divinity at this university?"

He earned some laughter, and a few of them expressed their skepticism.

"Very well. We won't use that word again. But it's an interesting bit of philosophy, and I'm glad I've learned to embrace it. Although, I must admit, it's not without hazards."

He snapped his head to look toward the back when Emilio called out, orating for the entire room, "That's because you're getting pulled into the next phase of all that. It's leading you deeper with a tight grip on your—"

"Careful," said Amos, "or you'll be lining yourself up for your fourth freshman year."

After Emilio had snickered with many of the others, he said, "Hey, I was going to say your nose. What were you thinking?"

Amos looked around for a second and saw that a lot of students were waiting for his answer.

He coughed once, then said, "Uh, my wallet? A tight grip on my wallet. What else?"

"Oh, okay," Emilio said, laughing a few times. "Yeah. Because of buying a hot tub, then planting it up on a frozen mountain. Stuff like that. Yeah, your wallet."

"So, philosopher Emilio in a psych class, you have once again claimed our attention for your own selfish aims. What is this next phase you've alluded to?"

"It's easy: you get a blast of div—well, that 'D' word that we can't mention—by feeling hot and cold at the same time. I could explain that, but we don't have that kind of time. I only have this lecture hall for so long."

Amos laughed along with the rest of them.

"Class," said Emilio. "Enough. Alright, the next phase is that you want more. You think that if that level of hot and cold was good, hotter and colder would be even better. You get greedy."

"And what," said Amos, "is the likely conclusion from that kind of greed?"

"You either freeze your ass off,"—he paused to look around, then smirked at having the highest level of their attention so far—"or it burns your ass to the ground."

The silence dragged on for a few seconds, then Amos said, "And what then, Mr. Philosopher? After my—I mean, after someone's ass is burned to the ground."

"Then," he said, pausing for the drama, "you can't stop—you want to burn even more."

Amos rapped his pen on the lectern to silence the snickering. "And you know this, how?"

Emilio shrugged and said, "Shit, I just make this up as I go."

* * *

"Shirley, never mind about what I'm wearing—I just like to dig into the closet sometimes. Did you finish up that report last Friday?"

Lenore stood beside her desk after just arriving at the office. She hadn't yet had a chance to sit, and Shirley, loitering in the open doorway, had a view of a skirt shorter than usual, heels higher than usual, and a blouse that had one more button ignored than usual.

"Hey, I'm just complimenting. Looks good. Uh, almost done with the report. Maybe I'll just, uh, get back to that."

"Thank you. We'll need that this afternoon. Oh, close the door, too, will you?"

"Sure."

"Thanks."

The light slamming of the door covered only the first few tones of the ringing of Lenore's phone, and she slipped it up out of her purse while sitting, grinning at the caller ID.

"Laura, I just got to the office."

"Too busy? I can call back if—"

"No, don't be silly. I mostly just boss people around here."

"And you should, Lenore—you are the boss. But I have to tell you, that's not what they want at the Frat Chat 2."

"The what? They're having another one at that fraternity house?"

"No, it's that other party I told you about. We just figured we'd call it that. Hey, we have to call it something. It's this Friday night."

"The Frat Chat 2. Sure, why not? So, go on, what are you talking about—about not being a boss?"

"It's just that, from what I've heard, you won't be there just for sex. I mean, yeah, you'll have more sex than you can imagine, but they—"

"Hmm. My imagination's getting better all the time."

"Maybe not for the Frat Chat 2 stuff, though. The thing is, they do this kind of ritual stuff, I think, and you'll be the offering."

"That doesn't sound so bad."

"Yeah, but like I said, it isn't just sex. They, uh, want to make it, um . . ."

"Oh, come on, Laura, you're not shy. Just say it."

"Alright. They want it to be degrading. They plan on a lot of sex, but they want their offering, uh, not treated like a princess."

"That, uh, sounds kind of ominous, Laura. Are you talking about some kind of abusive thing?"

"I think it's more like, well, like the offering is just a slave. Something they can do whatever they want with. Maybe humiliate her? Make her do stuff? I'm not sure."

"Yeah, I'm not sure either."

"Okay, listen: it's all for fun. They'll want you for all kinds of sex, but they want to spice it up, that's all."

"By abusing me?"

"That's probably not the right word. You know, Lenore, people pay for that kind of experience. You might find that it's the best sex you ever had."

Lenore crossed a leg, watched how that had forced her skirt up enough to show a lot of her thigh, then nudged it up a little higher. She was rubbing her thigh as she answered.

"Well, I don't even know what you mean. What kind of experience?"

"Oh, maybe just like them telling you what to do."

"That doesn't sound so bad."

"Maybe forcing you."

"Forcing me how?"

"I don't know, Lenore. I'm kind of curious myself. It's just that you wouldn't be bossing anyone around. No, you'll be the one bossed around. You wanted to feel like just an object, remember?"

"Well, I did, yeah."

"That's the deal. You're just an object to be used. You said you wanted to be used for wild sex, right?"

"Uh, sure, but I'm not sure about this, the way you're describing it."

"Okay, listen. They'll want you dressed up really nice. Now, imagine they make you strip down to just your high heels, then make you crawl from chair to chair, giving each of them a treat."

"Hmm, a treat. I could do that. That might not be so bad."

"How about if they're laughing at you, too, and calling you a slut?"

Lenore laughed and said, "Well, I would be. Uh-huh."

"How about a worthless slut?"

"Uh, that's one kind of fantasy, I suppose. Sure. What else?"

"I'm just making things up, but imagine they force you to wear a collar, and someone's leading you around on a leash too."

"Oh my gosh. You're serious?"

"You'd be just an object for whatever they want, remember? Ooh, you might have to kneel, and someone will tie your wrists behind you. Then, each of them—"

"They'd tie me up too? Laura, this is way more than a Frat Chat!"

"You should have taken my place at that, Lenore. Admit it."

"I, um, yeah, I probably should have. Things are spiraling down with Amos."

"The saint. You already don't really have a choice. You're doing the Frat Chat 2, Lenore."

Lenore laughed and said, "You're already bossing me around?"

"Uh-huh. And notice how you didn't get mad about it."

"I didn't. No."

"I think it's what you need, Lenore. You didn't do the Frat Chat and now, you're starving even more for sex. Any kind of sex."

"Any kind?"

"Mm-hmm. You're going to be degraded and abused and treated like nothing but a sex object. That's exactly what you need."

Lenore took several slow breaths, kept rubbing her bare thighs, and listened but didn't speak.

"Yeah," Laura finally said. "You're doing it—taking my place. You're going to do everything they force you to do."

Lenore breathed and studied her thighs as she crossed the other leg.

"You're going to be degraded, Lenore, and do you know why?"

Softly, almost breathlessly, Lenore said, "Why?"

"Because you're not just a total slut. What you want to experience most is being a worthless slut. Just something soft and sexy and there to be abused and degraded for their pleasure."

"Oh my gosh. Laura, I . . ."

More than a few seconds passed, then Laura said, "Uh-huh. Oh, they're going to love you. And you, Lenore, my nearly identical twin girl, are going to do absolutely everything they order you to do."

Chapter 4 – A Penchant for Drama

Nearly every one of Amos's students had already filed up the center row of the lecture room, then out through the open double doors. Only Lindsey was dawdling, fussing with her books, and she managed to get everything in order just in time to join Amos for the walk up and out.

"Good class today, Professor Amos."

"Why, thank you, Lindsey. Aside from periodic outbursts of philosophy from Emilio, we're making progress into the actual coursework."

"It's interesting. You're a good professor."

"Well, thanks again."

They passed through the doors and into a wide hallway with only meager foot traffic passing in each direction.

"I guess I'll see you next class," she said, smiling and beginning to walk away.

"Yes. No cutting of classes."

"Bye."

He watched her for only a second, her long brown hair shifting easily across her back, then turned when he heard, "Professor Riley."

"Yes?"

A robust man, taller than Amos, stood nearby. The olive skin of his face was smooth and free of whiskers and though his eyes were intense, he offered what looked like a practiced smile. His suit appeared tailored, and he wore it with an easy confidence.

He extended his hand and said, "I'm Michael. I don't believe we've met."

While shaking his hand, Amos said, "Uh, no, we haven't. Are you a parent of—"

Michael laughed and said, "Oh, no. I'm one of the regents here at the university."

"You are? I thought I'd seen bios for all of you."

"Oh, you have. Those are for the public. I'm sort of like a layer back, still involved in key policy and personnel issues but not so public-facing."

"Oh, I see. Well, good to meet you."

Michael looked each way, then said, "This isn't the best place to extend an invitation—certainly not the most formal. But I don't want to take much of your time, especially as it's lunchtime."

"Oh, here's fine. You said an invitation?"

"Yes. Your credentials, Professor Riley, are quite exemplary. We knew that when the university extended an offer to you. However, your goal—and our goal for you—is to move you up as quickly as is feasible and ready you for a full professorship here at our wonderful university."

Amos scoffed, then laughed, then said, "You're serious? I mean, thanks, but I haven't even had a chance yet to show my dedication to this."

"We know, and that's fine. Like I said, a lot of careful vetting landed you here, and the next step requires little more from you. You've already become a favorite of many students, and they give your lectures high marks. So, are you interested?"

"Well, yeah, of course. I can't thank you enough."

"It's not just me—oh, may I call you Amos?"

"Sure. That's fine."

"Terrific, Amos. No, I and the other unlisted regents are the true decision makers here, and we'd like you to join us for an unofficial event this Friday. It's kind of formal, and we partake of our share of rituals, just for the enjoyment of it. But the purpose is quite serious: we, all of us, just want to get an idea of your commitment to the university. So, what do you say? Are you in?"

"Yes, of course. Where and when? Not to be pushy, but are guests allowed?"

"We'll get word to you about the location. Just block out Friday evening, okay? Oh, and no, there's no 'plus one' for an event like this. I hope that's okay?"

"That's fine. Yes, whatever it takes. This is wonderful."

"It truly is, yes. So, Amos, plan on Friday, alright?"

"I will. I truly will."

"And Amos? Plan also to keep an open mind as you approach this. They're a good group but like I said, they have a penchant for drama with their own made-up ritual type stuff. It's all just for fun. Really, you'll have the time of your life."

"Sounds good. Yes, I'll keep an open mind. Thanks again, Michael."

"No, thank you, Amos. Until Friday, then?"

He didn't wait for an answer, and Amos watched him walking away for a few seconds.

"Huh. Unbelievable."

He checked his watch, then aimed his steps toward the exit closest to the park.

* * *

With her eyes on the closed office door, Lenore backed her chair away and stood, then began a careful, quiet walk toward it. Before engaging the lock, she twisted the mini-blinds wand, tipping them all closed and covering the only window that looked in on her private space.

She looked back across the tile floor toward her desk with her hands on her hips, then looked down and laughed.

"Oh God, Laura. You're too much sometimes."

Looking around again, she let her smile dwindle, then studied the clean flooring between her and the two compact upholstered guest seats off against the right wall.

"Still, you got me thinking . . ."

She stooped down, touching the floor with both hands and pausing there.

"Crawling, huh? No way. Not on tile. You can't make me, Laura."

She laughed at her own joke as she stood up again, then wiped her hands together and took steps toward the closest of the seats.

"They'd boss me around, huh? Make me do things? Hmm, you kind of started bossing me, too, didn't you, Laura? If you were there, too, would you be the one that did the bossing?"

Her eyes fixed on one of the small matching pillows, and she scoffed, then picked it up and set it on the floor near the chair.

After first staring up at the ceiling and pausing for a smile, she looked down at the pillow and said, in a whisper, "So, Laura, you're the boss at this party, huh? And you're telling me that I have to kneel for him?"

She looked higher, up at the seat cushion, then said, "Whoever he is? No, it's fine—a girl like me doesn't need to know who he is."

She knelt, keeping her thighs pressed together, then glanced behind her to see the pair of tapered heels, close together and pointing away. After a quick smile, she turned back to her assignment and reached both hands out, letting her imagination move them around.

But her hair got a rough grab, and she said, "Fine. Okay, I'll do it."

With both hands, she reached for the hem of her skirt, then grinned as she pulled it up, wiggling her hips to get it up and over. It took a few seconds to straighten out her panties, a tug to each side, and she held her cheeks for a second.

"Yes, I know they want that from me too. Mm-hmm, I want them to enjoy that. Oh, the same time?"

She giggled and added, "Hmm, both ends, huh?"

She got her hands busy with the trousers of the man who would be seated there, then paused as if holding something.

"Yes, I'm getting it out. Ah, there it is. Hmm."

She snapped her hands behind herself, crossed her wrists near her lower back, and gasped more loudly than a whisper.

"Hey, not so rough!"

Tipping her head forward, letting her hair fall forward on both sides, she said, in a strained whisper, "I'll do it. Oh, you want me to tell him why?"

Still pretending to have her wrists tied behind her, Lenore looked up higher, into the eyes of the imaginary stranger seated there.

"Because I'm a slut," she said.

She tipped her head back quickly and said, "Ow. You don't have to pull my hair—I'll say it right."

Imaginary Laura released her hair, and Lenore said to the stranger, "I'm a worthless slut. I'm not worth a damn thing except for this—being used for sex."

Her hair got yanked again, and she said, over her shoulder, "Okay!"

She leaned forward, worked her lips around for a few seconds, then looked up again.

"While I'm busy doing all I'm good for," she told the stranger, "tell me how worthless I am. Tell me how I disgust all of you, everyone that I'm going to kneel for and service. Tell me how I don't deserve any respect at all."

She leaned forward, almost kissing the cushion.

"Mm. Mm-hmm . . ."

A few moments later, she backed away from her task. Laura seemed to have released her from her bindings, and she wiped all around her lips, then sucked her fingertips.

"Mm, that was good. Better than I deserve."

Laura jerked her hair, turning her to face one side.

"Oh, a video. Okay. While the one behind me is still busy? Okay."

She sucked one more finger, then smiled at the camera.

"That's all I'm good for. Doing that for a stranger who's calling me a worthless slut. Mm-hmm, I swallowed it all too. I'm good for swallowing. A lot. I have to swallow a lot. They're all strangers too."

Laura gave her hair a pull, then left her alone.

Looking directly into her imaginary camera, she said, "My name is Lenore. I'm a fiancé of a professor and a local business owner. And whether I like it or not, I'm just . . . a worthless slut. I want everyone to know."

She got her hair yanked again.

"I'm soft and warm and smooth all over, and I'm only good for sex. Nothing else. Not a damn thing else—just sex."

Laura jerked her hair again, then left her to continue.

"And I don't deserve any respect. None. Because I'll do anything, no matter how degrading. No matter how abusive. My name is Lenore, and I'm nothing but soft and warm—just a worthless slut."

She stared into the camera for only another second, then laughed while restoring her skirt and pushed herself up onto her heels.

"Oh my goodness. Laura, no way. No way am I doing anything like that."

* * *

"Is that seat taken?" Amos said, coffee in one hand and pointing at the picnic table bench seat with the other.

"In a second, yeah," said Emilio. "Have a seat, professor."

While sitting, Amos said, "You really can call me Amos, you know."

"Alright, I will, Amos. Shit, we've been through a lot, and my freshman year is just beginning."

"Freshman. Yeah. Hey, we're still not talking about that one thing we've been through, right?"

"The Frat Chat? Sure, if that's the way you want it. We both remember it, though. God, that woman was hot as hell. So damn playful too. Just on her hands and knees, looking up at me with those big eyes while I held that wild blond ponytail and she serviced me. All on video, too, which is—"

"Hey! That's what you call not talking about it?"

Emilio laughed and said, "Told you. I tend to talk too much. Alright, I'll let that go. Just tell me, first, if you liked watching her enjoying what she was doing to me while you stuck it to her from behind."

"You're impossible. You really don't know when to quit."

"That's one incredible kind of woman, whoever she is. You can at least say that."

"I could. Fine, she's incredible. Uh, whoever she is."

"An incredible slut. She loved calling herself that too. You remember that, right?"

"Of course. Yeah, she did like saying that, but she's probably a lot of other things, like with a career, some kind of life, maybe even—"

"No, no, no. Forget all that, Amos. She said over and over that what she loves the most—the *most*—was being a slut. Whoever she is, whatever else she seems to be, down deep, she's mostly just a slut. Just acknowledge that, and we can move on."

"Fine. Whoever she is, she loves being a slut. More than anything else."

"Close, but no, not *being*. Try again."

"Sure. Fine. She *is* mostly just a slut."

"There. Now, on to other business."

"I mean," said Amos, "she could be quite an ordinary, endearing type of woman, right? Maybe that was the only time she did something like that?"

Emilio laughed, then said, "Right. She didn't really mean any of that. Shit, what an actress."

"Well, she might have a side to her like that, but she could just, I don't know, be that way at home, right? Like, if she's in a relationship, couldn't she just behave that way, like—"

"Like a total slut, one that loves being nothing but a slut?"

"Like that. Yeah. At home. That's all I'm saying."

Emilio turned enough to squint at Amos, then scoffed and said, "You sure are saying something. What that is, I might never know."

"Fine. We're done with talk of the Frat Chat."

"Right. If you say so. What's next on our agenda?"

"Hot and cold? That business?"

"Yeah, and I need to add some kind of corollary to that, something about how it's every man for himself."

"What does that have to do with the divinity of feeling those contrasts?"

"I don't know. Probably nothing. It might have to be a separate chapter altogether."

"Oh, in that book you're writing. Sure. What's the deal with every man for himself?"

"Just a general principle. Just one aspect of it is if I see some hot babe that I want, I don't give a shit about anything else. I'm going for it."

Amos scoffed and said, "That's probably more common than we think. Yeah. What else is going on?"

"Oh, nothing," Emilio said, and they both sipped their coffee and watched students and townspeople crisscrossing the park, most drinking their own coffee.

"All these hikes out here remind me: I saw you on your day off the other week, cruising through the park."

"Oh, yeah, around lunchtime. It's a day off, so I—"

"Got some fresh air. Yeah, good thinking."

"Hey, Emilio, did you ever hear of a guy named Michael—says he's high up in the university ranks?"

"Yeah, actually, I've talked with him. Why?"

"I just met him. He invited me to some kind of event Friday, and I told him I'd go. I don't want to sound like I'm boasting, but he says they want to check me out and get me a full professorship."

"Well, congrats. That's pretty cool, Amos. I wasn't going to bring it up because it's all kind of hush-hush, but I'm sort of involved with the logistics for that shindig."

"No way. You are?"

"Yeah, believe it. Since you're going, I'm not bound by my oath of silence."

"You took an—"

"No way, Amos. You know me—just adding some drama. So, you're going, right?"

"Well, of course. I'm a little in shock at being advanced so quickly."

"Well, shit, you're good, even though I break your balls a lot in class."

"It's fine—no offense taken."

"Your balls might say different. Speaking of balls breaking, there's another corollary to the hot and cold and divine bullshit theorizing. The thing is, it's a trap. That's going to be a separate chapter when I finally—"

"Wait, wait, wait. A trap? What do you mean?"

"It's like I started to explain in my lecture today."

"Your lecture?"

"Well, borrowed time. Your lecture too. So, you're feeling hot and cold at the same time, and you're grooving to it because it just feels right."

"Divine. Divinity?"

"Yeah, that. So, the problem is that you start thinking that if that level of hot and cold is good, well, shit, more would be even better."

"Uh, more divine?"

"Something like that. Yeah. So, you got a taste, and you want to up the stakes. Hotter, colder—maybe it would be more divine."

"And?"

"And you'll either freeze your ass into a block while going up in flames, or . . ."

"Or, what?"

"Or maybe you just see that scariness inside of yourself. You see a cold, dark place. A vengeful, bitter, frozen side of yourself."

"Sure. Or you see—"

"Or you see that you have a raging inferno in there, and you've gone and set it loose. You sparked it, lit it up, and it's going to blaze until it incinerates your sorry ass."

Chapter 5 – A Slut Like Me

The front door of Lenore's house swung in quietly, and Amos stepped inside, dropped his keys on the small wood table close by, then closed the door with a soft boom.

Some random clattering from the direction of the kitchen got him walking that way, and he paused at the entryway, observing Lenore facing away, working at the stove.

She wore her usual baggy blue jeans, long enough to bunch up around her white sneakers. He'd seen the flannel shirt many times, and he knew, without seeing it, that all but the top button had been fastened. It hung limply, giving no indication of the slender waistline hidden underneath.

Her long and thick blond hair was reduced to a tight nest, twisted and looped together and locked in place with pins and clips.

"Smells good," he said, then took more steps into the room.

Over her shoulder, without really looking, she said, "Hey. It'll be ready in a few minutes. You're punctual."

"Oh, you know me," he said, taking his usual seat at the table. "When that last class wraps up, I'm out of there. What's cooking? Besides you, I mean. Even in those clothes, your ass looks damn good."

She rattled the ladle into the pot, still didn't turn completely, and said, "Stew is cooking. Not my ass. Especially since I'm feeding you, Amos, you could try to show a little respect."

She turned, a steaming wide bowl in each hand, and began walking toward the table.

"If you want wine, go fetch it yourself. I'm not in the mood to be bossed around in our home."

"Hey, I'm just messing around. You can't blame me for wanting to hear you say those things again."

She stopped halfway there and stared, shaking her head.

"You know what else?" he added. "Forget that—don't say anything. Just walk around the kitchen in your panties."

She scoffed and said, "Just my panties, huh? You're out of your mind."

Before she'd finished delivering the food, as she still stared at him, he said, "True enough. Yeah, I forgot: panties and heels. Lenore, tell me you don't want to walk around like that."

He grinned as he waited for a response, but he saw no trace of a smile from her as she clunked his bowl in front of him, then sat across the table with hers.

"What are you calling me, Amos? You're still all ornery like last night?"

"Well, you're still gorgeous so, yeah. Of course. What am I calling you? You want me to say it?"

"You won't stop until you do. So, go ahead. Get it over with."

"I think you want to hear it. I think you want to traipse around the house for me wearing just—"

"Traipse around for you? Uh-uh. Forget it. Eat your damn stew."

"Who do you want to traipse around for, then?"

"Who said I want to traipse anywhere?"

"No one. I was just—"

"Just being an ass. Look, Amos, just say it. What am I? What do I love being more than anything?"

He pointed over his steaming bowl and said, "You love being a slut."

She kept her face a mask, showing no reaction.

"It's better when you whisper it to me, though."

"Huh."

"You want to smile. You know it's true. You want me to say it again?"

Still not smiling, she said, "Fine. It's not like I deserve any respect, so go ahead."

"Yeah. Lenore, you're a slut, and it's what you love the most. More than anything. You said so."

"People say a lot of things, Amos. I can say whatever I want just for fun."

"You're not mad? You don't look like you're mad."

"I'm not. You're just being stupid."

"No. Oh, no, that's not it. No, we're making progress here. I think you like hearing it."

"Stop it, Amos. Eat your dinner."

"This is more important. Lenore, you're right—you don't deserve any respect because you're just a slut. Lenore, you're a total slut."

"Stop. Eat."

"You want to walk around in panties and heels. You probably would at work too."

"You're crazy. Stop."

"A slut like you would probably even want to—"

"Amos, that's enough!"

She stood, rolling the chair away behind her, and pointed toward the front door.

"Take your stupid stew out onto the stupid porch, and sit your stupid ass out there."

"Lenore, I was just—"

"Last chance, Amos, then you're going out there without your damn dinner. Go!"

He didn't get up, but he did stay quiet and look down at his bowl, where he was using a large spoon to stir it around.

"I'll stop. Sorry."

She snorted out a scoff, reclaimed her chair, then sat and began eating hers too.

* * *

After several long quiet minutes of Amos and Lenore eating but not speaking, she splashed her spoon into what was left of her stew and said, “Changed my mind,” and pushed back her chair.

“What?”

“Wine,” she said while walking toward the counter.

“Always a good option,” he said and kept eating.

He scrutinized her form from behind the entire time, tipping his head and leaning to get a better view. She was still digging in a drawer for the corkscrew when he spoke out.

“Sorry, but I’m imagining you standing there right now in just panties.”

He watched her take a deep breath and sigh it back out, and she didn’t turn around.

“What about the heels? A slut like me should be wearing spiky heels, too, right?”

She turned enough to stare at him, without a smile, and he let his full spoon drift down into the bowl.

“Um, yeah. You know, Lenore, I’m just having fun. Sort of.”

“Yeah. I’m not going to argue: having yourself a kitchen wench wearing only panties and heels would count as fun.”

“Yeah. Um, but I’m kind of joking.”

“Amos,” she said while setting down the bottle and two glasses and the corkscrew, “just open the wine.”

“I can do that.”

She sat and watched his hands, sometimes shaking but making quick work of the uncorking, then the pouring. He set one in front of her, and she picked it up, held his gaze, and chugged half of it.

“Not long ago,” he said, grinning, “I would have joked about you swallowing so much.”

She scoffed and said, “Wine, you mean?”

His grin fizzled, and he drank a few sips, then set down his glass.

“Um, yeah. Wine.”

"You know, Amos, if I really am what I said for fun and you insist on repeating forever, it might not be wine."

He looked around the kitchen, eyes scanning the refrigerator door, then the cabinets.

"No, Amos. Nothing ordinary in a kitchen. You know what I mean."

"You, uh, you wouldn't, I mean, if you really—"

"You're stammering. You want me to be that? Fine. Like I told you last night. I can be that anytime I want."

She held up her glass and let the rim of it rest against her pursed lips for a few seconds.

"Mm-mm. Not wine."

"Lenore," he said, his voice showing less cockiness, "I've been stupid, saying that stuff. I don't have to keep saying it. I'll stop."

"So, you don't think of me as a . . ."

She watched his lower lip twitch as he waited, then she scoffed before continuing.

". . . that kind of woman?"

He shook his head quickly, then said "Modesty is good too. You know, baggy jeans and an old shirt . . . stuff like that."

"Oh, God, Amos, you need to make up your mind. Do you want modest or something else? You want me to say what that 'something else' is?"

"No. I mean, uh, no, there's no need."

"Fine. But I think you're going to keep playing this game, deciding on a whim whatever you want me to be at that moment."

"No. No, I won't. I, um, I like . . ."

"You don't know. God, Amos, you're all over the place."

"Uh, kind of. Yeah."

"How about taking your stew—for real this time—and being all over a chair on the porch?"

"Really?"

"Yeah, really. Go. Take your dinner outside. You can even take that bottle."

He stood with the plate in one hand and picked up the bottle with the other.

"I know how to work a corkscrew, too, you know. Go."

She remained in her seat, not eating, not fetching more wine, and listened to him shuffling toward the front door. She shook her head at the sound of him closing it as quietly as he could.

"Shit. I have to decide what I am too."

She stretched her arms to her sides, then fluttered her lips.

"Maybe Laura already knows. She seemed to know, didn't she? Maybe she's right about all of that . . ."

Chapter 6 – They're All Forcing Me

Lenore finished her dinner in silence, and Amos hadn't returned from his forced isolation on their front porch. She brought the emptied bowl to the sink, filled it with water, then reached for the other wine bottle on the counter.

"Well, why the hell not?"

Back at the table, she got it open, filled a glass, drained most of it, then refilled it.

"That's not bad. Oh, I feel that. Hmm."

She bumped back her chair and stood up partway, kind of in a crouch, and laughed as her balance abandoned her and she slipped back onto the padded arm of the chair.

"Oh, thanks, chair," she said, giggling softly with one thigh on each side of it.

She started to rise up, and the casters rolled too easily, letting the chair slip away just enough to cause her to stumble back onto it.

"Oh, maybe this is how to use this kind of chair. Hmm."

She chugged what was left of her wine, set down the glass, then held the table edge with both hands. She tried sliding herself along the soft padding, but that only got the chair rolling with every push and pull on the table.

"Uh-uh. Not like that."

Holding on with both hands still, she only rocked her hips forward and back, just a slight motion each way.

"Oh, that's it. Uh-huh."

She gave it a few more thrusts, then held still long enough to free up one hand for some wine pouring. Listening for an invasion at the front door, she set the bottle down quietly.

Leaving her hand around the stem, the glass stayed put as she gyrated her hips slowly and gently, rubbing against the arm of her kitchen chair until she laughed, then belched softly.

"Oops!"

She paused her self-pleasure long enough to take modest sips from the glass, playing with her lips against it, and kept going until she'd finished all of it.

Holding it out in front of her, she rubbed herself more, allowed the softest of moans, then gave that a rest as she tipped her head back and poured into her open mouth the few drops that were left in the glass.

She didn't look when she set down the glass because she was still facing up at the ceiling but not really noticing it.

Licking around her lips took only a few seconds, then she opened her mouth again, as if inviting something, maybe not wine, and rolled her hips forward and backward, forward and backward.

"Oh my goodness," she said as she stopped all of it.

A quick slide to one side planted her in the seat in its intended way, and she said, "This . . . isn't right. Amos, you're just too . . ."

With a groan, she leaned forward, grabbed her phone, and tapped Laura's number.

* * *

"Laura, I can't take this anymore."

"Well, hello to you, too, sexy girl."

Laura leaned back into her seat, kept the phone against her ear, and tapped the wine bottle against the table with a series of steady clunks.

"Sorry. Hi, Laura. It's just that sometimes, I mean, when I think—"

"Amos again, right? I already know it just by the tone of your voice. Lenore, you don't belong with some guy who wants to be a saint more than he wants to enjoy your delicious naked body."

Lenore laughed and left the bottle to rest on its own.

"Oh my gosh. My delicious naked body. You kind of summed up the situation here, though. Is it me? Or is it Amos? It's not me, right?"

"Give me some details. You know I always want details."

"Okay. He's obsessed with calling me a slut and wanting me to act like one. Just now, before dinner even, he was telling me I should walk around the house in just panties and heels. Can you imagine?"

"Mm. Yeah, actually, I can. I mean, I am . . ."

"Laura, stop it. This is serious. So, I play along for a while, then I get mad at him because he's being so smug about it."

"Does that stop him?"

"Yeah, like, too much. He snaps back to being a saint and wanting me to be all modest. God, he doesn't know what he wants."

"Yeah, that's your Amos. So, he's not around?"

"I sent him out to the porch, then I opened my own bottle of wine, then I . . ."

After a pause and listening to Lenore giggle for a second, Laura said, "Well, come on. Then, you what?"

"Oh, Laura, I, um, kind of had sex with a chair in the kitchen."

"Get out of here. Damn, I need some details on that. Come on."

Laughing first, Lenore said, "Alright. Um, I drank some of that wine pretty quick, and I kind of stumbled back onto the chair. But just, um, onto the arm of it. It's a nice width, and it's padded, and I—"

"You started rubbing yourself on it?"

"Yeah, exactly. I, uh, was—"

"You should say it, Lenore. Say how it felt good too."

"What? Laura, you're silly."

"Oh, come on. Try it."

"Fine. I was, um, rubbing myself, between my legs, and it, uh, wow, it sure felt good."

"You were rubbing yourself?"

"Mm-hmm. I was rubbing myself."

"Hang on. I'm visualizing it."

"Laura, stop. You're being silly. Then, I tipped my head back and poured the last few drops into my mouth."

"So, you were rubbing yourself, and you had your mouth open, pointing up?"

"Mm-hmm. Yeah, for the wine, which is really quite—"

"Forget the wine for a sec. Lenore, while you were rubbing yourself, your mouth was open like you were offering to . . . what?"

"Uh, drink wine, like I said. It was—"

"No, no, no. Pretend you did what Amos said—you're just in panties and heels—and it isn't some chair that's busy between your thighs."

"Oh, Laura. You're too much sometimes."

"I've heard that before. So, anyway, it feels good, what's going on between your thighs, and you've got your mouth open why?"

"Laura, I—"

"Remember, you're the center of attention. And at that Frat Chat 2, no one's even going to be nice about it. They'll have all that degrading drama going on, which I think you'll love."

"I will? Laura, I—"

"Oh yeah, I think you will. So, your mouth is open so you can . . . what?"

"Laura, I'm not saying it."

Laura laughed and said, "Oh yeah, you know what I mean. You should say it. You're being forced to . . . what?"

"Hmm. I have my mouth open because—"

"In just panties and heels, Lenore. Add that."

"Oh, Laura. I'm wearing only panties and heels, and I have my mouth open because they're forcing me to—"

The front door rattled and swung in, then closed with a soft thud.

"Laura, it's Amos—I have to go! Bye!"

She tapped the phone, then laid it down, not waiting for Laura to respond. There were only two footsteps, then silence and no sign of Amos yet.

Softly, to herself, Lenore said, almost in a whisper, "They're all forcing me to . . . oh, Laura."

She listened to the silence for a few more seconds.

"To . . . suck."

Her sigh was long and deep and led to a soft giggle. With one hand again on the wine bottle, she looked up and saw Amos looking back at her from the kitchen entrance.

* * *

Looking first at the empty wine glass in one of his hands, then at the bottle in the other, Lenore said, "Good. You saved some for me."

His eyes quickly took in the half-full bottle on the table, then turned up to hers again.

"You, uh, seem to be doing pretty well on that bottle of yours."

"Yeah, Amos, I, um, I've been sucking down my share of that."

"I see that. Well, it's quite good. May I?"

She tipped her head toward his seat and said, "Sure. Pull up a chair. These chairs are, uh, nice. Comfortable, I mean."

"Right," he said while sitting, then he placed his bottle beside hers.

"Lenore, I—"

"You should just make up your mind what you like. That's what you were about to say, right?"

"Uh, well, no. Um, it's, I'll admit, a curious and confusing situation, and one might say that it's even—"

"Amos. Pour yourself more, take a drink, then start again."

"Uh . . . sure."

He rattled the bottle on the rim of his glass as he poured it nearly to the top. It took some care to raise it up, and he allowed himself a few deep mouthfuls of it before setting down the glass.

"Better?"

"Uh, yeah. Uh-huh. It's just, it's like wine, in a way, when one tastes it and likes it, and one can—"

"Stop, Amos. Let's try questions and answers. Here's a simple one: do you like me being modest, dressed the way I am now or even all that pajamas and robe stuff?"

"Well, yeah, Lenore. It's adorable. Truly. It's a good, wholesome look, and it shows that you don't feel any need to display, uh, everything. I mean, anything. I mean, it covers up a lot of—"

"Stop. Next question: do you want me to be a slut?"

"Well, Lenore, I was just saying that because, uh . . ."

"Yeah?"

"Because you, uh, when you, you know, when you—"

"Right. You heard me through the door, when I was just messing around for fun. That's why? Because you heard that?"

"Uh, yeah. That's when. Yep. Through the, uh, door. The bedroom door."

She squinted at him and gave quick glances also to the wine she was pouring for herself.

"I see. So, you want me to be a slut."

"Well, I'm not actually saying exactly that, Lenore. I, uh, it's a fun word to say, and it's a fun word to hear you say, that's all, and you—"

She waved her hand, then let him stare for a second of silence.

"You just told me to walk around in panties and heels. Remember that?"

He laughed and said, "Well, a slut would—"

"So, you do want me to be a slut?"

"Uh, Lenore, dressing like that, for fun, doesn't mean you actually have to do any more than dress like . . ."

"Like a slut?"

"Uh, yeah, it's just—"

"What if I decide I want to act like a slut too?"

"Lenore, you, uh, would be a remarkable, one might say tantalizing, slut, whether you dress like—"

"So, Amos, you'd like me to traipse around the house, looking like a slut. But you don't ever want me to actually behave like a slut?"

"Uh, I guess. I mean, even if you did, like, just once—be a real slut—that doesn't mean you would have to keep—"

"What are you talking about? You're babbling, Amos."

"Uh, you wouldn't have to do like you said last night. You said—"

"I remember what I said. I said if I wanted to be a slut, I would. Anytime I wanted to. And you wouldn't even have to know."

She grinned at his blank stare.

"I mean, if you're pushing me to be a slut, Amos, I might as well be a total slut, right?"

"No one's pushing you to be a, um, slut, Lenore."

"So, you're pushing me to be modest all the time?"

"No! It's just that you're modest, like how you're dressed now, and I can imagine you being, well, slutty, like if you were—"

"Walking around in just panties and heels?"

"Yeah, that. Or if you—"

"Let my hair down too?"

"Uh, yeah, that would—"

"I'd want to look like a slut, too, wouldn't I, if I was the star attraction at a wild sex party?"

His jaw almost hit the table, and his blinks were slow and perfectly timed, his eyes focused on hers.

"Uh, a wild, um, sex party. Yeah. Like that."

"Okay, Amos, if that's what you want. I'll be the star attraction, a total slut, at a sex party that—"

"I'm not saying that!"

"What the hell are you saying, then?"

"I don't know, Lenore. It's just, you can be both, and both are, uh, something unbelievable, and you—"

"Amos, this is exhausting. You need to figure out what you want."

He stared down at his wine glass and said, "Uh, yeah. Maybe I'll just go, uh, do some preparation work."

"Huh? For what?"

"I got invited to a college event this Friday, Lenore. One of the regents invited me personally. It's all about a promotion."

"Oh, well, congrats. You deserve it—you're good at what you do. Should I plan to—"

"I asked, and he, uh, said there's no guest invitation. Sorry. I think it's just a boring university formality kind of thing."

"Oh. Well, sure. And you're preparing?"

"Just, uh, trying to get my thoughts straight on it. You know, trying to anticipate their questions."

"Good," she said while watching him refill his glass. "Run along and do some prep work."

He stood, met her gaze for a second, then turned and left for the living room.

Chapter 7 – Star of a Wild Sex Party

Lenore tiptoed toward the entry to the living room and leaned out just enough to see Amos, planted at his end of the couch and immersed in one of many sheets of notes.

"Good," she said while walking in, "my seat's open."

He looked up, laughed gently, and said, "Well, of course, Lenore. Always. Hey, I know I've been silly about all of that, uh, stuff. I hope you don't hate me."

With the remote control in her hand, wrapped in flannel pajamas and buried under the thick fabric of a long robe, Lenore plopped down at the couch's other end.

"I don't hate you, Amos."

She focused on the muted TV, clicking to and rejecting one channel after another. The clock, on the wall and patiently counting out the seconds of their lives, used the room's silence to show that it took its work seriously.

Her eyes remained on the quiet display of rapidly changing images, and she said, "It's confusing for me too."

"It is?"

She rattled the remote onto the end table beside her and turned toward him.

"Well, yeah. I mean, that's quite a pair of—Amos, look at me."

He grinned before taking his eyes from the soft mounds her breasts were forming under all of the modest layering.

"Quite a pair of *styles*—the modest and the, uh, other one—and you're not being at all clear what you like. You used to just want modest. That's what you'd plastered all through your profile, remember?"

"I remember. Uh, yeah, I did. It's just, uh, I saw you, and I heard you, and—"

"You said you heard me through the door. Sure. What do you mean you saw me?"

"Oh, uh, hmm."

"Amos."

"You, uh . . . when you dropped the blanket before, and your breasts were just, you know, they were—"

Lenore laughed and said, "That was hardly slutty, Amos. Kind of naked, sure, but not slutty."

"I guess you're right. It's just my, uh, imagination, then. That's all."

"Hmm."

She rose up, then turned and shuffled along between the couch and the coffee table until she was right in front of him.

"What are you doing, Lenore?"

"Shh."

Holding his gaze as he stared up at her, she loosened her belt enough that she could pull both sides of the robe down over her shoulders. She grinned at his eyes fixing on the large, round mounds under her buttoned-up pajama top.

"Lenore, you—"

"What's under this pajama shirt, Amos?"

"I, uh, your nightgown. It's—"

"Are you sure?" she said and started to unbutton it.

"You, uh, you always—"

"Maybe that's too modest for a woman like me."

She worked open another two buttons, and he saw the smooth skin of her chest and the beginning of her cleavage.

"Lenore, you don't have to, I mean, you—"

"Call me a slut," she said while holding both sides of the unbuttoned shirt.

"Lenore, I shouldn't joke about—"

"I'm a slut," she said. "Mm, it feels good to say it. I'm a slut, Amos."

"You, you're really—"

"Mm, take a look," she said and pulled the cloth all the way to both sides, baring her breasts completely. "This is what sluts do. Tell me I have to be your slut."

"What? Lenore, I never should have—"

"Tell me I'm not good for anything else—just sex."

"Lenore, you—"

"Do I look like the star of a wild sex party? Am I slutty enough?"

"You, you shouldn't—"

"Say it."

He swallowed hard as his eyes went from one to the other many times, then he looked up and saw her grin and serious eyes.

"You, uh, yeah. You're very slutty. You're a slut, Lenore."

"It's all I'm good for?"

He started reaching for her breasts, then let his hands drop onto his lap again.

"Yeah. Nothing else."

"Why aren't you taking what you want? A slut never says no."

"I can't. I mean, you—"

She scoffed and snapped her shirt together, hiding them away.

"Oh, Amos," she said as she stepped out from near his legs, "you don't know what you want. There, I'm all safe and modest again."

"Maybe we should just, uh, go to bed and—"

"You're in your bed—that couch. Have a good night, Amos."

While cinching up her belt, she left the room without looking back.

* * *

She'd made no effort to keep quiet the closing of her bedroom door, then the clicking of the lock. She paused there, her thick robe back in place and cushioning her as she leaned into the door and looked at the empty bed and soft glow of dim lamps on the twin nightstands.

A glance down at her hands reflexively tightening the belt further led to a scoff, then a laugh, then a determined tugging to untie it completely. And her quick turn to look at the door wiped the laugh away and replaced it with a frown.

"Dammit, Amos. You're pushing me. Oh, you're leaving me no choice."

She looked toward the bed, reached for the light switch, then paused before clicking off the lamps.

"Oh, you do want to see, don't you? All of you?"

Her hand left the switch to again hold one side of the loosened robe.

"You want to see your . . . slut?"

Her slippers got kicked off to the side, then she walked carefully toward the bed, stopping when her knees were pressed up against it.

"That's part of the fun, right? Watching your slut do all the things you're forcing her to do?"

Two palms on the soft blanket helped her rest her knees on the floor, and she worked the robe down over her shoulders, then off completely, and she let it drop off to the side.

"Oh, I don't think I should, but if you insist."

Still kneeling, she hurried to unbutton her shirt, then pulled it open, baring them entirely.

"Hmm, I suppose I could."

She twisted herself from side to side, watching as her breasts swayed to the left and right, then looked back up at the bed.

"Okay. I know I have to."

She eased the shirt down over her shoulders, then straightened her arms and let it drop quietly to the floor.

"Oh, of course. You'd all like that better."

Using both hands, she made quick work of removing every pin and clip and band from her tight lump of hair, then fluffed it all back.

"Oh, uh, okay."

She held her breasts, supporting them and lifting them slightly, pointing them toward her admirers.

"Like this?"

She paused to imagine their answers.

"Oh, I sure am on my knees. Uh-huh. I know what you're going to make me do."

They didn't dispute it.

"You can tell, can't you? That I'm a slut? Nothing but a worthless slut?"

She listened and nodded to their agreeing with that, then she looked lower, toward the lap of one whose legs were on either side of her as she knelt there, hair down and holding her bare breasts.

"If I have to. If you're making me."

She leaned forward, parting her lips and licking each one. But she paused, still holding her breasts.

"I have to say it too? Watching me do it isn't enough—you want me to say it too?"

That's what they wanted.

"You love degrading me, too, don't you?"

They sure did.

"Yes, that's all I deserve. I'm just a worthless slut. All I'm good for is . . ."

They waited, one obviously more eager than the rest.

". . . is sucking. That's all I'm good for—to kneel and suck."

She smiled at the unanimous agreement.

"Mm, and I'm so worthless that I'm going to suck all of you."

She listened to their laughter, then one voice more impatient.

"Oh, yeah, I should shut up. A slut like me should just shut up and suck."

Chapter 8 – I'd Have to Say What I Am

Tuesday morning's first light slipped quietly into the bedroom, unnoticed by Lenore huddled under a layer of sheets and blankets. The first round of soft rapping on the door caused her to stir, lick her lips and mumble, then only shift around in the warm pile.

The second set of taps, louder than the first, got her eyes open, and they focused first on the alarm clock on the nightstand.

"Oh, shit."

She stretched, arching her back and groaning, then mumbled, "Hmm, good dreams."

One loud knock broke her reverie, and she swung her legs out and stood, facing the mirror above her dresser.

"Now, see? That's how to sleep—no need to wrap everything up in flannel and—"

Amos gave the door another pound and said, "I, uh, have to get my clothes. I'm about to run out the door. Come on, Lenore."

"Coming."

On the way, she kicked aside her slippers and panties, then picked up the robe. She'd just started to drive an arm into a sleeve, then she stopped and laughed softly.

"Oh, what the hell."

Instead of wearing the long garment, she only held it in front of her, carefully arranged to allow the sight of skin, bare skin, on both sides of it.

A quick flick of the lock, a snap to turn the doorknob, and she pulled the door in just a bit and took a few steps back. Amos leaned his head into the room, and she scoffed silently at his eyes traveling all the way down, then all the way up.

"Work? Clothes?"

"Oh, uh, yeah. I'm almost late already. I'll just . . ."

He reached around for the hook, and she didn't hide her laugh at his hand fumbling around, missing all of it as he tried to take in more of her naked body behind a thick robe.

"Amos. You wore that yesterday, and you wore it last Friday too. Come on. Get something fresh and clean."

He gave up on snagging the hanging clothing and stepped all the way into the room.

"Uh, yeah. Two times is enough."

"Hmm."

"Oh, you're still—"

"A slut? That's how you're starting the day, Amos?"

"Uh, I was going to say you're still waiting to do the laundry."

"Hmm. Sure. Look, we should just get going. Grab some fresh stuff out of the closet."

"Uh, yeah. I should."

She leaned back into the dresser and kept the robe draping over most of the view, watching him quickly grab some items, then walk back toward the door.

He laughed weakly and said, "You, uh, you're not wearing that to work, are you?"

"Why, Amos, this old robe?"

She gave him a second, just enough time to tip his head.

"Yeah, just to cover the panties and heels that I'll wear around the office."

He scoffed and chuckled while looking down at the floor.

"I deserve that."

She let him continue looking down for a few seconds, then he held her gaze, squinting at her.

"Unless you're, you're not really—"

"Amos, get out. Go get dressed. Clock's ticking."

"Right. Uh, yeah. Okay."

He pulled the door shut with a soft boom.

"God."

She spun toward the dresser, still holding the robe in front of her, and snatched up her phone. A quick scroll got her to Laura's number, but she left it to view her photos.

Another quick scroll got her to the one that she'd sent to Laura, the one showing a lot of skin—bare breasts and more.

"Oh, hmm. I could do better."

She let the robe fall, then got the camera ready. The view in the mirror showed her entirely naked, as much as could be seen, and her hair down and wild from sleeping on it.

Holding the camera up, she pointed from the side, laughed at the difficulty of getting a shot with her face close but her breasts visible too. Holding it steady, she pursed her lips and wiggled an index finger in between them.

She held the pose, looking toward the lens, and said, "Hmm, that would be a good one. Or maybe this."

She tipped her head back, stuck out her tongue, then laid the wet finger on it.

But she didn't snap that photo either. She only laughed and put the phone back down, then bent to retrieve the robe.

"A video would be better. Ooh, a video at that party—the Frat Chat 2. I'd say my name. That would be kind of degrading, just that."

She brushed her hair back and looked into her reflected eyes.

"I'd have to say what I am and what I'm being forced to do. Hmm."

With a loud scoff, she picked up the phone again.

* * *

After a scroll to get to Laura's contact info, she typed out a text, saying how she almost took a racy photo of herself.

Seconds later, she tapped to take the call from Laura.

"Send the photo, Lenore. I need a boost to get my day started."

"That's a boost for you?"

"Well, sure. You're hot as hell. What kind of photo were you going to take?"

"Oh, Laura, I was, uh, doing something. Naked."

"Ooh, tell me more."

"I was, um, sucking my finger."

"You were sucking. Say that. Forget the finger."

"Laura, you're terrible. Fine. I was sucking."

"Mm, naked and sucking. Sure, it was just your finger, but how did that feel?"

"Like I was sucking a finger."

"No, try again. Use your imagination. Imagine you're at that party, the Frat Chat 2, and they're forcing you to do it. They'll probably make you talk about it too. They'll want to hear you say it."

"Hey, I never said I was going to do that party."

"You're thinking about it, though, right?"

"God, Laura, I can't stop thinking about it."

"Yeah, I know. That's why you're doing it."

"No, I don't think so. It's fun to imagine, but I couldn't."

"It's too late for that, Lenore. It's like an avalanche. No one can stop it—especially not you."

"What are you talking about? I turned down that Frat Chat, didn't I?"

"Uh-huh. Yeah. You started the fire, Lenore. Tell me you don't feel it. Tell me that you being used at the Frat Chat 2 doesn't sound inevitable."

Lenore lowered her robe, giving her a clear, unblocked view of her breasts, and she used her free hand to brush some of her hair forward, leaving waves of it on her chest, tickling her where—

"Yeah," Laura said after a few seconds of silence, laughing. "Uh-huh. We both know it."

"Laura, I, um . . ."

"Hmm, even that, the way you sound kind of hesitant. Oh, they're going to love you."

She gave one of her breasts a gentle squeeze, then said softly, "They, uh, yeah, I think they will. I mean, they would."

"Especially if they want you to talk, to say what they tell you to say."

"Oh, Laura, come on."

"Hey, pretend I'm one of them, and I'm shooting a video of you."

"Laura, stop. It's too early for this. I need to get going and—"

"It'll only take a second. So, the camera's on, and I'm telling you this: 'Say your name, then tell us what you love doing for all of us.'"

"Laura . . ."

"Uh-huh. You want to do this. Go on, Lenore."

"Fine. Um, my name is Lenore, and I—"

"You know we're getting a perfect view of you, right? Anyone who sees this will know who you are?"

"Laura, you're silly. Um, yeah, I want everyone to know that I'm Lenore, and I'm . . ."

"Say it. You want to."

"I'm Lenore, and I'm nothing but a worthless slut."

"And what are you going to do now, you worthless slut?"

"Laura, stop. Oh, fine."

Lenore cleared her throat, then said, "I'm just a slut, and I'm going to, um, suck."

"Yes, you certainly are. Everyone?"

"Mm-hmm. I'm going to suck everyone."

"Perfect," said Laura. "They really are going to love you. Wait, that's not right. They're going to love using you and degrading you, treating you like a worthless slut. I think you'll love it, Lenore."

"I, um . . ."

"Uh-huh. Oh, yeah. Hey, Lenore?"

"Yeah?"

"Are you still naked in your room?"

"Uh-huh. Why?"

"Before you get dressed for work, I'm telling you to touch yourself and watch in the mirror."

"Laura . . ."

"You'll do it. And when you really get things going, look yourself in the eye and say that you love being a worthless slut."

A few quiet seconds passed as Lenore studied her nakedness in the mirror, how her hair fell softly over her breasts, and how her free hand was already caressing its way down her belly.

"Mm-hmm. Yeah, Lenore. Have a nice day."

Lenore scoffed at the call ending, then set down her phone.

"I don't think you're wrong, Laura. Not about any of it."

And she didn't get dressed right away.

Chapter 9 – Crave Something You Don't Have

"Class!" Amos yelled to get himself heard over the clamor in the cavernous lecture hall. "We should get started."

Only a few of them seemed to agree, and Amos looked around at the continuing conversations until he met the calm stare of Lindsey in the front row. He gave her a wave and got a smile and wave in return.

"Okay," he said from his lectern at a focal point of the rising circular rows of seats, "let's give some attention to the reading assignment for today. One of the themes, which I'm sure all of you noticed, is the nature of self-reflection—understanding one's self. How if you devote some attention to calm study of yourself, you, as a natural consequence, have less attention to focus on others. Basically, you tend to leave them alone more. Maybe respect them more."

"A counterpoint," said someone high up in the back of the room, strategically close to the exit doors.

Amos looked up, scoffed, then gave Lindsey a quick glance. He only grinned at her shaking head, then looked back up at the young man in a t-shirt and ball cap.

"Yes, of course, Emilio. Where would we be without your counterpoints? No one in here believes you need my invitation or even permission so please, counter the points."

"Sure. Since you invited me and gave your—"

"I did neither. You have everyone's attention. Is it more from your eventual book, the theories on hot and cold and the like?"

"Ah, 'the like.' I believe you're onto something, professor. And yes, it's all twisted in with the hot and cold too."

"Remind us," called someone from across the room.

Someone else yelled out, "We don't remember all your nonsense."

"Nonsense?" Emilio said, then looked down at Amos.

Amos shrugged and said, "Could be, right? We'll figure it out as we go. Proceed, please."

"Yeah. It's like this: when you travel from too hot to too cold, it's a satisfying thing. You crave that cold after being so hot."

"Divinity," said Amos. "Which we're not permitted to mention at this university."

"Exactly. But it gets better. If you can manage to feel two contrasting conditions at the same time, like parking your ass in a hot tub on a frozen mountain, well, shit, then you got—"

He stopped to look around at a lot of them laughing, some shaking their heads, others mentioning his being expelled.

"Class," said Amos. "Yes, that language. Let's let him go, though. Emilio, proceed."

"Alright. So, the thing is, I can't be loyal to the cold, and I can't be loyal to the heat. You see that, right? If I park my, uh, self somewhere cold and never crave the heat, I'm missing out on any chance of soaking myself in . . ."

"Divinity?" said Amos.

"Yep. It's pretty simple: you have to crave something you don't have, and you have to let yourself reach out and grab it. That's it. That's the theory. There's no room anywhere for loyalty to anyone or anything."

Everyone sat silent, some turning to check Amos's reaction. His reaction was only to shake his head and stare up at Emilio.

"Well, that's a fascinating portion of convoluted rationalization," Amos said. "That could—"

"Wait," someone said in the front row, "I'm writing that down."

"What he said?" said Amos. "Or what—"

"What you said, Professor Amos," he said, still looking down and writing, then he looked up. "Got it."

"Well, that's, um, uh-huh. Alright. Emilio, I think you've got the essence of another chapter for your book."

"I agree. Maybe the chapters will never end, professor. Every time I blow off any kind of loyalty and take what I want, boom, there's another chapter."

"Uh-huh. Got it."

Amos ruffled around his notes, with many pairs of eyes studying him, then he looked up and said, "I have no idea what I was talking about."

From the back of the room, high up on the cascading rows, Emilio said, "We're out of time anyway!"

* * *

"My closet is deep, Shirley. There's no need to critique my wardrobe again."

"Oh, Lenore, I didn't mean anything by it. Can I compliment you, though? I mean, I could never pull that off."

"I'm sure someone could."

"What?"

Standing at the side of her desk, Lenore crossed her arms and scoffed.

"Nothing. You won't focus on your work until you've said your piece. So, let's hear it."

"That skirt is shorter than the one yesterday. It looks good, though, don't get me wrong. Still kind of professional and—"

"Kind of, Shirley? Come on. It's not that short."

"Oh, uh, you're right. And I don't think there's any accepted limit on how high a pair of heels can—"

"Shirley, maybe we should just get going with some actual business stuff, huh?"

"Right away. Uh, yeah. You want the door closed?"

"I sure do. Thanks."

Lenore watched the door get pulled shut and yield a satisfying latching with its mechanism.

"God," she muttered while tapping her phone. "Everyone's a critic and won't just leave me—Laura, hi."

"Hey, Lenore. You're at work?"

"Yeah, just got here. I just wanted to clear up that discussion about me, uh, you know, the Frat Chat 2. Laura, there's just no way."

"Hmm. Sure. Did you have fun before getting dressed?"

"Yeah, and I'm allowed. I can do that whenever I, uh, need to."

"Well, yeah. Of course. It's no big deal. What were you saying, though, while you were—"

Lenore laughed loud enough to stop her, then said, "It was just for fun, Laura. Oh yeah, I said some fun stuff. But really, alone in my room, just playing around is one thing. It's a whole different deal to be . . . you never even said where, did you? For the Frat Chat 2?"

"I can tell you more if you say you'll do it. Come on, Lenore, I know you want to. Remember who you're talking to? I've learned what makes you tick, and I've seen even more lately."

"Well, sure, you got me thinking about things. But Laura, doing all that with a bunch of strangers, being treated like—"

"More like mistreated. Forced, Lenore."

"Yeah, all of that. Look, it does sound exciting, and I'm probably going more crazy than usual from Amos. He can't decide if he wants a saint or a tramp."

"Tramp, as in a slut?"

"Fine. Yeah, a slut. I should try to keep this engagement alive, but I don't know what he wants."

"It's more about what you want. We both know."

"Laura, no."

"Think of the sex, Lenore. Ooh, so much of it."

"Laura . . ."

"I know you want to be used, too, like an object. You said so. Just something soft and smooth and not good for anything else."

"I did say that, but—"

"You need some wild times, Lenore. It's too late for you to even believe anything else."

She sighed loudly enough for Laura to hear, then said, "I, uh, yeah. Kind of. I'm obsessing about it."

"Well, if you won't do the Frat Chat 2, then you should give yourself a little wild treat anyway."

"Like what?"

"Well, the easiest thing is to have an affair."

"Laura, I'm engaged."

"Yeah, for now, but do it anyway. Ooh, hey, with two guys at once."

"Laura, I can't do that."

"Sure you can. Hey, on your own bed at home too. Middle of the day, two strangers show up, Amos thinks you're at work, and you're on the bed being told what to do and doing it like there's no tomorrow."

"Laura, stop!"

"You're thinking about it. I can tell by your voice. Hey, and somehow, you get Amos tied to a chair in the room, and he gets to watch."

"What? That's—"

"Think of all the stuff they're making you do, Lenore. And the whole time, you're watching him, telling him—when your mouth isn't full—that you'll never do any of that for him."

"When my mouth isn't—"

"Yeah. Uh-huh. He'll have to watch you telling these two strange guys, that neither of you know, how you're just a slut, a dirty little slut. You can see it, Lenore. I know you can. All naked, your hair wild, maybe some heels on, and you're romping on the bed, doing everything they tell you, even calling yourself a worthless slut while looking at Amos."

Laura waited, and the quiet seconds ticked past.

"Laura . . ."

A few more silent moments crept along.

"Uh-huh. Got you," said Laura. "Try to deny that you need something wild. If not that, then the Frat Chat 2. Right?"

When Lenore started to laugh softly, Laura laughed with her.

"Oh my God, Laura. How do you come up with this stuff?"

"Well, shit, I'm your best friend. I think about what I'd love to do, then I know you'd love it too. Tell me you wouldn't."

The line stayed quiet for many long seconds.

"Yeah," said Laura. "Uh-huh. There's no way even you can stop it now. And Lenore?"

"Yeah?"

"You need to pick one of those."

"I do?"

"Mm-hmm. My advice? You need everything you'll get at the Frat Chat 2. Go with that."

"Oh my gosh."

Chapter 10 – No Divinity for You

"I already bought you one," Emilio said, then tipped his head toward the coffee cup resting on the picnic table.

Amos held his up, shook it lightly, then said, "Picked one up. I'll use that as a backup plan, though."

"Hey," Emilio said, laughing while Amos took a seat, "if one was hot and the other cold, we'd have ourselves a real-world thing going on. You know, for those theories of mine."

"Wait a second," said Amos. "If I'm happy with this hot coffee that I have, why would I care about the cold one? I mean, if that one really was cold."

"You do raise a good point. How about if yours is too hot and you get burned?"

"Oh, okay. Then, I'll want that colder one for my burnt and disfigured face?"

"Easy, there. Let's not get into disfigurement, alright? Look, I'm just trying to make sense of my theories too."

"Because philosophizing is hard work?"

"Yeah. That. Expanding a theory to cover everything isn't easy."

"No, I don't suppose so. I'm still trying to get that other thing, about wanting the hot to get hotter and the cold to get colder."

"Yeah, I'll have to keep lecturing on that."

"Good one, Emilio. I'm not sure it makes sense with coffee."

"Nope. Hey, maybe we get back to the roller coaster. If fast is good, you'll want it faster. If the car has a cool paint job, you'll want it even cooler. See how that works?"

"Yeah, that paint job. That makes sense. You give that car some better paint, Emilio, and it likes it, so it wants it even nicer."

"It does? The car does?"

"It could, I mean. It might want a lot more pinstriping."

"Yeah, I could see that. Like, too much?"

"Yeah, way too much. It might go crazy with the paint."

"Uh, sure. So then, you'd want it all plain again."

"Well, maybe. Yeah, plain is good too. Sometimes, perfectly plain seems just fine."

"Amos," Emilio said, shaking his head, "that little old car can't be both. You're trying to style it up like crazy, then make it as drab as it can be?"

"Well, I mean, if the car is all painted up and it's getting hotter and hotter, like burning hot, then—"

"Whoa, wait a sec. You're mixing things up. You're heating up the car now?"

"Well, I'm not. It's got a life of its own, you know? It's threatening to get way more paint, and it wants to get so hot that—"

"Easy, professor! Hey, it's just some silly theory, alright?"

"It's not that easy, Emilio! Once the paint is flying and the fires are flaming, no one can control the thing. But you know what else? You can't just peel off all of that paint and pack it in ice somewhere. I mean, you could but then, you kind of miss the paint, right? And the heat? Right? Right?"

"Whew, Amos, I don't know, man. Let's level this all back down to something simple: hot coffee or cold coffee."

"Okay, I'm with you."

"About time. Okay, you obviously can't handle drinking both of them at once. Alright, that's not the best example. You can't have a hot, tricked-out coaster car and have it all dingy and cold too. You, professor, sir, can't handle both."

"Because I'm, I mean, I'm—"

"You just can't. It's just not in you. So, Amos, you'll have to choose."

"Which means . . ."

"No divinity for you, my friend."

"Dammit."

Amos chugged the last of his coffee, then stood, and Emilio tried handing him the spare cup.

"It's hot too. You can handle it."

With a snort, Amos took the extra coffee and turned to begin his hike out of the park.

"Damn," Emilio muttered. "What's going on with him?"

* * *

Emilio finished his coffee while watching Amos hike away down one of the many paved walkways snaking all through the large square park surrounded by university buildings. He spun his head around when he heard his name called out.

"Emilio!"

"Hey, Lindsey. Fancy meeting you here."

"I go to this school, too, you know. Don't be dumb."

"Fine. I just meant this exact spot, right by my picnic table."

"Yours. Yeah. Hey, I just wanted to say I'm glad you're easing up on Professor Amos a little. He's a good guy. You don't need to torment him every class."

"He expects it."

"By now, maybe. Today was okay, though. Can I sit?"

"Why, of course. Plant that sweet—"

"Hey, don't waste your time," she said and sat, leaving a fair distance between them.

"Sure. If you say so."

"I do. You going to the pre-season game Friday?"

"Not a chance—not my kind of scene. But the main reason is I have a gig Friday, sort of helping out with a party."

"Bartender?"

"No, not like that. More of just a delivery guy. Hey, I might know of a party someday that you'd want to attend."

"Maybe. What kind?"

"If we do it, it'll be at a frat house. We like to line up one totally hot, eager babe to be the star. And she, just her by herself, takes on every single—"

"Oh, get a clue, Emilio. That's not the demo I'd want, even if I was in the mood for a perverted scene like that."

He paused to look over at her, and all she did was shrug.

"Oh. Oh! You mean, you like—"

"Mm-hmm. Yeah. Don't tell Professor Amos—I think he has a crush on me."

"Get out of here. No way. Amos?"

"No, not really. He's just kind of sweet. Don't confuse the man."

"Shit, he's confused enough on his own. Alright, forget that party. We were talking about another kind of chat party, one where, again, a woman is the perverted star, and she takes on every *girl* that wants that kind of attention."

"What? What is wrong with people? That's a stupid idea, Emilio. Even the regular way, with her taking on all the frat guys. God."

He blew out a deep breath and looked around at the crowded park.

"So, I guess you're saying that your answer would—"

"Would be a big goddamn no. Yeah, you're guessing right. I think you're just messing with me anyway. This is a quiet college town, and nonsense like that doesn't happen here."

He coughed and said, "No, you're absolutely right—I mess with everyone. The concept is sound, though. Maybe we'll get something like that going someday."

"Doubtful. You can barely organize your ass out of freshman year."

"Point taken. Look, this conversation has about died a miserable death. But hey, if you ever see me here again, feel free to plant that sweet ass of yours right here and keep me company, alright?"

"Okay, look," she said, scoffing loudly. "It's sweeter than you can imagine, and imagining is all you'll ever do. I'm leaving. Keep dreaming about your dumbass party ideas."

* * *

He'd pulled the door open as smoothly and slowly as he could, but the tiny, vigilant bells mounted at the top tinkled anyway. And the clerk, the only living person in the liquor store at the time, looked up.

Right at Amos, who gave her a quick wave, then hurried over to his preferred shelves, where his and Lenore's favorites bottles were waiting patiently.

With one in each hand, he approached the young woman at the register and said, "Hey, me again."

He clunked them down while she said, "Yeah. You're more of a regular lately than the regulars."

"Uh, one might say that an employee here probably shouldn't offer such comments."

She shrugged and said, "Yeah. They even have a policy about that. Still, I'd risk this minimum wage paradise just like that."

She snapped her fingers high above her.

Amos scoffed but smiled, too, as he dug out his wallet.

"Rest assured that I won't file a complaint with management."

"Decent of you. Hey, you, uh, you teach over at the—"

"Yes. I'm a psychology professor. Kind of new."

She took a few bills from his outstretched hand and said, "Not like I'm spying or anything. Someone just mentioned that you know your stuff, teaching and all."

"Oh, well, that's a welcome comment. I do make an effort to be effective."

She'd been setting the bottles into a brown paper bag, and she nudged it closer to him along with his change.

"Uh, yeah. Wine helps with that, I'd bet."

"Hey," Amos said, laughing for the first time, "*that* I might report."

"Shit," she said, laughing too, "there goes my promising career selling booze to intellectuals."

"Nice. Well said."

"You take care, professor."

"If only it were just a matter of choice."

"I hear you. Hey, you can choose to give those damn bells on the door a good shake."

"I could. And I believe I shall. See you later."

Chapter 11 – A Pair of Red Shoes

Before pushing in the front door, Amos hesitated, then spun himself around to look out over the lawn, scanning along the row of houses across the street. It was only a second before he moved the brown paper bag between him and the door, then waved to a neighbor with the hand holding the keys.

Leaning backwards, he swung the door and stepped inside, then quietly set the keys on the high wooden table nearby. Before closing the door, he looked and listened, but there was no sound and no sign of Lenore.

Still listening and walking quietly, he entered the kitchen, saw signs on the table of Lenore having come home from her office, then placed the bag with two wine bottles on the counter and up against the refrigerator.

He was about to turn away, then he noticed the bottle from the night before sitting there, showing through its dark glass that it would take only minimal effort and resolve to finish it off.

With that bottle in one hand, while the other was wiggling out its loose cork, he walked toward the table and stood over the notebook, cellphone, and car keys that she'd left there.

He tipped back the bottle for a quick sip, then froze at a muffled laugh from somewhere in the house. His first step in that direction landed, but he froze again and leaned to look under the table.

Where a pair of red shoes with heels higher than Lenore would normally wear were lying where they'd been kicked off.

"Huh."

Still gazing at the shoes and swirling the bottle in slow circles, he paused at hearing what could have been a quick laugh again.

"Hmm."

The bottle got tipped back and left like that until it could offer no more, then he set it on the counter and began a silent hike toward whoever was in the house and unsuccessful at keeping their mirth contained.

* * *

A glance down the hallway gave Amos a clear view of their bedroom door. It was closed.

He trod carefully toward it, then locked his hand in midair before it could get a grip on the doorknob. Instead, he let his arm drop to his side, and he leaned close, giving an ear its best chance of gathering any info possible through the solid wood.

He held his breath at the absolute silence beyond the door, then shifted his ear closer, as much as he dared, at what sounded like Lenore's voice.

Steadying himself with a hand on each side, he leaned closer but couldn't understand anything she was saying.

But she did have some sort of pattern to it: she spoke a sentence, then paused as if listening, then spoke again.

"Huh," he whispered.

Lenore's voice had halted and hadn't continued in more than just a moment, then Amos heard the unmistakable creaking of the bed's structure and rustling of blankets.

And he didn't wait to hear any more that was said and especially not for any footsteps approaching the door.

He scurried just as quickly and quietly as he could back to the kitchen and as he neared the counter by the fridge, he heard the bedroom door rattle open.

After reaching for, then leaving alone the bottle that he'd just emptied, he then lifted up instead a skillet that had been drying in the rack.

He turned toward the entryway just as the footsteps halted.

"Amos. You're home."

Chapter 12 – I Want More

"Lenore. Yeah, I just got home, and I was, uh, going to see if I could, I don't know, maybe—"

After a sharp laugh, she said, "Amos, what exactly were you planning with that skillet?"

He stared at it even after he'd set it on the counter and said, "Uh, maybe not with this. Just, uh, putting it away."

"I see. Oh, I see what looks like more wine too. Good."

"Yes, I stopped on my walk home. One might say that a house can never have too much wine in reserve."

"Uh, yeah, one might say that. I'll take a glass if you're pouring."

"Well, sure."

He turned and rifled around in the bag, then stopped to listen when Lenore said, "Maybe take it to the table, and I'll get going on some actual dinner."

"Oh, that sounds good. Sure."

She leaned against the door jamb, giving him room to maneuver toward the table with an unopened bottle and two glasses. When he paused and leaned over, making it obvious that he was checking out her shoes under the table, she held her breath.

"We have days at the office," she said, hurrying to snatch them up, "where we're all encouraged to, uh, take it up a notch. In a professional way, still, of course."

"Of course," he said, a step away to give her room.

Standing, holding the shoes, she said, "Not the most comfortable, I can assure you."

"Oh, uh, one wouldn't think so, no."

She placed them on the floor near the exit, then said, while walking back toward the refrigerator, "Screw actual dinner. Frozen pizza sounds about right."

She flipped the oven knob to heat it up.

"Screw?"

"Well, you know. *Forget* actual dinner."

"Ah. Hey, here's your wine."

"Thanks."

She walked over, drank half of it, then set the glass back near the bottle.

"Good. I like that variety. We should mix it up, though—go through the shelves wherever you've been buying this stuff. You know, try a lot of different ones."

She was already unboxing a frozen pizza, then sliding it into the oven, and Amos sipped his wine and watched her. The oven door got thumped shut, and Lenore turned and crossed her arms.

"See? That's how a pro does dinner."

"I couldn't do it," said Amos, grinning. "I mean, I could probably get it in the oven."

"So, that's all it takes."

"Well, I mean, it might be upside down. Then, I'd burn it."

She was laughing and walking toward her seat when he continued.

"Then, I'd drop it on the floor too. No, I just, uh, couldn't."

"You sure can drink wine, though," she said as she sat. "Me too."

"I think that means you—"

"Want more. Yeah, Amos," she said, not looking at either the bottle or her half-empty glass, "I want more."

* * *

He poured wine into Lenore's glass, stopping as the level neared the top.

"More?"

"Mm-hmm. More."

He laughed and kept going, finishing with a slow drip to get it so full that it couldn't be moved without spilling it.

"You get what you ask for," he said, flashing a smug smile as he set down the bottle.

"Do I? Hmm."

She used both hands to hold her hair out of the way as she leaned forward, then touched her lips to the rim of the glass, causing the slightest of waves along the wet surface.

He scoffed when she fought to not grin while sucking at it, drawing down the level before backing away.

While she was lifting the glass, offering her own smug grin, Amos said, "That reminds me: out in the park, at lunchtime, having coffee with Emilio, we—"

"Amos," she said, the glass almost touching her bottom lip, "tell me that me sipping that wine didn't make you think of one of your students."

"Uh, he, um, no. Of course not. It's just that, the wine, it, uh, reminded me of coffee, and I—"

"Amos, relax. I'm just messing with you. Why would me doing that remind you of anyone? Stop being silly."

"Right. Yeah. Uh, never mind, then. It was just—"

"Amos, come on. What about your student?"

"Oh, you know, I'm always trying to learn my way around this town. The university, I mean."

He raised up his glass and finished a third of it.

"And, uh, he mentioned some kind of get-together that he said is kind of a regular thing. That's all. It just sounded, uh, kind of interesting."

"Well, it's a college town, Amos. Kids are probably having parties all the time."

"Yeah, uh, yep. This one had a memorable name, that's all. Kind of fits with the whole university scene, I suppose."

She raised her glass from the table but held it there and said, "What, pray tell, is the name of this particular party?"

"Pray tell? Uh, sure. He said it's called the Frat Chat."

She set the glass down slowly and carefully.

"It's just kind of an interesting name, Lenore."

"Uh, yeah, Amos. Frat makes sense. Chat, though?"

"Oh, that. Yeah. It's because there's a lot of conversation that goes on. Stuff like that."

"I see."

"You've lived here your whole life. Ever hear of something called a Frat Chat?"

"Huh. Um, I've heard of all kinds of things in this town. That sounds like a, I don't know, cultured event, so to speak."

"So, uh, you've heard of it? The Frat Chat?"

"You seem kind of interested in that party, Amos. What's going on?"

"Oh, nothing. I just, uh, you're from here, so I was just wondering . . ."

She kept her eyes on his as she emptied most of her glass.

"Well, everyone knows about the fraternities, so that's the 'Frat' part of it, right? And Chat? Well, Amos, you and I are chatting right now."

He stared at her calm gaze back at him for a few seconds, then scoffed and watched his hand slipping toward his own glass.

"Yeah," he said, looking down. "I've done some chatting."

"We chat all the time. Yeah. So?"

"I mean, at the Frat Chat. It's really a nice bunch of students there, and they—"

"Wait."

He waited, and the seconds crept past. The clock in the living room had ample opportunity to count them out.

"You're saying you went to that party, whatever you called it?"

"Oh, Lenore. You remember what I called it. Don't you?"

"Yeah, Amos. The, uh, Frat Chat. That's it, right?"

"Huh. Yeah, that's it. That's what they call it."

"So, how was it?"

"Oh, well, Emilio is quite a conversationalist. I think I've mentioned how he's kind of, uh, a philosopher. Or he wants to be. Or he thinks he—"

"Okay, I get it. He likes to talk. Chat, I mean."

"Yeah, Lenore, it's a, um, Chat."

"So, lots of good talk. It was good to have that Emilio character around then, I suppose."

"Uh, yeah. He sure does like to talk. Chat."

"You probably never let him out of your sight."

"Uh, what do you mean? He invited me, and I walked over with him, and we—"

"And you were with him the whole time?"

He tipped his head and squinted at her, then looked down and scoffed.

"Yeah. Sure. You already know that, though, right?"

"Amos?"

He looked up.

"How would I already know that? What are you talking about?"

"Oh, uh, just because I already said it. That's all."

"I see. He's so fun to talk with that you never let him out of your sight?"

"What an odd thing to ask. Is there some specific reason why—"

"Hey, I'm just trying to understand what this party, this so-called Frat Chat, is all about."

"Fine. Yes, and I think I've already said so. Yeah, I was with him the whole time. Anything else you want to say about the Frat Chat?"

"How could there be? Amos, you're acting strange, and it's making me uncomfortable."

She crossed her arms but kept from spilling what was left in her glass.

"Uh, yeah," he said, observing her hostile posture. "The porch?"

"Yep. Take the bottle. I'll call you when your share of the pizza is burned."

"Uh, burned?"

"To a crisp. Your share. Yeah."

* * *

Lenore held her wine glass close to her lips and listened until Amos had slammed shut the front door on his forced evacuation to the porch.

She chugged the remaining wine, clinked down the glass, and said, "Dammit, Amos. That was you."

Following a quick look at the clock, she jumped up and hustled toward the oven. After fumbling for a platter and a fork, she dragged the pizza off of the rack, then set the tray on the burners.

"No, dammit. You don't get any, Amos. You're never eating again."

She hurried to roll the cutter across it in several directions, then tossed the cheesy tool into the sink. A wide, steaming slice on a plate accompanied her back to her seat, where she refilled her glass before doing anything else.

Groaning at the hot cheese burning her lip, she laughed as she held her mouth open, blowing air in and out.

"Not the reason I want to hold my mouth open," she said, making herself laugh even more.

While still chewing, she gave a listen to the front door, which stayed quiet, then tapped her phone.

"Hey, Lenore, what's up?"

"Damn that Amos. That's what."

"What now?"

"Oh, I, uh, don't want to think about it. Trust me, though, he deserves a shitload of my wrath."

"Ooh, a shitload. Now, we're getting somewhere. He called you a harlot, didn't he?"

"Oh, if only. No, Laura, he—I'm sure that he—never mind. I just had to tell you how sick of him I am right now."

"But you won't say why?"

"Uh-uh. Maybe some other time."

"Right. Well, I'm happy to chat with you, doing some bitching about—"

"Chatting. Yeah. You said there's something called, uh, the Frat Chat 2?"

"Oh, there sure is, hot babe that could be my twin. Mm-hmm."

"I want to hear more but first, tell me about the first one, the original Frat Chat."

"What do you want to know? God, they really are sex-starved animals, Lenore. Each and every one just wanted to devour me. I've never had so much—"

"You said there was someone named Emilio there?"

"Uh-huh. He was a trip too. What a character. He sure did love what I was doing for him, though."

"It wasn't just him, though, right? You really did do two at a time?"

"Oh, I did worse than that, girlie. Try three."

"But the third, I mean, he had to—"

"Uh-huh. It's not the easiest thing to arrange, let me tell you. Oh, Lenore, you want to talk about feeling like a bad girl? Hmm . . ."

"You're unbelievable. Yeah, that would do it. But back to Emilio. You were blindfolded, and you were, um . . ."

"You really need to start using that word, Lenore. Say it. Say what I was doing to that stud."

Lenore laughed, then said, "You were . . . sucking him."

"Yes. Oh, I sure was. For a long time too. Damn, he was playing with me like I was the best sex toy he could imagine."

"Huh. You probably are."

"I'd bet you are, too, Lenore. Oh, mm-hmm. Yep."

"Okay, so, you're . . . sucking him, and you're blindfolded, so you couldn't see the other guy, the one that was with him?"

"Oh, you want to hear again what that stud did? Alright. I didn't want to go along with it at first, but Emilio wanted to take photos of me, um, in action."

"Oh my gosh. He really did, while you were . . ."

"Say it."

Lenore chuckled and said, "While you were sucking him."

"Yep. Like that. You know what else? He took that damn blindfold off of me. Lenore, he got my face as clear as can be, while I was . . ."

"Sucking him."

"Uh-huh. A video too. Oh, God, the things he had me saying."

"Hold that thought. I want to hear about that. But the other guy, what was he doing?"

"He was behind me the whole time, while I was on my hands and knees and getting used like a sex toy by Emilio."

"And when your blindfold was off, you saw him, right? The other guy?"

"No, I never did. That's kind of exciting, Lenore. To get screwed like that and never even see who it is. God, I'm such a pervert, I know."

"Oh, well, compared to everything else, what the hell?"

"Right? Anyway, no, I never saw him. Felt him, though. He seemed reluctant, so I teased him good. Wiggled my ass around until my cheerleader skirt dropped, then I stood up against the bed, kept my legs apart and straight—I know that's a sight—and he was just holding my waist."

"That's all he did? He just—"

"Oh, hell no, Lenore. He got a good grip on me and planted that thing as deep as he could."

"He did? He really did?"

"Well, what do you think, Lenore? That's the whole point, right?"

"Uh, yeah. Uh-huh. Then, what? They left, and more came in?"

"What can I say? I was a sex toy. You'll be a sweet sex toy, too, you know."

Lenore groaned, then said, "If I'd taken your place, yeah."

"Yeah, but you know that's not what I mean."

"Oh. The Frat Chat 2?"

"Mm-hmm. Seriously, they're going to just love you. Well, in a degrading kind of way."

"Degrading, huh?"

"Uh, yeah. Maybe sort of abusive too."

"Hmm."

"I don't hear you complaining."

"I'm so pissed at Amos right now, I can't even tell you. Even degrading sex sounds good."

"I think you even like the degrading part of it. I can tell, Lenore."

"I, um, I mean, just the thought of all that sex and—"

"And when you're there, you're there for whatever they want. You don't even think of saying no, right?"

"I don't want to."

"Good. And you'll play along with whatever drama they got going on?"

"Sure. I could."

"So, if one of them calls you a worthless slut, and you're down on your knees, what are you going to do?"

"Laura . . ."

"Say it. You know what you'll do."

"I'll, um, start sucking. If that's what I'm told to do."

"Yeah, you sure will, and you'll love it. And if there's a camera recording you, and they want you to stop just long enough to look into it and say what you are and what you like doing, what will you say?"

"Laura, you're too much sometimes. Fine. I'll, um, hold it close, so it's in the shot, too, and I'll say that I'm nothing but a worthless slut."

"And?"

"And all I'm good for is sucking."

"Because you're . . ."

"Soft and warm and wet and only good for sex."

"That was pretty good! One more time, and say your name."

"What? I'd never do that!"

"You're pissed at Saint Amos, right?"

"He's no saint. Just someone that's pissing me off so—"

"So, this is how you get back at him. Just feeling like that video might get out will be a thrill."

She gave Lenore a few seconds, but she stayed silent.

Without laughing, Laura said, "Good—still no arguing. Now, imagine I'm there, and I'm holding all of your hair, and I say this right in your ear: 'Do as you're told, Lenore, you worthless slut.'"

Lenore coughed once, then said, "My name is Lenore. I'm just a worthless slut, and I love, more than anything, to suck."

"That was good—you did what you were told. One more time. Remember, I'm holding your hair and telling you right in your ear. Oh, and Lenore, you're naked, right?"

"Well, yeah, I would be."

"You're naked, on your knees, and I'm holding your hair. And I'm up close, right in your ear, so close you can feel my breath when I tell you what to do, right?"

"Mm-hmm. Yes."

"Yes, that's how it would be. Now, naked sex toy on your knees, say it again."

Without any pause or clearing of her throat, Lenore said, "I'm Lenore, I'm just a worthless slut, and I love to suck."

"There you go. Just like that."

"Laura . . ."

"They're going to love you, in a degrading kind of way. I gave your number to Drake. He'll text you with the time and place."

"No, you didn't!"

"Lenore, stop playing like you don't want this. You're not fooling me."

"Not while you're holding my hair, no," she said, laughing.

"And you're naked and on your knees. That's right."

"What happened to panties and heels?"

"Ooh, you'd prefer that? Hmm, I'd prefer that, too, you bad girl. Both of us, then."

Chapter 13 – Like Someone Could Grab It

"Amos," she called through the front door that she'd just propped open. "Get your share before I take it all."

"Should I, uh, take a plate and come back out?"

"Oh, what the hell. Have your usual seat at the table."

She let the door swing shut, then walked back toward the kitchen. By the time he got there, she was already seated and chewing on a bite from her second piece.

Before he'd seated himself, she was already filling his glass.

"Have some wine. Drink up."

He plopped down and said, "Well, I think I will. Maybe it'll keep me from, uh, acting strange."

"Let's hope," she said, forcing her laugh. "Anyway, wine and pizza is a simple enough pleasure. We deserve some pleasures in our lives, don't we?"

"Well, sure. One might say that they're essential for a balanced life."

She used one finger from the hand holding her glass to point at him.

"Well said, professor. Pizza is one. Wine is another. I can't blame anyone for taking some pleasure in life if they have the chance."

"Well, I'm glad you didn't consume all of it, Lenore. I will definitely have some pizza and wine."

While he was taking his first bite, she nudged his glass closer, then said, "Don't forget the wine. It's even better than the pizza."

Speaking with his mouth full, he said, "Uh, I will. Yes."

He picked up the glass and with her nodding and smiling at him, he didn't wait until all of it was chewed and gone before taking a long drink.

"There. That's good. Oh, try some more. It's good."

"Well, sure. Okay."

He hadn't had the chance to set down the glass, and her coaxing got him to drink again. And her continued nodding and smiling didn't stop until he'd finished all of it.

Taking the opportunity to finish chewing his first bite, he watched as Lenore refilled his glass, then pointed at it.

"Wine's kind of pleasurable, isn't it?"

"One would, um—I'd have difficulty arguing with that. Very much, yes."

"Have some more."

"But the pizza's good, and I'd—"

"It might still be too hot, Amos. Go ahead. Have some wine."

"Uh, sure."

He drank half of the glass, belched softly, then said, "Oh my, um, that's more than I, um, usually—"

"Go ahead and finish that glass. We still have a few bottles hidden away. I'll even get more myself, without being told, if we need it."

"Without being told?"

"Uh, sure. Yeah."

"Oh," he said with the glass held close and ready, "you, uh, your hair is down still, from work, and it, uh, looks kind of—"

"Like someone could grab it?"

"Huh?"

"Oh, I just mean, it kind of feels that way. I'm not used to it not being up in a knot."

"Uh, yeah. Well, rest assured, Lenore, that I'm not likely to grab it."

"Nope. Not likely."

He'd leaned his head and was about to comment, but Lenore waved repeatedly, and he tipped his glass back for more.

"Yeah. Good. So, anything you want to talk about, Amos?"

"Uh, I'm not sure I can think straight anymore. I'm feeling a little, um, unprofessorish right now. Is that a word?" he said, then covered a light belch.

"No. No way, Amos. I know what you mean, though. Hey, tell me more about that party you went to. What was that called again?"

He laughed and pointed at her, then slurred his words a bit when he said, "Oh, Lenore, I think you remember. You tell me."

"I guess I do: it was called the Frat Chat, right?"

"Bingo. Yep. That's the one."

"Hmm, I'd bet. Parties can be kind of a pleasure, too, right?"

"Well, one would say that's kind of the point, huh?"

"Yes, one sure would. Was it?"

"I mean, the conversation was, you know, good. I don't know if anyone would say that was pleasurable, though. Oh, how about a refill?"

"Of course," she said and refilled his glass. "There had to be more to it than just talking, right?"

"You sure you want to hear? Yes, let's have that talk, Lenore. With all this wine circulating in us, we might as well, hmm?"

"Oh boy. Yeah."

* * *

He leveled a stare at her that contrasted with his twisted grin.

"You tell me, Lenore. Was there more? Hmm?"

"Huh? You were the one at the party, Amos. You tell me."

He spent a moment watching the glass he was tipping from side to side, sloshing around the wine that he hadn't yet swilled. Resting the glass, he looked up, still twisting a grin.

"Maybe I've had too much wine. You know, that must be it. I must have had too much because I . . ."

"You what?"

Laughing and unable to hold his head steady, he blurted out, "I, uh, thought I saw you there."

"What? Are you out of your mind?"

His grin shriveled down to nothing, and his lips fumbled around before anything meaningful was produced.

"You, uh, Lenore, I mean, I guess the wine is just—"

"You're not making any sense, Amos. And you can't blame it on the wine. So, it's your turn: what else happened at the party besides you imagining me there?"

"Uh, just a bunch of guys, you know, hanging around, uh, doing what guys do."

"Which is?"

"Well, talking is one thing."

"Sure. Anything else?"

"Um, laughing? I heard some of the, uh, guys, you know, laughing. Sometimes."

"Nothing else you want to tell me about this Frat Chat?"

He held her gaze for only a second before looking toward, then reaching for the bottle, which she hurried to yank out of his reach.

"You want the wine, Amos?"

"Uh, like you said, it's a pleasure, right?"

"It's one. Yeah. Here."

She shoved it toward him, and he got his hand around it.

"Let me guess," he said, his words dragging. "Back to the porch?"

She scoffed and said, "Anywhere out of the kitchen. I need to clean this up."

"But I haven't even, you know, had very much—"

"Take the bottle, and take the damn plate, and give me some space."

"To, uh, clean?"

"Yep. Go. Even the couch is fine."

"Uh, okay. Um, that Frat Chat thing, you really weren't—"

"Go, Amos!"

Chapter 14 – Oh God. Frat Chat 2.

As she carried the empty plate to the counter in one hand, she held a slice with the other and took a bite. A second trip brought the other wine bottle and her glass, and she leaned against the refrigerator with pizza and wine in her hands, staring in the direction of the living room.

She'd just taken another bite when her eyes rested on what she'd brought home from work—a notebook and her phone.

"Oh, shit."

She set all of her dinner down, then rushed over and snatched up the phone. A quick series of taps muted the ringer, and she put it back down.

"She did say he'd text. That . . . whatever his name was."

Before she could raise her glass and take a sip, she had to spin around and run back to the table to stop the vibrating phone rattling around on the wood surface.

"Shit," she whispered.

"Everything alright?" Amos called from the other room.

"Yeah, Amos. Just, uh, kind of clumsy in here—probably from the wine."

"I know the feeling. One might say that's kind of the point of, you know, wine."

"Yep."

"Sure you don't need any help in there?"

"Drinking more wine? No, I don't. Nice of you to offer, though."

"Uh, yeah. Okay."

She quietly picked the phone back up and gave it a tap to read the new text message.

* * *

"Oh my God," she whispered when she saw that the text was from someone named Drake. "It's for real."

Holding her phone at her side, she looked up at the ceiling, her face showing some tension.

But after a few seconds, the anguish gave way to the beginning of a grin, and she shook her head and whispered, "Frat Chat 2."

She read the message quickly, then again. Then, yet again.

Drake wanted her to confirm that she'd meet him the next day at a coffee shop some distance from the hustle and bustle of the park central to the university campus.

"Oh God," she whispered, again looking at the ceiling.

In the silent room, with a text from a stranger waiting for her reply, she whispered at the textured surface above her, "I can't, can I?"

She caught her breath when Amos clattered something around in the living room, then the TV started up, just noise and nothing identifiable.

"Oh, him," she whispered. "You're a liar, Amos. I know what you did."

With her eyes again scanning through Drake's message, she whispered to herself, "And I know what I'm going to do."

She typed the single word 'okay,' then hesitated with her thumb ready to send her reply and get the whole deal moving.

"I, um, can always just tell him no, right?"

She listened to the TV playing in the distance, looked around the room, then frowned, looked down, and hit "send."

Her deep breath followed a sometimes choppy course out of her as she stared again at the ceiling.

"Oh God. Frat Chat 2."

* * *

"Everything alright in there?"

"Oh God," she whispered, barely making a sound.

"Yeah, Amos. Just someone from the office, asking for the day off tomorrow."

She walked toward the living room, her phone silenced and stowed in her pants pocket, and leaned against the wall just inside. Amos looked up from his papers, a wine glass in his hand and a distinct laziness in his eyes.

"Good. You're a total—"

"I'm a total what, Amos?"

"A totally good boss. Oh, and a good pizza cook."

"Well, thanks, but you're still sleeping on the couch."

"I am?"

"Uh-huh. You and your bottle of wine. It's just been a long day, and I want the bed to myself. You can camp out here."

"I, uh—I could. Sure. Hey, about the Frat Chat, I, um . . ."

"Yeah? What?"

"Nothing. Just, uh, nothing. I'll see you in the morning."

"Yep. Good night."

The walk to the bedroom was direct, the closing of the door was swift, and the locking of it was done without hesitation.

Chapter 15 – What Laura Would Say

Lenore had piled on her flannel pajamas and robe, and her feet were cloaked in their usual white socks and floppy slippers, and she set a plate of breakfast in front of Amos.

"There you go. More coffee?"

"Yes, please. It's good. It's all good. Ooh, maybe not my head, though."

"Yeah. Wine. You way outdid me, but I'm still feeling it too."

She poured, and he watched her shaking hand.

"Whoa. That's good. Thanks."

She sniffed in a short breath, then poured more in her own cup and sat across from him.

"Eggs are good. Even the toast. Bravo, Lenore."

She scoffed with a full fork and said, "Bravo for breakfast? This isn't exactly some kind of performance."

"True. Still, though, I'm appreciative."

"You're welcome."

"Well, Lenore, we find ourselves with a day off. Wednesdays are good for that, being mid-week and all."

"It does break things up. I'm getting used to taking Wednesdays off myself."

"Oh, that call last night. That was, what, some last-minute instructions for the staff?"

She stared at him and chewed in silence for a moment, then sipped some hot coffee.

"You're quizzing me like your students?"

"Huh?"

"I told you last night that it was someone asking for a day off."

"Oh, of course. I remember now. No quizzing from me, Lenore, not on my day off."

He waited with a grin, which slipped away quickly at his not seeing one in return.

"So," he continued, "with no quizzing scheduled, and with us both having absolutely nothing to do, perhaps we can wander around town like we did two weeks ago?"

"Oh, we did, didn't we?"

"Yes, and it was splendid. What do you say? Tacos are on me."

"As tempting as that sounds, Amos, I do have a backlog of errands I need to get to."

"Oh? Like what?"

She rushed the next bite, a large one, then held a finger up while she worked on it. He waited patiently.

"Just the usual shopping kind of stuff. Maybe some odd groceries too. Nothing interesting."

"Well, even if it's not—"

"Didn't you have some yard projects that you've been promising to get to? I know those hedges always need work. Oh, but if it's too much, there was that young guy I had on the payroll before you came to town. Maybe I should call—"

"Well, no, Lenore. He won't be needed again. I can easily handle all maintenance and improvement projects around here."

"Good. I know you can, Amos. But I can see how it might be too much, what with all the university stuff. So, if you ever think—"

"Lenore, no, I can devote the entire day to my own backlog of tasks. The yard projects don't stand a chance against my resolve."

"Well, that's a bold claim. Alright. I believe I'll be surprised when I get back at how much you got done."

He stared for a few seconds, then said, "Yes, of course. Uh, yep."

* * *

Lenore had parked a block from the nearest university building and then walked to one of the few stylish shops the town offered. She only slowed, didn't pause, as she approached the store, giving a good look at the mannequins in the window, all of them dressed formally but in a very sensual way.

A gentle push opened the door quietly, and she was greeted with light instrumental background music and barely noticeable conversation between the staff and the few shoppers there on a Wednesday morning.

She looked all around, taking in the racks of clothing, then looked down at her newer, tighter jeans that she didn't wear around the house. The low black boots were seldom seen at home, too, as was the snug button-down blouse. Even her hair had escaped the usual clumping and binding and flowed like a thick, blond stream onto her shoulders and back.

"Can I help you find anything?"

"Oh, no, I don't think so. I just want to look around some. Thanks."

"Just call over if you need anything."

"Okay, I will."

After an hour of wardrobe changes, she'd found a short black dress and a pair of black shoes with high, sharp heels. Near the checkout, she looked through the add-ons and selected a tasteful silver necklace with black stones, and it was long enough, she knew by trying it on, that it would hang low enough to easily sandwich into the tight area between her breasts.

Before setting it all on the counter, she spent a moment at a table with underwear.

"Oh, new panties," she whispered. "Hmm."

She flipped through them until she'd found something thin and black and cut in a flattering way. Holding that, she sorted through the collection some more and partially lifted out another.

"I know what Laura would say."

The all-white panties had an almost excessive supply of lace and frills, and the sides tied at the hips with long, silky bows.

"Oh my goodness."

With her hand still out, caressing the fabric and tugging lightly at the bows, she noticed the engagement ring on her left hand.

She caught her breath, gave a nonchalant look around, then slipped the ring off and deposited it in her pants pocket.

She touched the lacy panties again, scoffed, stayed with her original choices, and paid for it all with cash.

Chapter 16 – What You Really Are

Immediately after entering the coffee shop, Lenore saw a young man seated in a conspicuous place and matching the description Drake had given her. He looked quite fit in a tight t-shirt, was absorbed in reading, and wasn't looking around.

"Oh, God."

She walked over, then leaned and waved, and Emilio looked up at her.

His eyes stretched wide, and he scoffed and laughed at the same time, then he pointed.

Lenore held her hand still, and he finally said, "You must be Laura."

"I must be," she said. "May I?"

He waved an upturned hand toward the chair opposite him and said, "I insist."

She sat and let her bags from the shop sit on the table between them.

"I have to check: that's your name, right? Laura?"

"Yes. I'm Laura."

"Yeah, of course you are. Thanks for showing up. I've heard some incredible things about you."

"Oh? Dare I ask what?"

He laughed and said, "How easily do you blush? No, I take that back. I'd bet you're not prone to blushing."

"Well, a woman like me, probably not. Thanks for texting."

"The thanks are all from me. Uh, right now anyway. Later, though? Huh. Maybe not just me."

She laughed, then pointed at him and said, "I know exactly what you mean."

"You do? I know you know all about the Frat Chats. I heard some about that. I do want to hear more, though. First, just some basics."

"Alright. I'm all ears."

He made no effort to hide his staring at her ample breasts filling out her snug shirt, then looked up with a smile.

"No, not even close. You have more delectable attributes."

"I don't believe I've ever heard a woman described that way."

"Hey, I have a way with words. So anyway, I'm just an advance scout, so to speak, to get you started."

"On my way to, oh, I don't know if it's really called that."

"What?"

"The Frat Chat 2?"

"That works. So, these folks throw a hell of a party, and they crave the best, well, entertainment that they can get for it. They don't want someone shy."

"I'm not shy."

"I've heard. That last Frat Chat. You certainly have the looks and the body for it. Tell me, how prone are you to saying no?"

"Hmm, like never."

"I've heard some of what you were saying at the frat house. I just need to hear some of that again. Why don't you ever say no, Laura?"

He waited with a smile, and Lenore only tipped her head and returned it.

"Because I'm just something soft that's made only for sex."

"Oh? You're a slut?"

"Uh-huh, I'm just a slut. It's all I'm good for. Just sex."

"Really? You must have some kind of life. None of that matters?"

"Uh-uh. Just sex. I'm just something soft that should be used for sex."

"Oh, used. Yeah. That's important for this event. You don't care about anything or anyone, just being a slut?"

"Mm-hmm. That's all."

"If I told you to crawl under the table right now, and you got down under there, what would you do, even without me telling you?"

She took in his playful smile and the twinkle in his eyes before answering, and she fought to not clear her throat or hesitate any longer than that small amount.

"I'd start sucking."

"Good. Good answer. Tell me, Laura, what you'd be sucking."

She didn't look away from his eyes and said, "Your cock."

He looked both ways, smiling, then said, "This is kind of part of this first test. Tell me, Laura, if you're so quick to do that, what are you?"

She swallowed hard but held his gaze, and her voice was less forceful than before.

"I, uh . . ."

"It's degrading, I know. That's the whole point. Look, maybe you're not right for this little party."

"No. No, I am. It's just—"

"I know. It's just lunchtime at a coffee shop. Hey, try laughing when you say it, like it's just a joke. You can do that, right?"

She shook her head at the sight of his smile, laughed softly, then said, "A cocksucker."

"See? No big deal. Try it again. If anyone asked you what you really are, what would you say?"

Listening to his laugh trailing off, and giving him her own big smile, she said, "I'm a cocksucker."

He leaned across the table, then gestured for her to meet him halfway, which she did. When he chuckled, so did she.

"Tell me what you are, Laura. Try it without any of that wonderful smile this time. Just those big, bright eyes."

It took a few seconds, but she erased every trace of a smile and looked into his eyes, so close that they could almost kiss.

"I'm a cocksucker."

"Worthless too."

Still maintaining a serious expression, she kept looking into his eyes and said, "All I am is a worthless cocksucker."

"Even if you're dressed all pretty and stylish, looking very proper?"

"Mm-hmm. Especially then—just a worthless cocksucker."

He let his smile reappear as he sat back, and Lenore sat back too.

"So far, so good. Hmm, I like the way you say that. I'd say you'll do just fine. Are you ready for the next phase?"

"The, uh, the party? Right now?"

"No, the real interview. This is just preliminary bullshit, fun as it might be."

"Uh, hmm. I, uh, would like, probably, to hear more about it first. Like, who's all going to be there?"

"Oh, sorry, that's not how this works. You're just a . . . what?"

She mouthed the words, "A cocksucker."

He pointed and said, "Yes, I believe you are. But the next step is for you to commit to starring in the event. Look, you seem unsure, so I'll give you an hour. Meet me back here in an hour and give me your answer."

"Uh, sure. Okay."

He rose quickly, grabbed his things, and made a determined walk toward then through the shop's door.

"Oh my goodness."

She sat still for a moment, then squirmed around in her seat, shifting her hips around, grinding her jeans into the cushion.

A smile appeared.

"Hmm. That sure was . . . degrading."

* * *

Enough of the midday sunlight slipped between the leaves above Amos to get a decent sweat started. The hand shears he wielded along the top of the hedgerow added to it, as they were dull and seemed to resent his efforts and push back just as hard as he fought with them.

When streams of that sweat on his forehead began to attack his eyes, he gave it a swipe with his forearm while also letting the clippers drop into the grass. And instead of picking them up, he slipped out his phone.

"Just for a break, Lenore," he said, laughing to himself as he tapped it a few times.

"Hey," said Emilio, "Professor Amos, isn't it your once-a-week day off from the stress of babysitting all of us?"

"Hey, Emilio. Uh, yeah, but I'm babysitting the yard instead. I don't know which is more demanding."

"Well, shit, I'll take it up a notch next class, that way you won't have any doubt."

"Decent of you. Hey, you anywhere close to the park? I might be losing my mind, but I—"

"What's left of it?"

"Yeah. I believe that more every day. So, I'm not loving the heat out in the yard, but hot coffee sounds good anyway."

"Yeah, you've lost your mind—significant slices of it, at least. It just so happens that I'm close to the park. In fact, I'm standing outside some lesser coffee shop, too, but the park guy's brew is way better."

"Any of it sounds good right now," Amos said, wiping his brow again. "As long as it's away from this yard."

"I'll meet you. It's a short walk. Oh, and I have some news for you."

"Like what?"

"Like someone I talked to. It's, uh, interesting. You'll find it . . . interesting. It's about someone you know."

"Huh. I'm intrigued. Alright, I'll lock up and get hiking. See you soon."

"Hey, wait a second. You're too hot in the yard, but you want hot coffee? That's what you're saying?"

"Uh, yeah. So?"

"Shit, it's starting. It's really starting."

"What is?"

"The self-annihilation branch of my theoretical ramblings."

"Uh, clear that up for me. Pretend I'm not a professor."

"I can do that more easily than you want to know. Alright, there's that bit about hot and cold at the same time. That's old news. The next step is that you start craving hotter or colder because, you know, more divinity. In your case, what with heatstroke and all, you're looking to burn your ass to the ground."

"I am? You can tell all that from me wanting a cup of coffee?"

"Well, shit, I don't know. I really do make this up as I go. See you soon."

"Right. See you."

Chapter 17 – Like It's Meant to Be

"Just like some regular school day, huh, Amos?"

Emilio was seated at their usual picnic table in the park, leaning against the table. He held a paper cup of coffee and beside him, another kept its steam trapped under a snug plastic lid.

Amos pointed at it and said, "My backup coffee. Nice."

"Hey, you said you wanted to burn your ass into oblivion."

"I did?"

"Alright, maybe you didn't. Either way, though, you got backup. Have a seat."

"Thanks. I'm not planning on staying long. I really do need to get some work done, but even a new professor deserves a break."

"A break without lecturing anyone—not even me. Hey, I told you I had some news."

"You did. Someone I know, you said?"

"Yep. Talked with her a short while ago."

"Who?"

"Well, come on, Amos. You know me—always about the drama. I can't just spill it without any lead-up."

"Fine, Emilio. Let's play it your way. What's the first clue?"

"It's a 'she.'"

"Okay. We're down to fifty-percent of the entire world."

"Oh, no, no, no. I said it's someone you know. You don't—"

"Know the entire world. Fine. We're down to half of the people I know. Still a large sample size."

"Spoken like a professor who's versed in statistics. Okay, it's someone you see often. I guess 'often' is accurate enough."

"Alright. It's a woman that I see often. Go on. What else?"

"It's probably something I should keep secret, but you know me, I—"

"Crave drama. Yeah. I know. So, who is she, and what's the secret?"

He leaned back and sipped his coffee, then said, "I'm not sure you want to know, professor. It might change your opinion of her."

"Well, so what? Come on, Emilio, I'm almost started on my backup coffee and when that's gone, I'm back to work in the fields of suburbia."

"I like that. Sounds quaint in a chain-gang kind of way. Alright, you asked for it."

Amos rested his backup cup on his leg and held Emilio's gaze, barely noticing his playful grin.

"It's . . . Lindsey."

"Oh, Lindsey. Yeah, from the psych intro class. I do see her fairly often. What about her?"

"Well, two things. Which one do you want first?"

Amos scoffed and said, "You pose an impossible choice. There's simply not enough data."

"Correct. Alright, I'll pick. I told her about the frat guys maybe someday having an all-female Chat."

"Seriously?"

"Yep. After she declined ever being the star of the standard Frat Chat format."

"She wouldn't want to be devoured by all the guys, you mean?"

"No way. She's hot enough, though, not that it matters."

"Huh?"

"Amos, you don't have to worry about her coming on to you."

"I wasn't worried about that. So, you mean, she has a boyfriend, or what?"

"Huh. Maybe a girlfriend. That's the other juicy detail: she digs chicks."

"Oh, okay. That's why you talked about the all-female Chat. No, I didn't know that about her. What did she think about the all-female version of it?"

"Not interested. But I'll run it by her again. You know me: I have to."

"Let me guess: you'll like the drama of it all?"

"Yeah, like the drama coming up on Friday."

"Oh, my promotion. Yeah, that's exciting."

"Not just that, Amos. I'm expecting hot and cold like we can't even imagine."

* * *

Holding the door until it had closed quietly, Lenore ventured back into the clothing shop. A glance around confirmed that no one was focused on her, but she still took a meandering path through the racks, lingering for a few seconds to study some garment or another, then ended up near the register.

"Oh, welcome back," said the same clerk who had just sold her the other items.

"Yeah, uh, just thought I'd take another look."

"You must have something special planned, am I right?"

Lenore laughed and said, "Uh, yeah, that's for sure."

"Well, if you need any assistance, just let me know."

"Thanks. Okay."

She watched the girl look down and continue with some paperwork, ignoring her again. So, she reached directly for the panties that she'd considered on her first shopping trip, the ones full of lace and frills and big, silky loops to tie them—or untie them—high on her hips.

"Hmm."

She pulled her hand back quickly when she heard the clerk say, "Oh, sorry, but I noticed you checking out that merchandise. I should have mentioned it before, but anything from that rack is free with the amount you purchased before. Sorry, I was too distracted."

"Free?"

The girl nodded, then pointed at the collection and said, "Any one of those, there."

"Okay, uh, thanks. I'm still deciding."

"It's quite an assortment. Just let me know. I have to run to the back for a second, but I'll be back."

"Okay."

Lenore watched the girl take her papers and hike around a corner and out of sight.

Focused again on the items, any one of which was free for the taking, Lenore gave one of the bows a gentle tug but not enough to undo it.

"Oh my goodness. Like it's meant to be."

Without letting it go, she took out her phone.

* * *

"Like usual," said Amos, "I have no idea what you're talking about."

"Hot and cold might not be the story for Friday. Maybe more of a plain coaster car getting tricked out like crazy."

"Yeah, like plain Amos getting pinstriped into a full professor?"

"Uh, yeah. Like that."

"I'm still surprised I'm being considered for a promotion already. Really, Emilio, I haven't even been here that long."

He laughed and said, "Long enough to tear through your first coffee, then start swilling—"

"Not that," he said, laughing. "At this university. It's only been a couple of weeks."

"True. I guess they know talent when they see it. So do I."

"That's quite a compliment. I didn't think—"

"No, get serious. I didn't mean you. Just, uh, women. I've got this talent for bringing out their dark side."

"Like Lindsey, you mean?"

"Sure. Yeah, Lindsey someday. But what I'm saying is that my instincts tell me when they want to get pushed and in what direction. And damn, I'm happy to push them right along, even when I should probably try to find a way to stop it from even happening."

"Lindsey? You're pushing her . . . where?"

"Forget Lindsey. I just mean, uh, in general."

He looked at his watch, then smirked before looking back at Amos. "Speaking of which, I have an appointment that I need to get to."

Amos scoffed and said, "Yeah, to push someone somewhere."

"You're catching on. Yep."

"Alright, well, have fun. I'm heading back to the house and yard and all that fun stuff."

"You do that. I'm planning for some fun stuff too. Way different, though."

* * *

"You called me a bad girl," Lenore said into her phone, turned away from the clerk's counter. "Last time we talked."

"Ooh, I remember. I was holding you by your hair."

Lenore laughed and said, "Uh, yeah. More than that."

"Uh-huh. You were naked and on your knees."

"And I was about to get, um, busy with a crowd of—"

"Huh. That, I don't remember. Weren't we alone?"

"Oh, Laura, you're impossible. Hey, I can't believe I did this, but I met with Drake."

"Good—he contacted you. So, you're all lined up and ready for the time of your life."

"No, I'm not. He gave me an hour because he said I didn't seem completely sure. I'm supposed to go meet him soon and give him my answer."

"There's only one answer, Lenore. You know that. Go tell him."

"Laura, I don't know. He, uh, kind of degraded me right there, like a test, I think."

"Oh, nice. How?"

Lenore looked at her watch and said, "I don't have much time, so I'll get right to it: he made me call myself . . . something."

"Like you've been doing. So, you called yourself a slut. That's a superpower, remember? You being able to drive them all crazy?"

"No, it wasn't that. It was something else."

"Clock's ticking, Lenore. What? Just say it. Tell me what you told him."

"Fine. I told him—"

"No, where's the fun in that? Just say it. Come on."

Lenore listened to Laura's laughter for a few seconds, then said, "I'm a cocksucker."

"You said that to him?"

"Uh-huh. Worthless too."

"Okay, again. Use my name, just for fun."

"Laura, you're impossible sometimes. Fine. Laura, I'm nothing but a worthless cocksucker."

"Oh, there you go. Yeah, that's a little degrading. Bet you hated having to say that, huh?"

Lenore bit her lip and held the phone close, ready to answer as a few seconds crawled past.

Laura laughed and said, "No, you loved it. You loved saying it."

"It was kind of exciting. It felt bad."

"Oh, and I know why. I know exactly why."

"Sure. Why?"

"Well, Lenore, darling twin that's taking my place, because it's true."

"I really am one of . . . those?"

"Hmm. A damn sexy one too. Let's add that."

"Huh? Add it to what?"

"You'll say that while you're naked, kneeling, and I'm holding your hair."

"You're too much, Laura. They'll all think—"

"Uh-uh," she said, laughing. "We're alone, remember?"

"Laura, you—"

"I got to go. Bye!"

Lenore took a look at her phone, then stowed it away.

"Oh my goodness," she said as she lifted up the fancy white panties.

"Oh, good choice," said the clerk. "Let me get a nice bag for that."

Chapter 18 – You Up for a Real Interview?

She saw Emilio right after she'd entered the coffee shop, seated again in the same place. But unlike the first time, he was watching the door and smiled at the sight of her. So, she smiled back and began walking toward his table.

"Oh God," she said softly to herself. "Frat Chat 2."

"Good to see you. Laura. Have a seat."

"Hi, Drake," she said and again left her packages on the table between them.

She hadn't seen him look them over at all and stared quietly when he said, "Ah, you made another purchase."

"You knew that?"

"I don't miss much. Yeah, a very compact package—just a slim little bag."

"Well, yeah, I did do a little more shopping. You really noticed that?"

"Uh-huh. Yep."

Still holding her gaze, never having looked down at her things, he said, "I saw that shoe box before, the first time we met. My guess, based on that, was that the other package contained some kind of clothes. So, should I throw out a guess what's in this new bag?"

Lenore was laughing before he'd finished speaking.

"Oh my gosh. Even with all my clothes on, I have no secrets."

"Hey, that's good. I like that."

Smiling, he leaned forward again, and one curling finger got Lenore to lean close again too.

"We can't dwell on this, so just get right to the correct answers, alright?"

She scoffed, never lost her smile, and nodded.

"So, Laura, what did you just buy?"

She shook her head just once each way and said, "Panties."

"Good. I won't ask you to confirm it, but I'd bet they're quite nice. Now, when you're wearing those for the party, it's because . . ."

"Hmm. Because I'm a worthless cocksucker."

"Yes. Oh, you sure are. A damn sexy one, though."

He leaned back, so she backed away too.

"Fantastic. I think you're saying that you're in for this little party?"

"Oh God. Yeah, I'm in."

"Hmm. I can see it in your eyes. It's like you're giving off some kind of scent."

"What?"

"That you're starving for sex. That Frat Chat you just did wasn't enough, was it?"

"Uh, the Frat Chat. Uh, no. No, I need more."

"You don't want to be treated like a princess, do you?"

"You know, I heard these people like degrading sex."

"And you're okay with that?"

She mouthed the words, "I'm a cocksucker."

"Hmm, perfect. Let's move you on to that next step I mentioned before. This has been fun, but it's not the actual interview. You up for a real interview?"

"Uh, sure. With who?"

"His name's Michael. He kind of runs the party, he and his wife, Eva."

"Okay, uh, do I call him, or what?"

"No, he needs to see you. Let's take a walk over there right now."

"Uh, a walk right—"

"You have somewhere else you need to be?"

"Oh, uh, no. Sure, let's go see Michael. Where is he?"

"A hotel room. I'll get you there. Hey, I'll finish up this coffee while you run that stuff out to your car."

"Okay, I'll do that. See you in a bit."

* * *

The first task Amos addressed was to get a fresh pot of coffee brewing. That started, he swung open the refrigerator door, snagged a slice of pizza, then leaned against the counter and began chomping into it.

He took a step toward the back door, where the shears and hedges were waiting, then stopped and looked toward the hallway.

"Huh."

After slopping the pizza onto the counter, a steady walk, with no effort at sneaking around, got him quickly to where he could look down at Lenore's bottom dresser drawer. He stared down at it, listening to the quiet of the house, then scanning the bedroom floor everywhere.

Stooping down, he yanked it open, dug roughly through the stack, and uncovered the neatly folded, recently cleaned cheerleader skirt.

"Dammit."

He touched it, then caressed it with his fingertips, then clutched it tightly in a fist.

"I know it was you. I saw the goddamn ring. You wore that, even with all that you were doing. God, you're such a slut."

He let the fabric loose, then smoothed it all back down like it was. He restored the stack above it, arranged it neatly, then stood and kicked the drawer to close it.

Standing with his hands on his hips, his breaths rapid, he kept staring at the drawer.

"I'll get you to admit it. You'll slip up."

He spun quickly, exited the room, and forgot all about the fresh coffee on his way outside and back to his work.

* * *

With her phone to her ear, walking from her car back to Emilio at the coffee shop, Lenore said, “Laura, this is getting out of control.”

“Hey, girl, it’s supposed to, right? Isn’t that the point?”

Taking quick steps along the sidewalk, pausing her words when anyone was close enough to hear, Lenore continued.

“But this isn’t even the actual party yet. Drake has me saying things and—”

“Things you like saying. Admit it.”

“Okay, fine, but now, he’s taking me to an interview! In a hotel room!”

“Lenore, there’s no turning back. You just make up your mind, right now, that you are a complete . . . what?”

Without any expression, she said, “A slut.”

“Uh-huh. And what else, that you just realized today while having coffee with Drake?”

“Oh my God,” she said, laughing. “I’m a cocksucker too.”

“Uh, yeah. There you go.”

“But Laura, I don’t—”

“Hey, if it helps, imagine I’m there, holding your hair. I’m holding onto it real tight, Lenore.”

Lenore laughed and said, “Oh, I guess that does help. Okay.”

“And you’re naked and kneeling.”

“Stop, Laura. You’re too much.”

“And it’s just us.”

“Oh my God.”

“So, Lenore, Frat Chat 2?”

“God. Frat Chat 2. I have to go. Bye!”

Chapter 19 – Just Play Along

Emilio hit the button and said, "We had to come in through that back door—the staff entrance."

"Okay."

Lenore stood with her arms crossed, watching the light count down the floor numbers. It arrived at their floor, the ground level, and the dinged and dirty doors slid apart.

"Here we go," he said and with a grip on her arm, he nudged her into the cab.

Still holding her, he spun around with her, and he hit a button for the fourth floor.

"Just a formality," he said. "The whole interview process, I mean. I think you'll do just fine."

"Well, thanks. I really do want—"

He quickly hit a button, stopping the car between floors.

"What's wrong?"

He turned to her, standing close, alone in the dim cube.

"We just both want you to do well at this interview. Am I right?"

"Well, yeah. Of course."

"And you're so eager to be a really bad girl, aren't you?"

"Yeah."

"No morals?"

"Uh-uh."

"Not loyal to anyone?"

She noticed his grin but held his gaze, pausing less than a second.

"No one. Not me."

"Huh. Me neither. I was just telling someone that. Turn around a sec. Face the wall."

"What?"

"Pre-interview, Laura. The wall."

Lenore turned her back to him and stood close to one of the walls of the elevator cab locked between floors.

"Hmm, nice hair too. Put your hands up."

She raised both hands about shoulder height, palms against the walls.

"Uh, no. Straight up."

She extended her arms all the way, still keeping her palms against the wall.

"Yeah, like that. You know, I couldn't help but notice that your breasts are quite nice. Very large. What do you think about them?"

"Uh, they're nice. Yeah, they're actually quite nice."

"May I?"

"What?"

"Seriously? I think you know."

"Uh, yeah. Of course."

He stepped closer to her and reached around with both hands, taking a breast in each.

"Oh, so soft. Your hair smells nice too."

"Thanks."

He started fondling them, squeezing and bouncing, running his fingertips over them, then said after a few seconds, "This shirt, though. Hmm."

She didn't move when he started unbuttoning her shirt, working his way to the bottom while saying, "Such nice breasts in there, I know. I just have to check, though. I know you don't mind."

She shook her head, and he smiled at her blond mane tickling his nose. He leaned in closer, almost looking over her shoulder, and both hands found the bra's clasp between her breasts.

"Ooh, it's kind of tight in there. So big and soft. Let's just . . . ah, there."

The clasp opened easily, and he used both hands to spread it apart, taking the shirt with it and leaving her breasts completely uncovered.

"Oh, that's nice. Hey, Laura, hold this stuff open for me."

She kept her breaths steady and did as he said, holding everything off to the sides. His warms hands started with a gentle squeeze, then he rubbed his palms all over, just lightly grazing her.

"Uh-huh. Like that. You like when they get attention, don't you?"

"Mm-hmm. Yes."

"Big, delicious breasts like yours should be played with all the time, shouldn't they?"

"Mm. Yeah."

He gave them both a tighter squeeze, then said in her ear, "Hands back up. Good. Just like that—way up high."

He fondled them for a few more seconds, then let his hands drop down along her sides until he was holding her by her waist.

"Oh, and a tiny little waist. Nice. Hell of a contrast. Hold still now."

He waited for a protest that never came.

"Good girl," he said, then reached around for her belt buckle.

He loosened that quickly, then popped the single button and unzipped her.

"Just need a little better look. I'm guessing there are some really nice curves hiding under all this."

Holding the waistband on each side, he shifted her jeans around, wiggling them and her panties down over the curves of her hips, and he stopped when it was all tucked below the bottom of her cheeks.

"And just like that, your ass is ready for some admiration. Wow, it's perfect," he said while holding up her shirt. "Hmm, perfect ass, tiny waist, big round breasts. Really nice."

She held still, largely undressed and with her hands high against the wall.

"Oh, look at you. Laura, you have some serious talent. You know that, don't you?"

She nodded and said, "Yes. Uh, I do."

Holding her hips with both hands, he leaned up against her and spoke in her ear.

"Tell me again what you are."

"I'm a, uh, total slut."

"Yes, one that's kind of undressed in an elevator too. Now, whisper to me what else you are."

She took a breath to answer, and Emilio rushed to say, "Oh, wait a second. Hold that thought."

He reached around to touch low on her belly, and he left his other hand low on her back. Then, he slid them both down far enough to touch whatever he wanted.

"Oh, you are a soft, sweet thing. Mm, you feel good. Do you like hearing that you feel so good?"

"Mm-hmm," she said, her breasts bare and her hands high above her as he felt her front and back.

"You're just made to be touched. Are you good for anything else?"

She shook her head, causing him to laugh softly as both hands took liberties with her. But he moved the hand from behind her up to her breasts, reaching around to touch her both high and low.

"In a second, you'll say what else you are, okay?"

She nodded and said, "Mm-hmm. Okay."

He turned them both to face the elevator doors, then hit a button to unlock it, leaving it free to travel again. While rubbing her breasts and letting his fingers explore other parts of her, they both watched a light come on above the door.

"Uh-oh."

Then, the cab began to move to the next floor up.

"Shh," he said in her ear. "Part of the interview."

He grinned at her very slight nod.

The door opened, and a young man with a variety of supplies in one hand began to take a step inside, then stopped, his eyes big and focused on Lenore's breasts.

Emilio made sure that the shirt and bra weren't blocking any of the sight, then said to the young man, "She wants to tell us something."

He nodded, still staring, while Emilio continued fondling her breasts and rubbing around between her legs.

"Go ahead," he said in her ear. "Tell us, you pretty little thing."

Lenore let a deep breath out, then inhaled again.

"I'm nothing but a slut."

Emilio quickly added, "Yep, one that likes getting felt up in elevators. Tell this horny young man what else you are."

"I'm . . . I'm a worthless cocksucker."

"Because you love to . . ."

"I love to suck cocks."

"Yes," he said to her, "Yes, you sure do. Good girl."

He looked up at the confused but excited man and said, "Hey, this car's taken. Get out, and wait for the next one. Go on!"

The young fellow stepped back, his eyes shifting rapidly between Lenore's uncovered breasts as each got squeezed, one after the other, Emilio's hands squishing them up.

The doors closed, and Emilio said, "That was good. Damn, you're good. Get yourself dressed—you look like a slut."

She dropped her arms and turned around, and they both laughed. Shaking his head, he hit the button for the first floor, and the elevator began to drop.

"You're a good sport about all of this. Nice job."

"Thanks."

"Michael's in 413. My work is done. Except for this."

He handed her a folded piece of paper.

"Your instructions for getting to the party. Follow them exactly."

"Uh, sure. Okay."

"Oh, and Laura?"

"Yeah?"

"I like your name. Laura's a good name for you."

"Uh, thanks."

The doors whooshed open, and Emilio got out.

"Oh my God," she said after the doors had slid shut.

She panted for a few seconds, then laughed and said, "Oh my . . ."

* * *

She got her jeans and panties yanked up first, but Lenore left that all loose as she hurried to clasp her bra, then button the shirt. While watching the lights above the door counting out the travel to the second floor, she smirked and giggled as she rushed the zipping, buttoning, and belting.

And just in time, she was able to brush back her hair as the doors opened and two staff members, one male and one female, got in.

When the woman was reaching for the buttons, Lenore said, "Oh, four, please."

That button got hit, but the woman had already punched it for the third floor. The couple exited, and the cab carried Lenore higher, to the fourth floor, where she had a pending appointment, as Laura, with a man named Michael.

* * *

The brass numbers on the door spelled out 413, and Lenore stood there, fully dressed, staring at the peep hole and fussing with her hair. She finally got it ready to her satisfaction, then reached up to knock.

But she scoffed quietly and let her hand drop.

"Oh, Laura. Yeah, you—the real one. I can't believe you got me into this."

The anxious expression gave way to a smile, and she looked down at how her deep breaths were pushing her breasts closer to the door.

Like she was already offering them up to whatever waited for her inside the room.

"What advice would you give me, Laura? I think I know: don't say no to anything."

She scoffed and said, "Well, what the hell. No harm in talking to the guy."

She knocked.

A few seconds later, the door swung in, and Michael held it with one hand and stood where Lenore could see him entirely. He appeared completely at ease in his dark pin-striped suit and subtle burgundy tie. His dark, serious eyes stayed locked on hers, and he looked from one to the other several times before speaking.

"You must be Laura."

"I must be."

He smiled and nodded and said, "My name is Michael. I was expecting you. Come on in."

"Hello, Michael. Thanks."

She had to turn sideways to enter, and he moved only enough to let her brush past. A few steps into the room, she turned to watch him close the door.

With his eyes on her and offering a relaxed smile, he engaged the latch. He smiled at seeing her paying attention to that, then unlatched it.

"Oh, sorry, force of habit. You should know that you're always free to go anytime you wish."

She sighed and said, "Thanks. I appreciate that."

"Later, Friday, you'll be the star in the drama of our party."

He waited, so Lenore nodded and said, "Uh, yeah. Friday."

"But now, Laura, we're just playing around with what can be called a practice session. Hey, in a way, you're interviewing me too."

She laughed softly and said, "Okay. That sounds reasonable."

"Good. And since it's a practice session, the best you can do is just play along. I think you'll find it quite entertaining if you do."

"Uh, sure. Okay, I will."

"Excellent."

Chapter 20 – So Pretty Kneeling There

"Please," Michael said as he gestured toward a comfortable sitting area with two chairs facing a loveseat, "make yourself comfortable."

"Thanks."

She led the way and took one of the chairs, and he sat on the small couch facing her. To her right was an end table with a lamp and a drink, but there was no type of coffee table between them.

"I've already poured some champagne for you."

He gestured toward the full glass on the table beside her. She got her hand around it, then looked up at him.

"So, Laura, I've heard very good things about you. From all of that, and the sight of you—you're quite attractive—I'd say you've already earned the invitation to be our special entertainer this Friday."

"Oh, well, that's all good to hear. Thank you."

"Before I give you any more details, what are your thoughts so far? Does it sound interesting enough for your, uh, expectations?"

"Yes, it does sound good. I believe I passed the pre-interview too."

"Oh, that young Drake guy. Yeah. He's exuberant. You must know, though, that you have the kind of sexiness that can make anyone kind of crazy."

"Oh, well, thanks."

"I've heard that you were quite the attraction at the Frat Chat recently. I have to let you know, though, that this affair Friday will be a bit more on the serious side."

"I've heard that. Serious, how?"

"I think the best word for it might be 'drama.' Can you handle some drama? We're all business owners, executives, even a few trust fund brats, but mostly, we fancy ourselves to be something like theater people."

"Mm-hmm. It sounds exciting."

"We'll make sure you get all kinds of attention, but you'll have to do as you're told. That's important."

"I can do that. I can be very cooperative and, um, willing."

"Ah, willing is good. At that declaration, let's consider the interview officially beginning. Stand up."

She grabbed the arms of the chair to help and stood in the narrow space between them. While still seated, he reached out to place a hand on each of her hips.

"Yes, good. Curves are good. It's kind of all hidden in these ordinary clothes, though."

"Well, you know—out running errands."

"Yes, of course. Life will be ordinary if we allow it."

He stood and moved his hands to her upper arms, and she had to tip her head back to look into his eyes. One of his hands moved to her chin, and he tipped her head each way slowly, studying her.

"Hmm. You're quite attractive, but you have the look of a woman that maybe expects a lot of respect at all times."

"Oh, uh, not me. Uh-uh."

"No?"

"No, I might look that way, but I'm just something that's made to—I mean, all I'm good for is being used for sex."

"That is what we need for the party. You're sure? You don't deserve any better than to be used for sex, possibly degrading sex?"

"Uh, that sounds exciting. That's what the party's about, right?"

"Mm-hmm. Yes, very much so. Drama, you know."

He brushed her hair back with both hands and smiled down at her. She only tipped her head and gave a weak smile back.

"On your knees."

* * *

Lenore stared for less than a second, made no effort at all to speak, then dropped quickly to her knees on the plush area rug.

"Good, Laura. You did as you were told."

"Yes."

He stood close, looking down at her with his hands on his hips. She kept her posture straight, which kept the generous mounds of her breasts out and very noticeable.

"I must say, you look good like that—on your knees. Do you like that? Do you like looking good when you're kneeling for someone?"

"Yes. Yes, I do."

"Very pretty like that, on your knees. It's where you belong."

"Yes."

"It's all you're good for, isn't it? Kneeling when a stranger orders you to?"

"Yes, that's all. I should always do what I'm told."

Touching her cheek gently while she looked up, her eyes big and not blinking often, he said, "Drake texted me what you like saying, something quite descriptive about yourself. Do you know what I mean?"

She nodded.

"Good. Say it for me, then."

"I'm nothing but . . . a worthless . . . slut."

"Hmm, yes, I do like hearing you say that. It is the absolute truth about you, isn't it?"

She nodded and said, "Yes. Mm-hmm."

"Good. I'm going to enjoy hearing you admit that while you're kneeling in front of me. Again, then, and no hesitations this time."

"I'm just a worthless slut."

"And you're not concerned with any nonsense like self-respect?"

"Uh-uh. None."

"You're good only for sex—even degrading sex?"

"Yes. Nothing else."

"You're doing very well, Laura. And you must know that you've never looked prettier. So pretty kneeling there."

"Mm-hmm. I like looking pretty."

"Maybe it's because of what you're about to do. Could that be it?"

She gave his trousers a quick glance, then looked back up at him.

"Uh, yeah. That could be it."

"Yes, of course. Now, keep looking up at me with those big, beautiful eyes, and loosen your belt and zipper."

She watched him as she did as instructed, leaving it all hanging open and holding up her shirt enough to show the smooth skin of her belly and just the top of her panties.

"Good. Use your left hand. Touch yourself, and don't stop unless you're told to stop."

She sighed and slipped her fingertips down over her belly, under the silky fabric, and found what she was told to touch.

He smiled at the change he saw in her eyes, even though she kept them focused up at his.

"That feels good, doesn't it? Such a soft part of you."

"Mm-hmm. It feels good."

"Perhaps your fingers should be wetter, though?"

He smiled as she nodded, slipped her fingers out, sucked them for a few seconds, then got them back to work.

"Mm," he said, "that was pleasant to watch."

He reached down for his belt, then his zipper, taking it all the way down.

"Keep feeling how soft and warm you are."

"Okay."

He worked himself out and left it pointing straight toward her, almost touching her lips.

"Look at me."

She looked up.

"You're a beautiful woman, on your knees and touching yourself, and you don't deserve any respect. I can tell just by looking at you that you're worthless. And now's a perfect time for you to tell me what else you are."

Still looking up at him, her lips almost touching what he'd just taken out into the open, she said, "I'm just a cocksucker."

He smiled and held both of her cheeks, keeping her lips close.

"Yes, you are a cocksucker, Laura. A worthless one. But you're quite good enough to be used, just used, as a . . ."

She couldn't contain her smile completely and said, "A cocksucker."

"Hmm, yes. Open that pretty mouth, you worthless cocksucker. It's time for me to use you in this hotel room."

She nodded and opened her mouth.

Chapter 21 – Is That What You're Offering Us?

"Oh, just like that," he said as his touch on her cheeks guided her closer. "Just a little farther. There, that's good for now. Close those pretty lips now and hold it tight. Good girl."

Lenore was on her knees in Michael's hotel room, holding him in her mouth and looking up at him as he fussed with her wavy blond hair on both sides.

"Yes, that's a sight. You look good like that, doing something you're meant to be used for. Are you happy like that?"

She nodded and took him along for the ride, her lips never letting it go.

"Yes, of course, you're happy. Remember that you're not good for much else. Keep touching yourself, and use your other hand, if you wish, to help you answer. Tell me, you worthless slut, what you're doing right now."

She held him with her right hand at the base and backed away just barely enough to speak.

"I'm doing what I'm told to do."

"Which is?"

"I'm sucking your cock."

"And?"

"Mm, and touching myself."

"Yes. Open again. There you go. Oh, that feels good in there. Your mouth is definitely meant for sucking."

He sighed with a glance to the ceiling, then continued playing with her hair, sometimes stretching strands out to the sides, then letting them fall.

"Hold yourself still, little slut."

He began slow, steady thrusts deeper into Lenore's mouth, and her lips squeezed him the entire time.

"Yes, like that. Good. We're just taking our time, in a public building with an unlocked door. So, it's perfectly safe for you to just play along. It'll be fun, okay?"

"Mm-hmm."

"My dear wife Eva concocted a new sort of drama for Friday's festivities. You have my word that I'd never let things go too far. But it'll be so fun and dramatic for you and all of us if you play along. Does that sound reasonable?"

She nodded.

"You seem to like playing along."

"Mm-hmm."

"Excellent. Now, here's a narrative that's fundamental for this drama: nobody in your life knows you're here?"

She shook her head only enough to be noticed, and he never slowed.

"Nobody knows what you're doing on your knees right now, being a sweet, darling little cocksucker for an absolute stranger?"

"Uh-uh," she managed to say with her mouth full.

He laughed and said, "Oh, so naughty. I don't think anyone even cares about you, do they? So sad—no one knows where you are, and no one cares."

She shrugged and kept accepting what he was feeding into her.

"Oh, that's adorable. Yes, that's an important part of being worthless—no one caring about you at all. Such a worthless thing. At the party, you're going to be degraded far worse than this. There's nothing you won't do, I hope?"

"Uh-uh."

"Of course. And while you're at the party, no one will know where you're being used and degraded. Before, during, and *after* we've had all our fun with you, no one will even miss you, will they?"

She used one hand to give herself room to speak, and Michael leaned out for a quick glance at her left hand moving in a steady rhythm.

"Uh-uh," she said slowly. "No one would ever miss me."

"That feels good, doesn't it? What you're doing for yourself?"

"Mm. Yes."

She'd just started up again, getting her lips around it, when he said, "No one would ever care enough to even come looking for you, would they?"

She backed away enough to say, "Uh-uh."

"Really, that's a main theme for this party. We'll all be doing so many things to you, and we'll enjoy it even more knowing that no one cares enough about you to even wonder where you are."

"No one ever will. Uh-uh."

"No one?"

"Uh-uh," she said, pausing as her hand kept busy in her panties. "No one would ever wonder where I am."

He got his hands around her head and pulled her forward, causing her to gag until he'd backed out some and got back to his steady pumping.

"Oh, yeah, that's exactly the kind of girl we need. You'll be perfect for our little party. Does that sound good to you, Laura?"

Free enough to answer, she said, "I want to be perfect for your party—a perfect slut."

"A perfect slut that no one cares about?"

"Mm-hmm. Yes. No one."

She made sure she had eye contact, then said, "Am I being a perfect cocksucker?"

He pulled her forward again, causing her to say, "Mm . . ."

"Almost, Laura. Yes, you are indeed a perfect cocksucker, and it's perfect that you can come to our party and no one will ever miss you. Keep your warm, wet mouth busy while I tell you more, alright?"

"Mm-hmm," she said, holding still as he slipped it back between her lips.

"Shh, now. Just listen, then say what you know I want to hear because you know that's part of the fun—we just love the drama."

He paused, then smiled at her nod.

"Laura, are you offering to be a *disposable* cocksucker for our fun?"

She snorted out a breath but didn't try to get away and only looked up at him with a few quick blinks, her eyes big and bright and her lips squeezing him tightly.

"Laura, we want a perfect little girl, a cocksucking slut like you, that's not just worthless. We want her dressed up pretty for us to play with, in any way we wish, and she must be a *disposable* little darling too. Is that what you're offering us?"

He pumped for a few more seconds as she looked up at him from her knees. He held her cheeks, thrusting smoothly into her mouth, and her wet lips held him coming and going.

"Yes, it takes some pumping in your sweet mouth for you to realize it. Let's just give your wet mouth some more, you keep touching that soft, wet part of yourself, and you'll start to accept what you truly want to be for us."

Still holding her cheeks, he slid it in deep, then back out almost all the way, then back deep—many times while she continued rubbing inside her panties. Then, he backed it away.

"Remember that we're just having fun, so just play along. Are you ready to say now what kind of cocksucker you want to be for our fun?"

It took another second, then she nodded and said, "Mm-hmm. Yes."

"Hmm, that's a very good start, pretty thing."

He gave her another deep pump, held it there, then he pulled it out and said, "Tell me, then, what you'll be for us."

"I'm disposable."

"Yes," he said while giving her a few more pumps, holding her cheeks gently. "Tell me again."

With it touching her lips and her fingertips doing a skillful job between her thighs, she stared up at him and said, "I'm disposable. I truly am disposable."

"Good," he said and pushed just the end in and out a few times, smiling at her lips conforming and holding him tight the entire time.

"Say it all, pretty little party girl. What do you want to be for us?"

"I want to be a pretty, disposable girl for your party."

"It feels good to just play along, doesn't it? Just say things for the fun of it?"

"Yes."

"Good. So, pretty girl, you really do mean disposable?"

"Mm-hmm. Yes."

He laughed gently, then said, "And you know exactly what that word means, don't you, pretty party cocksucker girl that no one will miss?"

She looked up, her eyes big and calm as she nodded gently.

"It has a very definite meaning. Do you know what that is?"

"Mm, yes. I know what that means."

"A pretty thing that's disposable, just something to be bagged up like any other trash? That kind of disposable?"

"Mm-hmm. I'm that kind of disposable. I want to be a pretty, disposable girl for your party."

"And what do you expect we'll do with a disposable thing like you, a thing that no one will ever even look for?"

Her left hand picked up its pace.

"Mm, I should be bagged up like any other trash."

"Is that because after we've had our fun, you'll be our soft, naked, used-up trash?"

She quickly pulled in part of a breath, then relaxed and let it out.

"Soft, naked, and all used-up?" he said again. "To a pretty thing that knows she's worthless, that does sound reasonable, I know."

He grinned at seeing her arm moving for more concentrated rubbing.

"Mm-hmm. Mm, soft, naked, and all . . . mm, all used-up . . ." she moaned as her rubbing picked up.

"Yes, and it's important that you think of the contrast: you'll be so soft and warm, naked and vulnerable for anything we want. And the entire time, you know that you're also just a disposable thing, something to be bagged up like any other trash. Think for a second how you'll be both. Imagine how it'll feel that you've surrendered yourself for that, at the exact moment that you realize it's too late to turn back."

He pushed the end in and out between her squeezing lips, smiling at her big eyes closing as she began moaning at what he'd just said and from her busier left hand.

"Yes, it's a sweet contrast when you surrender yourself to that drama. You feel right now, from what I'm doing with your mouth, what a soft, vulnerable little girl you are, and you know you're just trash—getting all used up from our fun. Yes, so soft and *all* used up."

Her moaning increased, and he watched her big eyes just start to roll up, then they closed.

"Yes, now you see it. It'll feel so good when you surrender to our plans for you."

He smiled at her continued moaning and eager rubbing.

Patting her hair gently while she was still moaning, he said, "Yes, Laura, such a good girl now. It'll feel good even for you to say it again. It feels so good because you know you're just a . . ."

He slipped it out and nodded at her eyes staying closed. Her lips were wet all over, and the soft pink tip of her tongue was showing itself.

"Mm," she said, pausing quickly just to rub her lips together, "I'm a soft, naked thing to be used up for sex. Mm, all used up just for sex."

"Soft and so vulnerable for anything at all. And are you trash, too, little girl?"

"Mm, yes" she said breathlessly, her eyes still closed. "Mm-hmm. I'm also just trash to be bagged up."

"Yes, all at the same time. That feels so good, doesn't it?"

"Mm-hmm. Oh, mm-hmm . . ." she said, her eyes still closed as she began to shake lightly.

"Good. You're a very good, soft little girl. Yes, just enjoy how that feels. Be a very good, disposable little girl and open up for me. You'll always feel even softer and more vulnerable when you're forced to suck cock."

She parted her lips, licked them both, then said, "Mm, yes. I'm so soft when . . . I have to . . . suck . . ."

"Just a soft and pretty, disposable cocksucking girl."

"Mm-hmm. Disposable . . . cocksucking . . . girl . . ."

"It feels good to be nothing more than that, doesn't it?"

Her mouth opened in a quiet gasp for a few seconds, her lips quivering, then she said softly, "Mm-hmm. Nothing more . . ."

He gave her lips what it seemed they wanted, and they closed, wet and warm as she continued to shake softly.

"Suck, soft little girl. You're being forced to suck the cock."

He touched her hair lightly on both sides, then caressed her cheeks, feeling the increasing shaking and smooth warmth of her skin.

* * *

After just a minute, Lenore had sighed and stopped shaking, and Michael said, "Oh, I'm getting close myself. Yeah, I'm just about there. That mouth of yours is so warm and wet . . ."

"Mm-hmm."

He sighed, then tipped his head each way, studying her face.

"You've fixed yourself up quite nicely, and I know it's just for this. You have a very pretty face."

"Mm."

"Even prettier with something hard and thick between your lips."

She opened her eyes slowly, nodded, and said, "Mm-hmm."

With one hand still holding her from behind, he touched her lightly under her chin, getting her to tip her head back and more easily see him.

"Yes, that's quite a pretty face. Just lovely."

He pressed up on her chin more, and she tipped her head back farther. She was losing her grip, so he held it with one hand and wiped the end of it from one side of her lips to the other, then back again.

"Pretty lips. So perfect for sucking. Not good for a damn thing else."

"Mm-mm," she said, still looking up at him.

"And it's so perfect for our party guests that you love being used. Such a pretty thing that knows she deserves only to be degraded."

He pushed more on her chin, said, "Just a bit more," and she was facing nearly straight up at the ceiling.

"That's such a nice view from up here. Such a pretty face on such a worthless cocksucker."

"That's me," she whispered.

"You really feel like a worthless cocksucker right now, don't you?"

"Yes, I sure do."

"Don't stop touching yourself, pretty thing."

"Uh-uh. I won't."

"You know what I'm about to do, don't you?"

He'd begun steady, long strokes with one hand while he held her head with the other.

She nodded gently, her big eyes looking up into his, and said, "Mm-hmm. Yes. I do know."

"Your makeup is just perfect—you spent some time on that. You know that your face looks very pretty right now, don't you?"

"Mm-hmm."

"Your big, beautiful eyes are stunning. So perfectly done. You know I'm going to ruin that, and you know how, right?"

"Mm. Yes," she said, "I know how."

"Such a degrading thing to do to such a pretty face."

"Yes. Mm, so degrading."

She nodded and kept looking up at him, and he gave her chin another gentle touch. She was tipping it back far enough to be as horizontal as possible.

"There. That's perfect. Just hold that pretty face very still, okay?"

"Mm-hmm. I'll hold my face very still for it."

"Yes, you will. And try to imagine that right now, while you're patiently waiting for what you know is coming, one of our male guests is taking you unmercifully from behind."

She gasped.

"Oh yeah, he ripped your panties down and sure is pumping you. He's penetrating you so deep."

"Oh, hmm . . ."

"When he's done, the next will penetrate you even deeper. Very deep."

He got a tighter grip on her hair and made sure she knew it.

"And that next one won't be . . . in the same place."

"Oh God . . ."

"And you won't dare to complain at all."

"Uh-uh. Mm, no, not me."

"You won't try to get away from what he's doing to you."

"Mm-mm. No."

"You'll beg for him to go even deeper."

"Yes."

"Yes. You'll be a very good girl for whatever any of us want. Right now, we're going to ruin that very pretty face, make a real mess of it just like a thing like you deserves."

With his free hand, he brushed her hair aside, taking his time, until it all fell toward the floor behind her.

"Bet you'd like a photo of this, huh? The way you're posed so obediently, face still perfect, accepting that you'll be degraded?"

"Hmm, yes."

"Are you worthless?"

She nodded.

"What else? More importantly, what is so wonderful and adorable about a worthless girl like you?"

"Disposable. I'm disposable."

"Yes," he said, and her eyes followed his hand when he reached to one side and brought into view a clear plastic bag. She squirmed just enough for him to notice.

"Shh, now, pretty girl. Remember, it's all for fun, and you're free to go anytime."

She held still and looked at his eyes, then the bag.

"There. That's better. Be a good girl for this too. You are disposable, aren't you?"

She nodded.

"Yes, you're so soft and warm and just trash at the same time."

He held her with his left hand and pulled the open end of the bag over her head, just far enough to keep it snug and cover her hair.

"Keep touching yourself, Laura, and tell me again what you are. It's just for fun."

She relaxed and said, "Mm, I'm disposable—a disposable cocksucker."

"Yes. Yes, you are. And isn't that the wonderful thing about a worthless girl—that she's disposable?"

"Mm-hmm. Yes."

He laughed and said, "And you sure are quite a good cocksucker. Mm, that mouth of yours. Do you want what's going to happen next, Laura?"

"Mm-hmm. I do."

"You want it all over your pretty face?"

"Yes. I want it."

"Tell me what you deserve."

"I deserve to have it all over my face. My pretty face deserves it."

"Keep going. Convince me," he said, and he picked up the pace, holding it directly over her.

"It's what I deserve," she said. "It's all I deserve. I'm worthless, and I have to get it all on my face."

"Even if you didn't want it?"

"Mm-hmm. Even if I begged you not to."

His pace quickened more, and he said, "Beg for it, Laura. Beg, you disposable, cocksucking slut."

She gasped, said, "Oh . . ." then smiled.

"Oh, you like hearing that. Yes, it's very exciting to be so soft and vulnerable. Laura, I want you to beg for it, like the disposable, cocksucking slut you are and always have been."

"Mm, please. Please, spray it all over my face. It's all I deserve. I deserve all of it on my face."

"Yes . . ."

She pursed her lips like blowing a kiss up to him, then said, "Because I really am just a disposable, cocksucking slut."

"Oh, good girl—that sounds so sweet. Tell me again."

"It's all I want to be: a worthless slut—a slut that kneels and sucks cocks."

"What else?" he said, holding the plastic bag too. "Most importantly?"

"Mm, I'm disposable—I want to be soft and vulnerable and disposable. And I deserve it all on my face."

"Oh, damn, here's what you deserve."

His first dose lay heavily between and across both of her eyebrows, then along the right side of her nose, ending just above her upper lip. And he nudged the bag down to cover most of it, leaving her eyes in the open.

"Mm," she moaned, rubbing herself more vigorously, "on my pretty face . . ."

"Yeah . . ."

She got her left eye closed just in time and from leaning back, it collected into a sticky pool that sagged just enough that she could open her eye again, but her eyelashes had collected a lot of it. He quickly shifted the bag lower until it covered her eyes and the edge rested near the end of her nose.

"Mm-hmm," she whispered, much of her face hidden behind plastic, "I'm just trash . . ."

"Yes . . . and your face. Your cocksucking face."

The next stream lay from one cheek to the other, across her nose and almost on the plastic, which he tugged down to cover her nose but leave her lips free.

"Mm-hmm," she said, breathless as she rubbed between her thighs, "my pretty, cocksucking face . . ."

"Ah . . ."

He left a thick deposit between her lips and nose, like a sticky mustache, and it began running down her cheeks on both sides.

"Do like you're kissing, you sweet, disposable girl. Hold your lips."

She hurried to purse her lips, and he stroked and dabbed all around, like icing a cake.

"Ah, there you go . . ."

He gave himself several more tugs, covering her lips entirely and leaving several wide trickles speeding down on both sides, soaking far into her hair and gathering around her ears.

"Mm," was all she could say with so much on her lips.

"There. A perfect little girl. All that careful effort to get your face so pretty, and look at it now."

"Mm."

"Now, you're ready."

* * *

He breathed deeply, let out a relaxed laugh, and held her head again with both hands.

"No, don't move, Laura," he said while sitting back on the couch right in front of her. "Hold your sticky face very still."

Lenore didn't move anything except her left hand, which had settled back into a contented, rhythmic rubbing. Michael gently pulled the bag lower, then lower still, and she still didn't move.

"Shh, soft, disposable little girl. Shh. Very still for this."

He kept going until the edge of it was just past her chin. He smiled at the sight of her swallowing hard but holding herself still, cooperating.

"So much prettier already. You're really just a disposable cocksucker, aren't you?"

The entire bag nodded with her, and she sped up her left hand, stretching her panties with the increasing efforts.

"Mm, you do like hearing that. Because you know it's true: you are nothing but a disposable cocksucker."

She moaned softly and kept rubbing herself.

"Just a cocksucker. And so disposable."

"Mm," she moaned, still rubbing.

"Yes, of course, you are. You love how it feels to be disposable. You see that now."

The bag was long enough that when he pulled it more, it bunched up on her shoulders and rested loosely on her chest. Any more nervous swallowing wouldn't be seen again.

Her excited breaths were puffing it up and then letting it relax, over and over, even as he chuckled and pushed on the plastic, touching it to the sticky patches on her face and getting it to stay there.

"Mm, such a disposable thing. Just a sticky piece of trash now, huh?"

She nodded and said though the plastic, "Mm-hmm . . . just trash."

"Shh, now. Be good and just hold that sticky face still for me."

He used both hands to hold her around her throat, not tightly, but enough to start gathering the bag all around.

"Doesn't it feel good to be so soft and vulnerable and just sticky trash too?"

She rubbed herself harder and moaned a soft gasp inside the bag.

"Mm-hmm. Yes. Very good."

"You're still rubbing yourself?"

"Mm-hmm. I'm so . . . soft."

"Yes, very soft. Remember, we're just playing, okay?"

She nodded and said, "Yes."

"Tell me you want me to squeeze this tight. Say for me what all of us will want to hear you say at the party."

She hesitated for only a second, then moaned and said, through the plastic, "Yes, squeeze it tight. I'm just trash—sticky trash."

"Are you sure that's what you want?"

The bag shook lightly with her nodding, and she said, softly, "Yes. Squeeze it . . . very tight."

"You must know that it might never loosen again. You do know that?"

In the second of silence before she answered, he grinned at feeling her swallow again.

"Mm-hmm. Yes."

"And you're still begging for it to get very tight?"

"Mm-hmm," she said with her left hand even busier. "I'm begging. Mm . . ."

"Good girl. Yes, all of us will want to *keep* it *very* tight at the party. You'll be so soft, Laura, and so used-up. It'll feel so good that way, won't it?"

"Mm-hmm. Mm . . ."

She nodded and the bag shook from her rubbing between her legs.

"A little bit tighter for the sticky trash."

He tightened his grip so that no air could pass in or out, and she watched him with big eyes through the plastic as the bag inflated and deflated, no longer allowing any fresh air.

"For a piece of used-up trash, you're quite beautiful now. Tell me you love being beautiful like this."

It took only a second, then she smiled and said, muffled, "I love this. Mm, I'm so beautiful now."

"Good girl. Such a good girl now."

The bag continued puffing, Lenore breathing the same air repeatedly, and shaking from her intense rubbing.

"We both know that no one will ever miss you or wonder about you."

She nodded gently.

"So, you can tell me you don't ever want me to stop."

She stared for a second, not answering but still rubbing herself.

"Tell me," he said with his hands around her throat and trapping in the only air she had.

"Mm, don't stop."

She panted, puffing the bag.

"Don't ever. No one will miss me."

"No, nobody will. You've never been a sexier girl than now, when you're about to be all used up."

She nodded, gasping into the stale air.

"What you're doing feels so good, doesn't it? Like never before?"

"Mm-hmm . . ."

"Good girl. Here, this is what you insist I do. It's what you're begging for."

He squeezed hard enough that her gasp was silenced instantly. But her left hand didn't stop, and her mouth locked open, quietly gaping behind the plastic.

"You're so soft now, all hidden away behind the plastic. Such a pretty, disposable little girl."

She shook with her orgasm as it peaked just then, her lips gummy and clinging to the plastic.

"Yes, just like that, little girl. It feels so good to be pretty and all alone in plastic."

She jerked inside the bag, her fingertips gliding rapidly up and down.

"Just pretty, sticky trash that no one will ever miss."

He kept his big hands tight around her throat, smiling as she watched him through the plastic, unable to make a sound but still rubbing, stretching her soaked panties.

Her lips moved the plastic as her eyes closed slowly and her mouth opened and closed just enough, like a fish out of water, to make him smile.

Then, she relaxed, and a weak smile appeared.

He let a few quiet seconds pass, his hands gripping her throat.

"There. A perfect orgasm for you."

He gave her a big smile and fluffed open the bag, then he held her head with both hands.

"You must know that that was how you looked your best."

She gave only the slightest of nods while taking quicker, deeper breaths.

"Mm-hmm. I know."

"You'll be so beautiful at our party. Such a pretty, soft, used-up thing."

"Yes. Mm-hmm."

Laughing once, he said, "Besides, it's all you deserve."

And he saw only a hint of a smile through the clear plastic as she stayed careful and still and only said, "Mm-hmm. Nothing more."

"Here," he said, and he helped her ease herself back toward the chair, and he gently laid her head back on it.

"Stay. Let's let that dry a little. You'd like that, wouldn't you?"

"Mm-hmm."

"Good, just stay still," he said, then he started fondling both breasts through the buttoned shirt, and Lenore didn't move at all.

"Bet you'd like this fine pair sprayed on, too, huh? Can you imagine that, seeing them all sticky, things dripping off?"

"Hmm, okay. Yeah."

"While you're bagged up so nicely, like the disposable cocksucker you know you are?"

"Mm. Yes."

"Hell, we'll coat your naked body. Just a worthless, sticky cocksucker, bagged up like trash."

"Hmm," she said, still weak from her orgasm. "I deserve that too."

"Here," he said and grabbed the bottom edge of the bag. "Let's get you out of this. Now, you know what kind of fun we'll have at the party."

"Mm. Yes."

He shifted it around, got it up off of her face, then off of her head, and let it fall off to the side.

"Oh, wow, it's all gumming up in that pretty blond hair. Huh. That won't clean up easy."

He pinched some of her hair and pulled it across her face, then dragged it up and down over her coated lips.

"Open for me, slut. I want to degrade you just a little more."

She parted her lips, and he worked the thick strand of hair in, into the mess that he'd left there, then pulled down on both sides, leaving it deep in her mouth.

"Good, Laura. Close up now. You just hold onto that."

She held her lips tight, keeping her hair and the mess he'd made inside.

"A little bit more. You're just so much prettier now."

"Mm."

"You see how it's all just for fun? It's just some drama that you can enjoy playing along with?"

"Mm-hmm."

He took some hair from the other side, then laid parts of it across her face, working it into the sticky areas and leaving it all there.

"Well, you sure are a pretty mess. And it's all kind of set now. Good. Here, let me help you."

He supported under her arms and helped her to stand, then brushed aside the rest of her hair that he hadn't stuck to her face.

"See, Laura, this is just a taste of how we do things. I hope I haven't scared you out of the time of your life."

"Uh-uh," she said, unable to open her mouth but shaking her head.

"Just adorable. Worthless but adorable, and we didn't even need to undress you."

Lenore couldn't speak, even when he took her arm and began coaxing her toward the door.

"You're just perfect for being degraded."

He stopped her, turned her to face him, and held both of her arms. Before continuing, he studied his artwork, a mix of drying streams and drops and hair, a lot of it tucked tight between her lips.

"You might not have known that before, Laura, but you do now. You crave it. It's the only kind of sex you'll ever want again."

She only looked at him with her right eye.

"I need you to admit that. You know it's true. Just a little nod."

He waited, smiling, and Lenore managed her own smile and nodded.

"Yes. Perfect. We're going to have so much fun with you. The last step, now, for your interview. Step out into the hall, as beautiful as you are right now, and stand there for five minutes. Let anyone that passes see what you are."

She groaned and started prying her lips apart.

"Go ahead, try to talk. None of that is going to clean up too easily now anyway."

He was still laughing when she struggled to say, "No, I can't do that! What if I know someone that works here or is visiting?"

"Oh, well, that sure would be degrading, wouldn't it?"

He fluffed out the hair that he could, then swung in the door.

"At least, admit it to yourself, Laura. You've loved every bit of this."

He gave her a push out into the hallway, then pointed close to her face and said, "Five minutes. You're going to show me that beautiful blond mane for five minutes through the peep hole."

Then, he fluffed the unstuck hair back behind her, chuckling, and slammed the door.

Lenore spun around and pressed her head up against the small port in the door, then turned to her right and saw two women approaching.

"Oh God . . ."

Chapter 22 – God, What an Experience

"Laura, things are already so far out of control! I was just in his room and God, the things he made me do! Then, he made me stand out in—"

"Whoa, Lenore! Take a breath, alright?"

Lenore was at her kitchen sink, watching through the window as Amos, his shirt off in the warm sunlight, was still battling with the unruly wall of hedges. Clouds of insects swarmed around him, and he could barely manage to clip once before swatting all around madly.

"Okay," Lenore said and took another deep breath. "Okay, I breathed."

"Good. You sound better already. Now, nice and easy—tell me what's going on."

"I don't think I can do it, Laura—that party with those bizarre people who are probably all freaks like—"

"Hey! Start with the easier stuff before you have a heart attack. First, where are you right now?"

"I'm at home. I'm standing in the kitchen, watching Amos work in the backyard. I circled the block, saw him in the back, and sneaked inside."

"Okay, that's good. So, you can talk. Now, don't jump to anything that happened, but tell me where you were before you came home. Just that, Lenore. Just answer that."

"A hotel room."

"Oh, a hotel room. Was it nice?"

"Uh, I guess. Yeah," she said, then laughed softly. "The rug was soft anyway."

"We'll get to that. Okay, so you weren't there alone. Who was there with you?"

"He said his name was Michael."

"Yeah, that's the guy. Uh-huh. And yeah, he's on the freaky side. I heard he's almost like a hypnotist or something."

"He sure as hell might be. When he was talking, I couldn't—"

"Hey, slow down. Tell me about that in a second. Michael's wife, Eva, though, is even more extreme. Gorgeous but outrageous too. Okay, so you met him there. I suppose that was your interview for the party?"

"Yeah, I guess you could call it that—the main one. Oh, Laura, you weren't kidding—even the damn interview was degrading."

"Mm. Well, of course—he wanted to check you out. Still, you told him you'd do the party?"

"I did say that I would but now, I don't know. I mean, it'll be even more bizarre."

"More bizarre than what? Come on—it's time for details, Lenore."

"Okay. He kind of lured me in by leaving the door unlatched, making it a point to tell me I was free to go whenever I wanted."

"Yeah. That seems fair enough. So, you didn't run out of there?"

"No. Why, when he's being so nice?"

"Okay, then what?"

"He, uh, he wanted me to say that I didn't expect any respect, that I was only good for degrading sex."

"Ooh, that's making you nothing but an object. And you said it, right?"

"He really was like a hypnotist. And besides, he said it's all for fun, and I should just play along."

"And it sounds like you did play along?"

"Oh, yeah. Then, he told me to get on my knees."

"Ooh, and you did?"

"Uh-huh. Real quick. I was all psyched up to do anything anyway. I mean, I made up my mind I'd do anything."

"That's the right approach. Uh-huh. Okay, so—oh, that's why you said the rug was soft?"

"Mm-hmm. Yep. So, I'm kneeling for him, and he told me I looked good on my knees, and I had to say that I belonged there. Then, he made me keep looking up at him and say what I was."

"And what's that?"

"I said I was nothing but a worthless slut."

"Ooh, Lenore, that's sexy. I'd bet he loved that."

"Oh, he sure did."

"Who wouldn't? Okay, then what?"

"Laura, he got me to start masturbating, right there while I was kneeling for him."

"And you did, right?"

"Yeah, and it felt good, maybe because the whole thing was so different."

"I can picture it."

"Then, he, um, took it out. God, he was ready."

"Well yeah, a sexy thing like you, down on her knees. Okay, he got it out. Then, what?"

"Before he made me, uh, you know . . ."

"Oh, come on. Just say it."

"Okay. Before he made me suck it, he made me talk about how worthless I was, how I was just a slut. I had to say a lot how I was nothing but a cocksucker."

"Damn, that's sexy—you really were just a sexy object."

"You know, I did feel sexy, Laura. God, what an experience. So, I'm, uh, sucking, and he's making me say that no one cares about me, I'm not good for anything else, even that no one would ever miss me because I'm so worthless."

"Yeah, that's what that party's about. They want to own you. Okay, keep going."

"It got kind of scary, then, but I was rubbing myself, and it was such a weird thing to be ordered to do that. God, that felt good, and when he wanted me to say I was disposable, a disposable cocksucker, I did. I said that a lot."

"Disposable? Lenore, that's crazy."

"Uh-huh, but it all felt so good. He made me say that I knew exactly what that meant. And I even agreed that I was so disposable that I should be bagged up like any other trash."

"Lenore! Oh my gosh!"

"Alright, here's where it got even more, uh, different. I'm busy with him, and he starts tipping my head back, telling me I have a pretty face."

"You do. You're gorgeous. I'd tip your head back too."

"Oh, Laura. So, he's complimenting me while I'm sucking him, telling me how pretty I am, even how I must have spent some time with the makeup, stuff like that."

"Oh, shit, I think I know where this is going."

"Uh-huh. He asked me if I knew what was about to happen. And he asked me if I wanted it—all of it on my face."

"And did you?"

"God, Laura, right then, yeah. Damn, that felt so sexy."

"Yep, just an object. So, he did, right?"

"Not right away. Laura, remember the disposable part? He found a plastic bag, and he got it started over my head."

"No way. Really?"

"Yep. I knew exactly what he wanted to do to me."

"Yeah, I know too. Go on."

"He wanted me to tell him that I was a, oh, maybe I shouldn't—"

"Lenore. Just say it. What did you say? What were you right then?"

"Hmm. I was a disposable, cocksucking slut."

Lenore listened to the silence coming from Laura. A few seconds passed.

"Laura?"

"Oh my God, Lenore. Whew, you are so sexy. Mm. Say it again. Not past tense."

"What? Laura, no."

"Oh, come on. Just say it. For me."

"I'm nothing but a disposable, cocksucking slut."

"You sexy little thing. Damn. That Michael's got a good act going on."

"And that's exactly what I felt like. So, he got me good. I mean, everywhere on my face, Laura, even covering an eye. He worked his way down, spraying me until it was all running down into my hair and sticking there."

"Oh my God, that's sexy as hell, Lenore."

"So, my face is covered, and he pulls the bag so low that it's down by my breasts. He's telling me how beautiful I am like that, just a disposable cocksucker and Laura, God, it really felt that way. Even when . . ."

"Go on. What?"

"He got his hands around my neck and squeezed the bag. Not enough to close it, but it was obvious he sure could have. Then, he got me to say that I wanted him to squeeze it tight because I was nothing but trash. And I did!"

"And he tightened it up?"

"Oh, he sure did. I was trapped in there, my face a mess, and I'd asked for it. He told me how beautiful I was right then, and I agreed with him, and then my orgasm crashed like crazy. Oh my God, Laura!"

"Perfect timing. Obviously, it was all just for fun," said Laura. "He let you go."

"Yeah, he did. It really was just this crazy drama thing, and that's what they want to do at the party. He said so."

"Wow. Hell of a party. You'll be the sexiest thing ever."

"Yeah, if I go. He took the bag off, and there was a lot of it stuck on my lips. He pushed some of my hair in there, too, and made me hold it in."

"God, he really degraded you. Lenore, you really were all the things you were telling him."

"I guess I was. But it gets even more degrading. He played with my breasts just to let all of that dry up some on my face."

"And did it?"

"Oh my gosh. Yeah. Everywhere, even all over an eye. He'd made a real mess of me."

"I'd bet that took some time to clean up."

"Oh, but he wasn't done with me. He made me stand in the hotel hallway for five minutes. He said he'd better see my blond hair through the peep hole the entire time."

"God, that Michael. What a freak. He loves degrading you."

"Yeah, so I did. Thank God it was mostly deserted."

"Mostly?"

"Just two young women walked past, and man, did they laugh. They both called me a slut and kept walking."

"Then, you what? You couldn't drive home like that."

"No, I went to a restroom, and, uh, when I was checking it out in the mirror, I, um, masturbated. Again."

"Oh, Lenore. That's hot. You had it all over your face?"

"Mm. Mm-hmm. And I was licking at what I could, feeding what I could from my fingertips, and giving myself a giant orgasm."

"You are so ready for their party, Lenore."

"Oh, now that I'm home, I don't think so, Laura. It was fun being that Laura for a while, but I don't know . . ."

"Okay, listen. Imagine not just one guy doing that to you. What if it was one after another? Tell me you don't want to try that just for kicks."

"Laura . . ."

"Oh, and they'll do way more to you than that. It sounds like you didn't even undress for Michael. Imagine a lot of them doing all kinds of things to you, and you're naked and helpless for them. God, Lenore, remember what you said you are."

"I remember."

"Say it again. Right now."

"Laura, I . . ."

"You want to. I can tell, sexy girl. Say it."

"I'm nothing but a disposable, cocksucking slut."

"Yes. That's you. And you're doing that party we call the—"

"Shit! Amos is coming! Bye!"

* * *

Lenore kept watch on Amos taking his time in traveling toward the house, stopping often to wipe sweat and swing at insects.

She jammed the phone into her pants pocket, then said, "Oh God!"

In the drawer next to the sink, she found a small hand mirror, which she held up to inspect her face. She saw that she'd missed some of Michael's contributions when cleaning herself up in the hotel bathroom.

"Oh, come on," she said as she scraped at some stubborn crust near her right temple, dried thoroughly on the skin and fingering deep into her thick hair.

The back door swung in, and Amos stepped inside without any hesitation. Lenore turned enough to keep her right side out of his view.

"Amos. You're working in the yard."

"No. I was. Now, I'm in the kitchen."

"Right. Nice. Well, it's good to see things improving out there."

Walking toward the sink, he said, "Sure. Damn hedges. Damn bugs too."

He began washing his hands, wringing them together under the running water, and Lenore scratched around, sending small flakes to the floor until he shut off the faucet and turned, grabbing a towel.

"You alright?"

"Yeah," she said. "Why do you ask?"

"No reason. You just seem different. Get your errands done?"

"Oh, you could say that. Yeah."

"Did you already take a shower? Your hair is kind of wet."

"Oh, no, there was just some frizz, so I wet it. No big deal."

Still drying his hands, he yanked open the refrigerator and took out a beer.

"Oh," said Lenore, "when did we get that?"

"I picked it up the other day. I can have beer if I want."

She stared for a second, still turned to her right, and said, "Well, sure, Amos. No one ever said you couldn't. I might have one later too."

Leaning against the counter while twisting off the cap, he said, "One what?"

"Amos, what do you think?"

He tipped it back and swallowed a few times before looking her way.

"Beer. Of course. It's a joke."

"Yeah. Funny. Hey, toss that towel in the basket when you're done, alright? I should probably get some laundry done."

He scoffed, took another quick drink, then said, "Probably that cheerleader skirt again. Yeah, have to keep that thing clean."

"I told you, Amos, it helps things last longer if you—"

"Always ready, huh?"

"What? My cheerleading days were years ago."

He scoffed and kept staring at her, swirling the bottle in lazy circles.

"You're being weird, Amos. Those hedges need you more than I do right now."

He mumbled, "You need something . . ." then tipped the bottle high to pour the rest down his throat.

"What did you just say?"

"Nothing," he said and clinked the bottle on the counter. "Don't forget that skirt for the laundry."

She shook her head but not enough to show him her right side. He only gave her a quick glance, then exited the room, slamming the house's back door on his way to tend to the overgrown hedges.

"Shit."

Chapter 23 – You Need More of It

Lenore took up her post at the kitchen sink again, watching Amos walk without enthusiasm back toward the dense jungle at the rear of the property. It wasn't until he'd picked up the shears that she took out her phone.

"I think I hate him."

"And you should, Lenore. You deserve better."

"Huh," she said, laughing. "That's not what Michael wanted to hear."

"Oh, that's right. You're worthless, you don't deserve any respect, that kind of stuff. I know that's all kind of—"

"Laura, no, whatever you're going to say. That was what made all of that so fun—the way he was treating me."

"Like an object. That's what you wanted."

"Yeah. I was a worthless object, and he wanted so bad to hear that no one cared about me. It was kind of scary when he was talking about no one even looking for me. God, I really felt worthless and good for nothing but sex."

"Well, that's the whole point. That's their thing. Hey, how was that orgasm in the bathroom after, huh?"

"Oh my goodness. Probably the best ever."

"You were remembering all that he forced on you—made you do?"

"Oh, yeah. With him, I timed it just right, and I got there just when he started on my face. Oh, Laura, that was a big one—I was still rubbing, and it felt so, so good."

"Damn. I like what you're turning into, Lenore. So sexy."

"I, uh, don't know that I'm turning into anything. It was just a weird interview thing for a party."

"Uh-huh. Keep telling yourself that."

"What, you think I'm really changing?"

"Huh. I think you're just figuring out what gets you going the best."

"You're too much sometimes, Laura. I think the party would be like that but even more. That's some crazy drama that they want."

"Yeah. So, you're doing it, right?"

"I don't know. Maybe. I know it's worse than the Frat Chat, but I'd like to hear more about that."

"Alright, I like talking about it. The first two were easy and quick—I think they were shy. But they got the shirt off of me, and wow, they loved my breasts."

"Well, of course."

"You like my breasts, Lenore?"

Lenore laughed and said, "You're being silly. Yes, they're nice. Of course, I like them. Then, you did someone named Emilio and someone else that you never saw, but he got you from behind."

"Yeah, that was a high point. That Emilio, God, he was getting me to say so many things. It was weird at first, then I really got into it. That's how you'd have to be at the party."

"I kind of was at the interview. Yeah, I was saying all kinds of stuff."

"Good. So, Emilio and his unseen buddy finished up, and they both got their share. And it went like that for a while—two at a time. You'll probably do a lot of that at the party."

"Uh, two at a time? Michael was talking about that, while he was doing my, uh, face."

"Uh-huh. Yeah, someone getting you from behind too."

"Laura, he said there would be more than one, and the second guy wouldn't get me in the same place. I know what that means."

"That's exactly what it means. I told you I was taking three at a time at the Frat Chat, didn't I?"

"You were serious?"

"Oh, heck, yeah. It's almost a comical thing until it's all set up."

"Doesn't that kind of hurt?"

"A little. At first. But it's something, Lenore, to have three studs acting like starving animals on you all at once."

"I'd imagine so."

"Be ready for it. Don't you dare say no to anything."

"Well, if I agreed to the party, if I really went to that thing, I'd have to make up my mind to—"

"Hey," Laura said without a trace of laughter. "Lenore, enough with the talk about not going. You *are* going. You're going, Lenore."

* * *

"Look, Lenore," Laura continued as Lenore still watched Amos through the kitchen window, "enough fooling around. You are doing the party. You *are* doing it."

"Laura, stop it. Stop being so serious. Sure, that was a wild fling at the hotel, but I can always decide what I want to do and when I want to stop."

"No, dear girl, you don't understand. I don't have firsthand knowledge, but I think Michael and the rest are serious about their fun but kind of on the shady side."

"So?"

"So, Michael doesn't know that I'm sending a substitute. Drake is the only one that knows. Michael is lining up the same entertainment that he heard was so good at the Frat Chat. Lenore, no way does he want a stand-in."

"You can just go do the party, then, Laura. You're the one they wanted, right?"

"You still don't get it. Michael has already seen you. He's already had all kinds of fun with you. You're the one he wants, but he has to keep believing that you're the one from the Frat Chat."

"This is getting too—"

"Lenore, stop. This isn't up for debate. Complicated? Is that what you were going to say? It'll get way worse if you don't follow through. If Michael gets pissed, he'll find out from Drake who I really am. Oh, shit, they won't be too nice when they come after me."

"They'd do that?"

"I don't know! Maybe? I sure don't want to take that chance."

"Laura, I'm sorry, but this is just getting too weird. Sure, it was exciting to be that way at the hotel, all degraded and disrespected—God, I've never done such things. It surprised me what a turn-on that was. But that doesn't mean—"

"You still don't see it. Lenore, that's you. You weren't just playing. That is who you are. I've thought so for a long time."

"What? No, you can't mean—"

"Oh, I sure do mean it. It's you. And you need more of it. You want what that party will give you. Lenore, you have to go. Mostly for you but for both of us."

"Laura. Stop. I'm not doing the damn party."

The phone went quiet, and Lenore waited, watching Amos punching ineffectively in all directions.

"Fine," Laura finally said. "I'll make sure Amos finds out what you just did in that hotel."

"You wouldn't."

"Oh, you don't think? Yeah, I will. You think he's difficult now, wait and see."

"Well, if I'm ending this engagement anyway, maybe it doesn't matter if—"

"How about your office people? Think they'd like to know all about how you spent your day off?"

"Laura, how could you? I thought we were friends!"

"We are, Lenore. The best friends. Shit, we even look alike. But you have to do this. It's the only thing that'll keep us both—"

"Oh, there's another call," said Lenore.

"I hear it. Go. Make the right decision, my gorgeous twin girl, and remember: we're still friends."

Lenore saw a number that she recognized, scoffed while tapping her phone, and said, “Drake?”

Chapter 24 – Get Yourself Sexed Up

"Hi, Laura. Yeah, this is Drake. From the elevator?"

"Hey, you think I don't remember that? Even that part of the interview was—"

His laughter stopped her.

"What?"

"No, that was unofficial and just for my own amusement. Damn, you're quite a treat."

"You just did that on your own?"

"Uh-huh. Every man for himself. That's a philosophy that works."

"God, this is so out of control."

She scoffed silently at the sight of Amos swinging his arms around, then dropping the shears and swinging even more.

"Yeah. You don't have any control," Emilio said. "That's the whole point."

"Okay, I get it. What do you want?"

"I'm just checking that you didn't lose the info on the where and when and how to get your sweet self there. Then, you can—"

"Wait. Hold up a second. You—"

"You're right—there's something more important first: which part of our fun in the elevator did you like the best?"

"What? Oh, come on."

"Your breasts are unbelievable. Damn, what a nice handful."

"Uh, thanks, I suppose. Yeah, they are pretty nice."

"Just pretty nice? Oh, and then, slipping your pants down and just checking things out. Damn, such nice curves."

"Is there a point to this? Why don't you get back to why you called?"

"I will. In a second. Here's what I want to know first, and be honest: that guy that opened the doors and saw all that. Do you remember what you said to him?"

"Yeah, Drake. Yeah, I do."

"I don't. What was it again?"

She smiled at the sound of his laughter.

"You're impossible. Fine. You're kind of relentless."

"Yep."

"Okay. I told him that I was a worthless cocksucker."

"While . . ."

"While I was kind of stripped and getting felt up. There, you happy now?"

"One more thing: what did you say to him next?"

She scoffed and watched Amos almost dancing near the back hedges.

"I told him that I loved to suck cocks."

"Plural. That's very important. You're the one that made it plural."

"Drake, you—"

Amos tossed the shears to the ground, waved his arms around frantically, and began a sprint toward the house.

"I have to go!"

"Why? Wait, just another—"

"No, I, uh, there's another call."

"I didn't hear anything."

"The phone's broken. Bye! I'll call you back!"

She just got her phone put away when the back door swung in, and Amos stood there, bug bites dotting his face.

* * *

"You look terrible."

He smirked and said, "At least the hedges are looking better. That's what matters."

She squinted at him as he stepped toward the refrigerator, and he took out another beer.

"Don't try to stop me—I deserve this."

"Why would I try to stop you? Everyone should get what they deserve."

While twisting the cap loose, he tipped his head and squinted back at her.

"Even if," she continued, "they never knew that's what they deserved."

"What? What are you talking about, Lenore?"

"Nothing, Amos. I just have a lot on my mind. About work, I mean. Hey, you have spots all over your face."

He leaned to look more closely at her, and she held her breath and rotated slightly more to her right.

"You don't. You weren't out getting bitten up."

He sneered and pointed at his own face.

"You wouldn't want anything all over that pretty face of yours."

She stared, turned more to her right, and said, "What an odd thing to say, Amos."

He looked down at his work boots and said, "Well, I, uh, just mean, you're lucky you're not out there where you'd get all bit up."

"Maybe you should put on some bug spray or something."

"That's just what I need: to have stuff sprayed on my face now too."

"Oh, um," she said, then swallowed hard, "yeah. Maybe not a good idea. For you, I mean."

"Huh?"

"Uh, we're talking about you. Now. That's all I mean."

He turned his head for a lengthy look at the opened wine bottle on the counter, then back at Lenore.

"One might think you've been drinking, Lenore. Just pouring it right in there."

"Right in there. Yeah. Hey, you're the one drinking. Maybe you should chug that and get going while there's still daylight."

"I was going to. I don't need you to tell me."

While he had it tipped back, finishing what remained, she said, "No, of course not. Not everyone likes being told, uh, what to do."

He shook his head while setting down the empty bottle, then scoffed and walked back outside, letting the door slam on its own.

"Oh my goodness . . ."

* * *

Amos had just left, and Lenore had already taken out her phone. She glanced up from it only long enough to see him walking away from the house, then she hit Drake's number.

"Good, glad you took care of that other call."

She let him laugh for a few seconds, then said, "Well, I'm back. Look, I don't—"

"Friday, 6:00 pm. Follow the instructions."

"Drake, I'm starting to think—"

"This is important: wear some sunglasses and maybe something with a hood. It's for your own privacy, so no one has any clue what kind of sleazy antics you're up to."

"You're not listening. Seriously, I've been—"

"Just do what I wrote out, and that'll get you right to the party room. Doesn't that sound good? The party room?"

"Yes, I mean, no, I mean, it's—"

"Oh, and even though it's written out, I need to stress this: dress yourself up nice. Really, fix your hair, do it all. They'll like you even better. Hell, you'll even like it better. You want to look good for all of them, right?"

"Well, yeah, I always want to look good, but I—"

"I'm not completely sure, but Eva, Michael's wife, will probably see you as like a personal toy and want to dress you up her own way."

"What? No, you can't be—"

"Look, just dress yourself up nice and if Eva treats you like a doll that she—"

"I can't do it."

"What are you talking about?"

"Drake, I just can't. It's too much!"

"I'll tell you what the hell is too much: you thinking you have any choice. Oh, hell no, Laura. You're doing exactly as you're told."

"But I—"

"You already said you would. There's no going back."

"I am going back! Forget it—just forget the whole thing!"

"Alright, you listen to me: I don't know if there's anyone in your life that you value. I mean, you did say you're worthless. But if you do have someone, I'll tell him or her, in great detail, about every little thing you let me do in that elevator."

"You wouldn't."

"Oh? Try me."

"It's my word against yours. I won't even admit that I was anywhere near—"

"I recorded it. Hey, what can I say? This is a pro operation. Do you remember the fun things you were saying?"

"Yeah."

"You might not remember, but your voice, Laura—you sounded like you were enjoying the hell out of everything. Shit, there's even the sound of the elevator doors opening, then you saying to someone what you love to do. Remember that?"

"Yes," she said, her light sobbing carried along with the word.

"You even made it plural."

"I remember."

"Hey, it isn't all that bad. Be there at 6:00. Get yourself sexed up."

With one hand over her mouth, Lenore shook from the sobs that she tried to keep quiet.

"Laura?"

She ended the call and stuffed the phone roughly into her pocket.

"Dammit . . ."

Chapter 25 – We Also Play for Keeps

Staring out the kitchen window with eyes blurry from tears, at a man without a shirt losing his war against hedges and buzzing insects, Lenore nearly jumped when the phone in her pocket rang.

She gave it look and didn't recognize the number.

"Please, be a wrong number!"

She took the call and said, "Hello?"

"I recognize that voice. Do you recognize mine?"

"Yeah. Uh, it's Michael. You got this number from Drake?"

"Yes, right after he just called me with a disturbing development. Do I really need to define that, or can we simply deal with it?"

"There's, uh, nothing to deal with. Look, today has been incredible. I just, uh, think I'd rather not actually, you know, do your party."

"Oh, that's nonsense, Laura. At least be true to yourself. It's what you want."

"No, I just want to do some laundry, then maybe read for a while and—"

"No. Stop it. We both know you need way more than that."

"We do?"

"Yes. Being in a private hotel room with a stranger, having no choice but to do what he demanded of you . . . that's what you want. You loved all of it."

"Oh, uh, Michael. Look, I did play along with all that, but I think—"

"You weren't 'playing along' with anything, Laura. I know acting when I see it, and that wasn't acting. Not at all. That was all you."

"You think so, huh?"

"Can you promise me just one answer with complete honesty?"

"Uh, sure. Why not? What's your question?"

"Laura, do you deny that you get a perverse thrill from being called a disposable, cocksucking slut?"

Lenore gasped quietly, and a few seconds passed in silence.

"That's what I thought. Your silence was your answer. No, Laura, you're not even fooling yourself. You loved everything today, and it's making you crazy to have to wait for whatever else might be lined up for you. Tell me I'm wrong."

She bit her lip and frowned at Amos giving no sign that he was about to return to the house anytime soon.

A few seconds passed.

"You think I couldn't tell that you climaxed while that pretty face of yours was getting itself so sticky? Hell, it was so obvious. Tell me you didn't adore all of that."

More silent seconds passed.

"Exactly," he said. "You liked everything I said to you and everything I did to you. You want more. You want a lot more."

"No, really, I . . ."

"Yes?" he said, then laughed. "You really can't even pretend, can you? No, you can't. Do you know when you showed the most excitement in your eyes today, Laura?"

"Uh, no. When?"

"You felt such a dark streak of excitement when I was quizzing you about if anyone cared about you. You said no. You got even more excited when I wanted to hear that no one cared enough to ever come looking for you. You loved being called disposable, and you loved saying that you knew what that meant. Oh, that touched a nerve and made you feel like such an object. Tell me you didn't love drama like that."

She winced and began forming a reply, but she stopped, then tried starting again, but she couldn't find—

"Yes, you see? Friday, Laura. Oh, and tell me this doesn't give you a nice little spike of anticipation. Are you ready?"

"Uh, sure. Go ahead."

"Simply this: be sure to do your makeup very nice. You'll want to have a very pretty face. Do you remember what you liked me calling your face?"

"I, uh, yeah. I remember."

"Humor me and say it."

She cleared her throat, checked Amos again, then said softly, "My pretty, cocksucking face."

"Yes, that's it. It's so very pretty, especially when it's sucking a cock. I'm certain that you adored knowing how pretty you looked and how defiled it was going to be. That anticipation, Laura—you crave it."

"I do?"

"Oh, yeah. Follow Drake's instructions, and we'll all be so eager to—"

"No. Michael, just . . . no. I can't."

"Hmm. Alright. Hey, Laura. Do you remember a special moment when you held your head back, pointing that pretty face up, and I fussed with your hair to get it all hanging down so elegantly?"

"Uh, yeah."

"Do you remember what I asked you, right at that moment, after I'd made sure that no hair was blocking your face?"

"Oh, God. You didn't."

"Oh, I sure did. We like to play, and we also play for keeps. I had you kneel in the exact spot where the video camera would get the best shots of you. I've scanned through it a bit, and my goodness, you're absolutely stunning."

He laughed and added, "And you're so enthusiastic about being a cocksucker. Laura, you begged for it on your face. Oh, I won't apologize, but I will surely make that public in many ways."

She let the tears trickle down her cheeks, and she kept her sobs quiet.

"Exactly. Yes. Follow Drake's instructions. Oh, I just can't help myself: you're quite pretty, and you look sophisticated, but you're really a worthless, disposable, cocksucking slut."

His laughter continued until the call ended.

* * *

She'd just hid away the phone and began wiping at her cheeks when she saw Amos returning to the house. A towel was close, so she used it for a few quick blots, catching the last bits of tears, then threw it back down just as he entered.

"What?" he said, standing in the open doorway.

"What, what? Nothing."

"You alright?"

"I'm fine. Just, uh, maybe some seasonal allergies or something. Maybe you kicked up some pollen back there."

He stepped all the way inside and slammed the door.

"Yeah. My fault."

"No, Amos, I didn't mean it like that. Come on."

"Fine, Lenore. I've had enough of the damn hedges for a lifetime. Maybe we should call that young yard guy you had on the payroll."

"We could. Sure. He could probably use the money."

"That's what it's for—to be used."

She stared at him.

"Anyway, I'm going to get cleaned up before dinner."

"It's not for a while."

"Yeah. I know. You want me to cook tonight?"

"You? No way. Didn't you say you had some notes to go over, something about that school work function thing you have to attend Friday?"

"No, that's not what I said."

"Well, excuse me."

"What I said was that I wanted to take some time to consider my answers to whatever questions might be asked of me. This could be a big advancement in my career, Lenore."

"Sounds boring to me. But yeah, I hope you do well. Weird that they don't allow any guests, don't you think?"

"Huh? No, uh, it makes sense, I think. It's just a university thing, kind of boring, probably. Boring. All business."

"I see. I won't be that bored Friday, having a glass of wine with Laura."

"Oh, Laura. Yeah. I still think it's interesting how you two look alike."

"We kind of do."

"And even your names are similar. It's just weird."

"Uh, yeah. Sure. Um, you go study or whatever. I'm going to lie down for a while because of, you know, allergies. Or whatever."

"Fine. I'll study. You're taking the bed, one should assume?"

"Who talks like that? 'One should assume?' God, Amos, you're so much a full professor already."

"I'll take that as a compliment. Don't oversleep. I'm threatening you with my haphazard and likely hazardous brand of dinner prep."

"I'm begging you not to."

"Who talks like that?" he said, pointing at her and grinning. "Like you'd ever beg for anything."

"Uh, yeah. See you, Amos."

* * *

Lenore leaned her back into the bedroom door to close it, and she made no attempt to keep her locking of it quiet. The nightstand lamps weren't on and with the sun falling behind the trees, the room welcomed her with a comforting lack of light.

"Oh my God . . ."

She walked right to the bed, crawled up just a couple of steps on her knees, then lay flat with her face in the soft quilt.

"What am I going to do?" she whispered.

A few tears flowed easily into the cloth, absorbing instantly, and she raised herself up on her forearms, looking down at the faint wet spots.

She laughed softly and said, "I'm a wet thing. Even like this."

Rolling over toward her own side of the bed, she stared up at the ceiling and paid no attention to where her arms had ended up.

Until she rested both palms on her thighs.

"Those people," she said, scoffing then smiling. "God, the things he wanted. Things that . . ."

She rubbed her face with both hands, then fluffed her hair out to the sides.

"God, I should just admit it. I liked it. All of it."

While she kept her right hand making minor hair adjustments, she slipped her left down closer to her breasts.

She squeezed one, then the other, then she rubbed all around on them.

Her left hand then found a warm, tight place between her thighs, and fingertips were sliding up and down.

"I kind of have no choice. I have to do their party."

She got her right hand to finish what her left had started with her breasts.

"Hmm, and I know Michael will insist—all of them will—that I—hey, I don't even know how many."

She left her breasts alone long enough to cover a quiet giggle.

"So, what he said about, uh, different places. Oh my gosh. And what he did on my face. How many times at the party?"

She giggled quietly again and whispered, "God, I'd have so much on my face. They'd love doing that to me."

She lost the smile but kept rubbing herself and staring up at the ceiling.

"And even though it's just for fun, I'll have to say I'm disposable for them. Hmm, that felt different just saying it. God, what an object I'd be for everyone."

She licked her lips and rubbed harder.

"What did Michael say? Oh, mm, just soft, naked, used-up trash. Oh my goodness . . ."

She got her hand up under her shirt, then slipped it under her bra and continued, touching her breasts all over, doing everything with them.

"Hmm, my face covered by so many, and I'll just be pretty and hold still for all of them. Just soft, naked, used-up trash. And Michael will make me beg for it."

Her breathing had sped up and so had her hands.

"I might even have to beg Eva for it all over my face. And she'd probably laugh right while one of them is . . . penetrating me. So hard. So deep."

She kept touching herself and arched her back, tipping her head back.

"And what if he was serious about being disposable? That's the drama, right? Because I won't know for sure, and I'll just be . . . just . . ."

She groaned and rolled onto her side as she reached a peak almost as strong as when she was almost soft, naked, and used-up trash for a stranger in a hotel room.

Chapter 26 – Quite Good at Following Orders

"That worked better," Lenore said, seated at the kitchen table with a steaming cup of coffee.

Amos had just stopped himself in the doorway, and he looked down at his clothes.

"The, uh, you mean—"

"Yeah. I got up earlier so you can get in there and grab your clothes instead of hooking them off the back of the door."

"I have been hooking them a lot lately."

"Yeah. Coffee's hot."

She pointed toward the pot, and he started toward it.

"There's eggs in the pan too. Probably still warm. You'll have to make some toast if you want any."

"I do. Uh, I will. Uh, the toast."

"Amos, are you alright?"

"Yeah, I'm, uh, maybe a little nervous about the, uh, university thing. Tomorrow."

She scoffed and said, "Yeah. Tomorrow's a big day."

"It is?"

Holding his gaze, she said, "Amos, you just said so. Get your breakfast. Don't be late for work."

"You neither."

"I'm the boss. I'll be fine."

"That's good. You make a good boss."

He had his back turned, shuffling through a bread bag, when she said, "Oh, I don't know. I think I'd be quite good at following orders too."

"Uh-uh," he said, still not turning around. "Not you, Lenore. You expect a certain level of control at all times."

"I do?"

He spun around, cup in one hand.

"Well, I guess. I don't know. What do you think?"

She scoffed, shook her head, and said, "Amos, I just said that I'd probably be good at doing what I'm told, didn't I?"

"Oh, uh, yeah. You did. I'm just, uh, a little distracted."

"Tell me about it."

He stopped his tipping of the pan and the sloshing of eggs onto a plate.

"You too?" he said. "Why?"

"Oh. Um, just work stuff. There are always decisions to be made."

"One might say that you're excellent at making decisions. Always have been. I'd say, Lenore, that you should just trust your feelings. Your feelings, Lenore. They'll point you in a direction that—"

"Amos. Your eggs are getting cold. Grab your toast, sit down and eat, and get yourself to work on time."

"See? Like a boss."

"Oh my goodness. Yeah. It gets old."

"It does?"

"Oh, uh, no. I don't know what I'm saying. Eat. Or don't."

* * *

Amos had made his slamming of the front door obvious on his way out to walk to the university. Lenore had been holding the bedroom door closed, then she opened it, tiptoed out to look through the living room window, then scoffed at the sight of him walking away through their neighborhood.

Checking her wristwatch while hurrying back toward the bedroom, she began to smile and took quicker steps. In the room, she fished around in stacks of boxes and bags in the closet until she'd found her recent purchases.

She dumped her new clothes on the bed, then stepped back to look. The black dress was crafted from a thin material, and it looked short even just lying there flat. She set the new shoes up near it and shook her head at the height of the heels.

"Oh, can't forget that."

She dug into a small bag for the necklace, then started to lay it over the dress. But instead, she dropped it over her head and tugged down on it, easily confirming again that if her breasts were bared, those bare breasts would find a way to trap it there.

"Oh, that too."

A separate small bag held the new panties, and she lifted them up for a closer inspection. She scoffed at the sight of all the lace and frills, so innocent looking, but there were also large, silky bows that tied the flimsy garment together on the sides.

"Not so innocent."

She looked at her watch again, then quickly got out of her robe and pajamas, which she tossed across the bed. More than a few moments were spent playing with the necklace between her breasts, seeing how pulling up on it didn't get it free too easily. With her eyes on the new purchases, she slipped off the panties she was wearing, then stepped into and pulled up the new ones.

After a second or two of fussing with the bows on the sides, noting how they lay so gracefully across the smooth skin of her hips, she added the dress, then sat to finish the shoes with the delicate ties around her ankles.

A quick, impatient turn got her facing the mirror, and she caught her breath.

"Oh, that does look good. All of this."

Looking toward the edge of the dresser, at her phone, she said, "No, I shouldn't."

Laughing, she snatched it up and said, "But I'm going to."

She took a few photos of herself, reviewed them, then aimed it for another one—one from the side while she held the dress high and revealed the dainty loops holding on her new panties.

She hit the send button and said, "Take that, Laura. Unless I'm Laura. Oh my God."

The reply came back immediately.

"You want more obscene? Huh. I guess I've done far worse."

She rushed to get the dress off, fussed with her hair enough to get it looking wild, then snapped a photo from the front, one that showed not only her thick mane of blond hair and her smile but also her breasts, in their entirety, as she passionately held tightly the new necklace.

"Oh, what the hell," she said and sent it.

Expecting a quick reply, she held the phone and waited. The seconds crawled past, despite the normal ticking from the clock in the living room.

After a few minutes, Lenore sent a text that said only, "Laura?"

The reply was quick, and she read, "Oh my God. Lenore. You're gorgeous."

"Aw, thanks," she typed, then hit send, then set down the phone.

She gave the phone a glance, squinted at its silence, then faced the mirror. Her hands didn't hesitate as she raised them to hold both breasts, pointing them at herself.

"Hmm. He said soft, naked, and what?"

She giggled and added, "Oh, used-up."

She fondled them and forgot the phone, her eyes never straying from the sight of how large and smooth they were, and how her hands had no chance of containing them.

"They sure would use me. Say it, Lenore. Okay. I loved being used like that. I do want more. Oh, God, what's happening to me?"

She squeezed them together, then looked into her eyes.

"What am I? A disposable, cocksucking slut. Ooh, I'll admit: I never had an orgasm like that one when I knew what he was going to do to me. Holding my face still for it, imagining someone behind me, all of it. Mm, that was . . ."

She sighed and let them go, then picked up her phone to check the time.

"Shit."

* * *

She'd folded the dress and got that packaged up again, then reached for the new shoes.

"Oh, what the hell."

She left them there, left the panties and necklace on, and grabbed a short black skirt from the closet. A bra got settled into place, clasping in the middle in front, and she rushed herself into a thin white blouse.

"And just like that, I'm good to go . . ."

She spun toward the door, then came to an abrupt stop and again studied herself in the mirror. Listening to the far-off ticks of the clock on the wall, she devoted a moment to distributing her hair, letting thick bunches of it fall forward and down on her chest.

"Go where? Where is my life going? Ending an engagement to a saint, for one thing."

She put her hands behind her back, then studied the size of her breasts, the large round shape of them.

"God, they're all forcing me do the party. All of them. Even the real Laura."

Shaking her head, walking out of the room, she said, "I might as well be their soft, naked, used-up girl."

Chapter 27 – You Need to Be Ready

"Thanks, Shirley," Lenore said from her seat at her desk, "just anything from the taco place would be fine."

Shirley, standing in the open doorway, said, "We're sending one of us in about a half hour. I don't think I've seen that necklace before. It's very nice."

"Oh, you really don't miss much. I just dug this thing out of the closet this morning. I like it too. Can you swing that door shut when you go?"

"Sure, Lenore. You'll get your bag soon."

"A bag? What?"

"Lenore, what? A bag from the taco place, what else?"

"Oh, I was just thinking of, I don't know, that maybe their food was in boxes."

"It never was before."

Lenore met Shirley's stare for a few seconds, then flicked her fingers and said, "I need to make a call. Thanks, Shirley."

"Anytime."

The door was shut, and Lenore had a view of the employee through the open blinds as she strolled back to her desk.

"Oh God. Distracted? Huh. A little."

She stared at her computer screen for a few seconds, then scoffed and said, "Who am I kidding? I'm doing the damn thing."

Holding her phone to her ear, she said, "Yeah, hello, Laura. So, nice new underwear, huh?"

"Yeah, with the ties on the sides. Very nice. Hey, sorry about threatening you about that party. It's just that I'm kind of involved, too, you know."

"I know. You're forgiven. This whole thing is just out of control."

"Yeah. Wild times."

"You know what, though?"

"What?"

"I'm doing it. I'm going to be their entertainment."

"Oh, good call, Lenore. Is that my fault? Because I—"

"It wasn't just you. Drake threatened me and so did Michael. The only one that hasn't is Saint Amos."

Lenore smiled at the sound of Laura laughing.

"He is kind of a saint, isn't he? Well, sorry everybody's ganging up on you about—"

It was Lenore's turn to laugh.

"What?"

"Ganging up on me? Come on, Laura. Tell me you didn't mean it that way."

"Oh my God! No, I really didn't. That sure is what you're going to get, though."

"Oh, it's not just that, Laura. They have this whole theater drama play worked out, and I get to be the star."

"Ooh, a sexy star. You do need to go, Lenore."

"You really meant what you said before?"

"Uh-huh. I've always seen a much wilder side to you, but you've been making an effort to stay respectable. Got to respect that."

"Well, thanks. But I don't want to be a saint."

"After what you've already done?"

"Oh my God. Yeah. Wow, that was just the interview. So, I don't know what to expect when I get there. What if there are more questions first, and I'll have to keep acting like it was me at the Frat Chat?"

"Oh, yeah, for the Frat Chat 2. You'd need more details about what I did, right?"

"Yep. So, if you have a few minutes, could you—"

"Lenore, no. Sorry, but you need more help than just a few comments over the phone."

"I do?"

"Uh-huh. Hey, can you sneak out of the office for lunch?"

"Uh, probably. I just ordered some taco take-out, though."

"Someone else will eat it. I think you should meet me at your house. There's just too much to go over."

"Really? That much?"

"Lenore, this Frat Chat 2 is important. These people are professionals, whatever else they are. You need to be ready."

"Huh. Yeah, you're right. Okay, I'm leaving right now. Just stop by when you can."

"Okay, twin girlie. See you in bit."

Chapter 28 – In Very High Heels

Lenore closed the front door and reflexively reached for the lock, but she grinned and left it alone. Instead, she strutted toward the kitchen, still smiling but at the sound of her new heels on the hardwood flooring.

She set her notes and work things on the kitchen table, then got out the coffee to get a pot started. But she stopped in her tracks at the sound of the front door opening.

"Oh, no. Amos?" she whispered.

She glanced down at her attire, whispered, "Shit," then walked, unable to stop her heels from announcing her arrival, toward the living room.

Turning the corner, she gasped, then let out a relieved laugh.

"Laura. Oh, thank God. I thought somehow Amos had come home."

"Nope. Just me. Shit, it's like I'm looking in a mirror."

Lenore scanned Laura from top to bottom, smiling at her tight, short black skirt and largely unbuttoned black blouse. Her bare legs ended in black heels that were almost as high as her own.

"Something special going on?"

"Helping you, yeah. No, Lenore, I was just trying on stuff when you called—playing dress-up. I didn't waste any time and hurried right over."

"But we kind of match."

"Huh. Well, we look alike, so it was bound to happen someday with the clothes too."

"Well, come on in. I'm getting some coffee started, and we can—"

Laura had closed the distance and put a hand on Lenore's arm.

"Oh, Lenore, I don't think so. Coffee at a time like this? Uh-uh. Wine is what we need."

"We need wine? Really?"

"Uh-huh. You do have some, right?"

"Yeah. The saint and I have—what?"

"It's just funny," Laura said, still laughing. "Sorry. Go on."

"We've been drinking more often, Amos and I, but I'll open a fresh bottle."

"Perfect. I'll just warm up a seat on the couch."

"Good. I'll get it and be right in."

Only a few seconds had passed, and Lenore strode into the room with a bottle and corkscrew in one hand and two large wine glasses in the other. She set it all down on the coffee table while pretending to not notice that Laura had seated herself in the very middle of the couch.

"Have a seat," she said and tapped the cushion beside her. "I'll even do the honors with the bottle."

"Don't mind if I do. It's so nice to skip out on work like this."

She sat to Laura's right, and their thighs were pressed together.

"Oh, yeah, Lenore. It's for some important business too."

"Hmm. Very important."

Laura made their skirts rub together as she leaned forward, fussed with the wine bottle for a moment, then sat back and handed a glass to Lenore.

"Cheers, pretty girl."

"Cheers, equally pretty girl," Lenore said. "Michael was calling me that at the hotel."

"I want to hear all about that," she said, leaning farther back into the couch and keeping their arms touching too. "And about him. What was he like?"

"He was, uh, something. A real take control kind of guy. Tall, dark-skinned, neat. Handsome like a romance book cover. It would take a while to go through it all—damn, we did a lot in that hotel room."

"Sounds like it. And that wasn't even the party. Lenore, can you even imagine all you'll have to do there?"

"No, I really can't. I don't even know how many would be, um—"

"How many would be using you? Degrading you? Fun stuff like that?"

"Mm, yeah. So, maybe I should start at the very beginning. When I knocked, he—"

"No, wait. We can get back to that. Tell me what you thought of holding still for him, knowing he was going to spray all over your face."

"Oh, that. Oh my goodness."

"You didn't expect that at first, did you?"

"Uh-uh. And by that time, there was no way I could say no."

"Lenore."

She turned to look at Laura and raised her eyebrows.

"You didn't want to say no. You wanted that."

"What? Laura, I never would have guessed that—"

"Hey, I'm just teasing, Lenore. That must have been some kind of experience. While you were waiting on your knees, you were masturbating?"

"Mm-hmm."

"Because he ordered you to. And you were climaxing when he was squirting it on you? All over your face?"

"Oh, and he got me good—all over. A lot of it even ran down and got messed up in my hair. I had to—"

Laura was turned enough to rest her elbow on the couch back, and she brushed back and held Lenore's hair, then leaned closer to look at it.

"What?"

"Oh, just checking. You sure you got it all?"

They both laughed, and Lenore said, "Actually, no. It was all gummed up in there."

Laura leaned even closer and said, "Was there some around here? On your skin here?"

"Yes. There too."

"I should have been there to help you, you poor thing."

"Help, how? Give him another target?"

She gave Lenore a quick kiss on her cheek, then backed away just a small amount and said, "Like that. I could have kissed it away for you."

"Laura, you're being silly. Drink your wine."

Laura still held her thick hair back, away from her neck and cheek.

"Oh, I will, but I might have missed a tiny drop," she said, then kissed her again.

Lenore grinned and looked up at the ceiling, but she didn't move away.

"Laura, okay, yes, that would have helped."

"Mm-hmm. I would have been happy to help when my best girlfriend was in so much trouble. Some horrible stranger in a hotel room squirting it all on her face."

"Hmm."

"Not just tiny little drops either."

She gave her a longer kiss on her cheek, then stayed close to whisper in her ear.

"Lenore, you said you had an orgasm when he was leaving that all over your face?"

Lenore still didn't move away, and she only nodded and said, "Oh my God. Yes."

"Mm, that's nice. What was he saying to you again?"

Before Lenore started to answer, Laura had placed her left hand on Lenore's thigh, then moved in close enough that her nose was gently rubbing around on her ear.

"So you don't have to say it too loud—don't want the neighbors to hear."

"Hmm. He was telling me that I was a disposable cocksucker."

"Oh, a cocksucker. And a disposable one too? God, just a cocksucking object, huh?"

"Yeah. Well, I sure was."

"Mm," said Laura. "A girl just special for sucking cocks. What else?"

"Soft. He kept saying I was soft."

"Mm. You are. And he was pumping it onto you?"

"Oh, yeah. He said I was soft and vulnerable."

"Oh, vulnerable too. Hmm. And you didn't try to get away?"

"Uh-uh."

Laura leaned in closer and kissed around her neck.

"And he sprayed it all over your face, maybe even here?"

Lenore had a very short, very soft laugh, and said, "Hmm, yeah, my cocksucking face, he called it. I called it that too."

Laura let go of Lenore's hair and held her waist with both hands, and Lenore turned enough to face her.

"Say it again, Lenore. I'd love to hear you say that."

"You would?"

"Mm-hmm," she said, then leaned close enough to rub noses.

"Laura, he was spraying my . . . cocksucking face."

"Mm, a cocksucking face. You do have a cocksucking face, Lenore."

"Yeah, he sure found that out. A pretty, cocksucking face, we both called it."

"Mm, it is pretty. And he must have sprayed some on your lips too?"

Lenore was holding herself quite still, her big eyes looking into Laura's big eyes that could have been her reflection.

"Yeah. Yeah, Laura, he sure did."

"Just a little?"

"Oh, no. He made me pucker up, and he really focused on my lips."

"Oh, you even puckered up for it. Like you were kissing."

"Uh, yeah. It was like that. He got them good."

She focused on Laura's lips when she said, "I would have helped you with that. Would you like that, Lenore? Get some of that sticky stuff off of those pretty lips?"

"Mm-hmm," she said, her soft laugh more of a moan. "Off of my cocksucking face?"

"Mm, yeah, your cocksucking face," Laura said as she pressed her lips into Lenore's.

Laura kept the kiss going for thirty seconds, then backed away just enough to speak, still holding her trim waist.

"And you never told him no, did you?"

"Uh-uh. Never."

"And you won't now either."

Laura stood and lifted up Lenore's hands with her.

"You have a little bit more there, Lenore, and you really need my help. Come with me, and I'll try my best to clean up what that horrible man did to your . . ."

Lenore laughed and said, "My cocksucking face."

"Mm-hmm. Such a cocksucking face you have, Lenore."

"Uh, Laura, I—"

"Shh. You can't say no. I won't let you."

"You won't?"

"The bad man at the hotel didn't let you. Neither will I. We're both just telling you what you have to do."

Lenore, looking up with big eyes, didn't smile. But she didn't argue either.

And she stood, close to Laura, who put her arms around her waist.

"You're taller than me now," she said.

Lenore finally smiled and said, "Oh, it's just a little bit, from the heels."

"Mm-hmm. Love them. Come on, you soft, pretty cocksucker in very high heels."

Lenore shook her head with a gentle giggle, and Laura leaned closer for a quick kiss.

"Hmm, you liked hearing that. Lenore, you're a soft, pretty cocksucker in very high heels."

"Oh my goodness . . ."

"Mm-hmm. Yeah. I'm taking you to your bedroom, Lenore. It's either that or you promise to do the party."

Lenore only sighed and shook her head, and Laura grabbed and pulled out her new necklace.

"Oh, this is nice—convenient too."

She turned, held it like a leash, and began leading Lenore toward the bedroom.

Over her shoulder, she told her, "No, I changed my mind. You're doing both."

Still leading her, holding her necklace, Laura smiled at Lenore not offering the slightest protest.

"And I'm sure, my pretty cocksucker girl, that you got that sticky mess all over you."

"I did, huh?"

"Mm-hmm. Everywhere. It even got on me too. I'll show you exactly where."

Chapter 29 – It's Not Life or Death

At Amos's loud sigh from his end of the couch, Lenore stopped flipping channels on the muted TV and dropped the remote on the end table beside her.

"What, Amos?"

"One might say that there's nothing there that's worth seeing."

She watched him staring at the TV, his back straight and barely using the cushion behind him. A second later, he turned toward her.

"You're not making some kind of comment about my nighttime attire, are you, Amos?"

He glanced down at her usual thick robe, tied tightly, over long flannel pajamas that grudgingly gave a thin view of her floppy white socks before the ragged slippers ended the ensemble. No skin was visible.

"Oh, uh, no, Lenore. Of course not. You're, uh, dressed modestly, that's all. No, I meant the TV."

"Huh. Okay. Were you thinking about calling me a slut again?"

He shook his head vigorously and said, "No, you don't like that. You don't want to hear such talk. I accept that. One might say that I must accept that."

She scoffed, then laughed before saying, "Oh, you're ready. For whatever happens."

"What? What do you mean?"

"Your little university party tomorrow. You forgot about that?"

"Well, no, it's on my mind, to be sure."

"I'm just saying that you're ready for whatever happens. You'll be a full professor before you know it."

"Well, I appreciate your vote of confidence. It's just lightly unnerving to not know what to expect. For a class, I know quite well. At social functions, especially one where my career future might be determined by my words and actions, I'm less confident."

"Oh, you'll be fine. Just forget about it. At the party, just say and do what feels right. That party won't be life or death, you know."

"Well, no, I should say not."

"Go ahead."

"Huh? Oh, wait. Ah, that's funny, Lenore. You can be quite comical at times."

"Funny. Disposable too," she said to herself, grinning.

"What's that, Lenore? Besides funny?"

"Oh, I was just, uh, joking, saying that I was, um, quotable too."

"Hmm. Okay. Well, yes, you are. Quite."

"One would think?"

He laughed and said, "And now, I'm being mocked. Quite appropriate, one might—I would think."

"Alright, well," she said and tossed the remote toward him. "I'm going to bed. It's been some kind of day."

"Do you want to talk about it?"

"Not really. You just get comfy out here again."

"I thought maybe tonight might be the night when—"

"Amos, I'm all worn out. I just want to sleep."

"I won't even move. I'll just lie completely still on my side of—"

"Oh, um, it's not just that. I'm kind of, uh, overdue with washing the sheets and stuff. You're better off waiting."

After a few seconds of silence, she turned toward him and saw him staring at her.

"I don't believe our conversations have ever broached such topics before."

She shrugged and said, "Well, first time for everything. For a lot of things."

"Huh?"

"Nothing, Amos. There's the remote,"—she pointed at the device near him on the cushion—"unmute the thing unless you want to listen to that damn clock ticking all night."

He looked at it and said, "Damn clock? Why, Lenore, it's a very—"

"Amos," she said while standing, "I'm just being silly. Get some sleep. I'll see you in the morning."

He watched her shuffle out of the room, covered in thick cloth and with her hair locked up tight in a ball. The scuffing of slippers on the wood floor faded, then the bathroom door thumped closed softly.

"Huh. The damn clock?"

Chapter 30 – My, Uh, My Urges?

"It's fortunate," said Amos, "that I didn't stop at the beverage shop after classes. I would have missed out on this very early dinner."

Lenore had just set a plate of hot food in front of him at the kitchen table, and she was walking back to the counter for her own. When he saw her also reaching for the open wine bottle, he stopped her.

"Lenore, none for me, please. I have that university function in a short while."

She finished her grab of the bottle and brought it back to the table.

"Right. You wouldn't want to get yourself in any kind of trouble."

"Well, no, of course not. I tend to not look for trouble. One might say that that's good advice for anyone."

He held her gaze for a second, until she scoffed, then he lifted his fork.

"I'm not one of your students, Amos. Don't get in the habit of lecturing me."

"Hmm. Lenore, it was just a bit of good advice that I believe would be useful for anyone, including you."

"You're so damn helpful."

"Yes, well, it should apply equally well to situations that should be brought out into the open rather than leaving them veiled in secrecy."

"What on Earth are you talking about? Try eating. Try that."

He took a bite, then continued while chewing.

"I can say quite clearly of what I'm speaking. Just a moment ago, when I was—"

"'Of what I'm speaking?' Oh, come on, Amos. Just be normal. I know you can do it."

"I intend to be an above-normal professor. You should know that as well. Now, may I finish?"

"Finish your dinner? Yeah, get busy with it."

"That's not what I meant, and you know it. Very well, I'll proceed without your expressed permission. Before entering the house today, the neighbor next door and I chatted for a minute. He told me something that was news to me, and I felt somewhat befuddled."

"Befuddled. Nice. What about?"

"Only that he noticed you enjoying an afternoon away from your office yesterday. Yes, I believe that's the way he characterized it. It took some concentrated effort to leave him convinced that I knew all about it."

She stared, chewing.

"But of course, I knew nothing about it. It's good that you allowed yourself some respite from the rigors of work. I just, uh, had no idea."

"Well, I'm the boss, Amos, and if I want to give myself a break to relax around the house—"

"With your friend, Laura? I believe that's what our good neighbor meant by someone of similar appearance."

"Oh, yeah, she did meet me. We just kind of, uh, did some, uh, chatting. It was a nice break from work."

He scooped up another large bite and chewed while continuing.

"I think I know exactly what that was all about, Lenore."

"You, uh, you do?"

"Mm-hmm. I can summarize the activities in only several words. There's no reason why I shouldn't, is there?"

"Um, no. Go right ahead, Amos. Dammit."

"Oh, profanity. Yes, that fits."

"Just get to the damn point."

"And again. Very well. Lenore . . ."

He paused to look from one eye to the other as Lenore stared back, the food in her mouth ignored.

"Lenore. Drinking wine in the middle of the day with a friend is the first step in what could become a sharp decline."

"Oh," she said, laughing and covering her mouth with the hand still holding her fork. "Yeah, you got me there, Amos. We sure did sit around and drink some wine."

"Lenore. Even if you're able to control your urges in the future, you—"

"My, uh, my urges?"

"Yes. For alcohol. I thought I'd made that clear?"

"Oh, you did. Yep. Go on, then."

"My advice to you is that you should—"

She pointed as she stood, letting her fork clatter onto her plate.

"Advice? I'm trying to enjoy my damn dinner, and you're spouting all of your professor advice at me?"

"Well, I'm not exactly spouting. But my advice would also include the recommendation that you sit back down and—"

"Oh, this is getting good. You just stay in your damn seat."

She grabbed the wine bottle and her glass, strode to the counter and poured it full, then turned, leaned back, and pointed at Amos.

"Tell me about Emilio."

"Emilio? Why, he's, uh, one of my psych intro students, and we often have coffee in the—"

"God. The Frat Chat, Amos. Tell me about the damn Frat Chat."

"Lenore, I suspect your increased drinking is leading to more aggression and anger and—"

"Whoa! You really need to stop with the advice. Come on, Mr. Talkative Lecturer. Tell me what happened at the Frat Chat."

He watched his hand setting his fork onto the plate, the food on it undelivered. Then, he laced his fingers together in front of him, used them to push his plate away, then held Lenore's gaze.

"You tell me, Lenore."

"What?" she said. "I wasn't there. You were, though, so why don't—"

"Come on, Lenore. It's time to admit to more than sneaking wine with a lookalike friend on a workday afternoon. Admit that you were there."

"Amos, you are so wrong. Why would you think—"

"I saw you. Oh boy, did I see you. Huh. A side of you that—"

"You might have seen someone that resembled me, Amos. How about that? Do you know of anyone like that?"

He began blinking his eyes, and his lips fumbled around. After a few seconds of enduring a blistering stare from a woman holding a glass of wine, he scoffed and looked at his plate instead.

"I, uh, saw you, Lenore. I saw the ring."

"Oh, the ring," she said, then laughed. "Wow. And you didn't check to see for sure if that was me wearing that piece of junk?"

"Now, wait a minute. It's a quite nice and pricey piece of—"

"Keep it, then! So, whoever that was, she got some of your horny attention? Oh, just admit it, Amos."

"She, uh—that had to have been you, Lenore! I wouldn't have done anything, except that—"

"So, you admit it. Good. You were alone with her, Amos? Just you and her?"

"Oh, uh, no. That, uh, other—"

"Emilio? Is that the name your professor brain suddenly can't recall?"

"No, my brain can—I can recall. Yes, that's the fellow. He, uh, he was in there too."

"Watching?"

"Uh, yeah, you could say that he was—"

"Oh. Not just watching."

"Um, no. He, uh, I mean, you were, um, when he—"

"You thought that was me sucking him, Amos? And you thought what the hell, you might as well screw me while I was sucking one of your students?"

"I might not be proud of my behavior, Lenore, but—"

"Might not?"

"What I mean is, there was, uh, whiskey involved in this whole—"

"Let me see here. You got liquored up with a student, then you decided, what the hell, let's both have sex with my fiancé?"

"No, I never said that to him. I only—"

"You said, 'Hey, Emilio, my fiancé is a cocksucker. Have at it?'"

"A what? No, I didn't say anything remotely like that either, Lenore, when—"

"Call me a cocksucker, Amos. Go ahead."

"What? Lenore, I—"

"Or should I just say it? You want to hear me say it? Amos, I'm just a—"

"Lenore! Like I said, it's nothing to be proud of. You seemed to be enjoying the whole—"

"It wasn't me! Oh, God, Amos. You're helping me drink as much wine as it takes, and we're talking through all of this bullshit right now, or it's over. No fancy university bullshit interview party for you tonight."

He laid his palms flat on the table and looked toward her as she continued to lean against the counter, her wine glass emptied.

"We can schedule a time for us to discuss the entire sordid—"

"You're still going to that stupid thing? God, Amos. Really?"

"Well, uh, it does mean a promotion. And since you seem determined to blow up this—"

"Funny. Blow? That wasn't me, remember?"

"Uh, yes. Bad choice of words. But if our engagement is already in jeopardy, I'd rather be turned loose as a full professor. Sorry, Lenore, but I do have a practical side to me."

"Practical. Uh-huh. Screwing your fiancé while some other guy is getting serviced by her? Oh yeah, that's practical."

"Lenore, you're forgetting that whiskey is a formidable substance that can—"

"Amos. You know what? Go to your stupid party. I'm for sure meeting Laura for a glass of wine. Maybe two at once. How about that, huh? Two at once—sound familiar?"

"Well, Lenore, I—"

"And before I'm done, Amos the professor who loans out his fiancé for sex, it'll be way more than two. Way more."

Chapter 31 – Both Doing Fun Stuff Tonight

"You need this bad. Here."

Emilio held out a bottle wrapped in a brown paper bag from where he sat at their usual picnic table in the park. He'd been leaning back, elbows up, shaking his head at Amos after he'd walked over, then only stood and stared down at his shoes.

And Amos kept staring.

"I'll flunk you real fast, professor," Emilio said, chuckling. "Take it."

He shook the package around, and Amos reached out and took it.

While rustling the paper around and twisting off the cap, he said, "Hot and cold. Sometimes too cold. Sometimes too damn—"

"Now, wait a second," said Emilio. "Get some of that in you first. You'll start seeing that there's no such thing as too hot."

Amos tipped it back for a deep swallow, then tried to hide his brief choking spell.

"That's how you know it's working. Have a seat, Professor Amos."

Amos sighed and sat like Emilio but leaving plenty of space between them. He took another quick sip, then handed it back.

"And I mean professor," said Emilio. "Ready for your coronation?"

Amos scoffed and stared out at the grass lawns spreading out all around under the graceful, well-trimmed tree branches. The sun was setting and with classes finished much earlier, the foot traffic was light. No one noticed or cared about the two men drinking whiskey out of a bag.

"Yeah, I'm ready. Maybe more than ever. It might be all I have left."

"Hey, parties are great but not that great. Don't you have some kind of engagement going on too?"

"Some kind. Sure."

"Expand on that, as a professor would say."

Amos laughed and reached for the bottle, but he only held it on his leg and kept gazing straight ahead.

"Nothing lasts forever, Emilio."

"No, don't tell me it's over."

"I'm not telling you that, and it isn't. It's just—hey, things aren't easy. You think you want cold, then hot, then both, and you end up not having a damn clue which one you actually have."

"Shit. I'm way behind on that book. That's a whole 'nother chapter you're spouting."

"I do tend to spout. And lecture."

"Tell me you didn't try that on your fiancé."

Amos finally took another drink, then handed back the bottle.

"I, uh, yeah. But I thought I knew something about her. I was wrong."

"Ooh, not cool at all. You accused her of stuff, and she's innocent."

"Yep."

"What stuff?"

"Just, uh, nothing important. I made a big deal about her having wine in the middle of the day."

Emilio shook the bottle around in front of Amos until he laughed.

"Yep. Should have been whiskey, like professors do."

"It's not the middle of the day, Emilio."

"Point well taken. Besides, this is a proven elixir for getting a usually mild-mannered, though insanely intellectual professor ready for parties. Like—"

"Like the Frat Chat. Yeah. That, uh, blonde was quite attractive."

"Wasn't she, though? No one could blame you for what you couldn't stop yourself from doing."

"My fiancé does."

"Oh, I think I saw her that Wednesday when you were in the park. Was that her with you?"

"Yeah."

"Wait a second. She knows about you at the Frat Chat?"

"Somehow, yeah. So, I'm a rat. She wanted me to stay home tonight to talk through it, to save our engagement."

"Wait another second. She, your fiancé, was planning to stay home tonight?"

"Don't sound so alarmed. What's wrong with that, Emilio?"

"Oh, uh, nothing. That's commendable of her. But you're going to your college thing anyway?"

"I'm a double rat. Yeah."

"And she's, what? Staying home?"

"No, she said she's meeting a friend for a drink."

"Oh, good. I mean, good for her. Alright, you're both doing fun stuff tonight. It's shaping up to be a hell of a Friday."

"It is?"

"Oh yeah," he said and passed the bottle to Amos. "Drink up. We're going to an insanely special Friday night party, professor, sir. I mean, Amos."

"If you're that eager, you must be expecting a fair level of drama of one sort or another."

"You're so damn right. Maybe more levels of drama than either of us can count."

Chapter 32 – Any Tasty Drops

Tipping her head back to take the streaming hot shower spray, Lenore said several times, "Damn you, Amos."

She backed herself away just enough to let it hit her chest and breasts instead, and she watched the water strike her skin, reflect off of her in random ways, and trickle and drip off of every part of her.

"Hmm," she said while holding her breasts up, meeting partway the rapid spritzing, "that feels good."

She smirked and said, "Who knows what will be all over them soon?"

As she was reaching for the shutoff controls, she glanced at the soap dispenser mounted to the shower wall.

"Oh, I might as well."

She backed out of the brisk streams, then gave the small spout a series of quick upwards hits, filling her palm with the thick, white soap.

"Huh. Why didn't I think like this before? That's Amos's fault too—oh, better stay modest, he'd say. Or 'one would say.' Dammit."

Looking down, she smeared the creamy white goo all over her breasts, using just a fingertip to help accumulate it on two specific areas.

"Oh, no," she said, feigning alarm, "no more, please!"

Her hand showed her urgency as she collected more, then applied it, thickening the coating, almost covering all of the skin. She kept the fingertips of both hands busy tracing swirling patterns, closing in tighter, then getting slick grips and pinching and pulling lightly.

"Ooh, that's so slippery," she said, rubbing her hands all over them, then holding them from below, lifting them.

"Huh," she said, then leaned forward as far as she could, smiling at her lips being so close.

"Hmm, I really could. If that wasn't soap. They might even make me do that. After they all . . ."

Scoffing, she let the water finish a thorough rinse, then got herself partly dried off before stepping out onto the floor. Holding the damp towel loosely around herself, she tapped her phone with her free hand and put it on speaker.

"Laura, it's me."

"Hey, Lenore. It's a memorable Friday night for you, isn't it?"

"It is now, for sure. Damn that Amos. He admitted what he did at the Frat Chat. Laura, he admitted he screwed you at that damn party."

"What? What on Earth are you talking about?"

"That was him with Emilio. Laura, that was him."

"Oh my God," Laura said, then laughed. "Well, shit. That dirty cheater. Sorry, Lenore, I didn't know."

"Oh, Laura, I'm not mad at you about that. How could I be?"

"Well, thanks. That really is all his fault."

"Yeah, so the hell with it—I'm doing the Frat Chat 2. I just took a shower, and I'm going to—"

"Just now?"

"Uh, yeah. I'm still drying off. I'm about to—"

"Hmm, hold on a second, pretty girl. You're still naked, and you're still wet, and you called me?"

"Oh," Lenore said, then giggled. "I guess I did."

"Do you know why?"

"Mm-hmm, because I wanted to let you know that I was definitely going to the Frat Chat 2."

"That's not the only reason."

"No?"

"Uh-uh. It's because you're my pretty little girl, and I should come over there right now and lick every water drop off of you."

"Oh my God. Um, you'd, uh, you'd really—"

"Mm-hmm. Next time I threaten to publish those videos and force you to meet me at home during the day, guess what we'll be doing."

"Oh my goodness. Showering?"

"Hmm. Hey, Lenore."

"Yeah?"

"Are you touching yourself?"

"Oh, um," she giggled before saying, "I am now. Mm, it feels good."

"You've definitely crossed some kind of line, haven't you?"

"Mm-hmm."

"All you want is for it to feel good, isn't that right?"

"Mm. Yeah."

"So, we'll have that shower soon. We'll lick each other dry."

"Oh my gosh. I have to?"

"Yeah, you have no choice. But right now, it's a last-minute coaching session for you. You're going to dress real pretty for all of them?"

"Yes. A new dress, those heels I wore here for—"

"For me. Uh-huh. Ooh, those are nice."

"Hmm. And new panties too."

"You're going to be such a pretty little treat for all of them, Lenore. Maybe especially for the women. Oh, they're going to have so much fun with you."

A few seconds of silence passed.

"You're still touching yourself, aren't you?"

"Mm-hmm. Laura, this is so out of control."

"Yeah, and it's a wonderful thing. I'm glad I can get a taste of that."

"Mm. You're quite the blackmailer. I can't talk much longer. I need to do an extra good job with my makeup."

"Why?"

"I think I mentioned that. Michael made a big deal about how pretty I'd fixed myself up. And Laura, he made me plead to have him spray all over my face."

"Oh, damn, that's right. Lenore, he'll do it again, won't he? Maybe all of them?"

"Mm-hmm. And this is weird, I know, but I want to be as pretty as possible for that, just for the contrast."

"Yeah, you should. The prettier you are, the more obscene that is. He made you beg for that? Really?"

"Oh, yeah. I told him I deserved it sprayed all over my pretty, cocksucking face."

"Ooh, I love you saying that: your cocksucking face."

"And he really did make me say, more than just once, that I was nothing but trash. He liked saying that I was disposable and made me say that I knew exactly what that word meant."

"Oh, those people—theater people, Lenore. They're just playing, saying things like that."

"Oh my God, I had a giant orgasm when he was telling me I was disposable. I was rubbing myself then, too, like I was in a trance."

"You are so damn sexy, Lenore. So, you know that they like to play like that. You be sure, at the Frat Chat 2, that you play along with everything, no matter what."

"Michael said that all of them at the party would want me to say the right things. God, I got chills when he was calling me soft, vulnerable, and used-up trash. I told him, too, that I wanted to be used-up and bagged up like any other trash."

"That's the definition of an object, isn't it?"

"Mm. Yeah, an object just for sex."

"Lenore, that's some wild stuff. Make sure you play along with all of it."

"I don't think I can help myself. My orgasms never felt so good. I want even more like that. He wanted so bad to be sure I had no self-respect, that I was just a worthless slut."

"How did that feel when you were saying all that?"

"Mm, sexy. It was weird but yeah, I felt sexy."

"You really will be used-up trash with all the orgasms waiting for you. I'm jealous. I want to try bagging you up too."

"Laura, you're being silly."

"Am I?"

"You, uh, you'd really want to play like that?"

"Mm. After I clean you up real nice in a hot shower. Oh yeah, plan on it, my pretty little girl. I'll make sure I clean you real nice first, then bag you up."

"Laura, you—"

"And you'll be a very quiet little girl for me, all wrapped up, hidden away while I check with my tongue for any tasty drops that I still need to lick up."

"Oh my goodness . . ."

Chapter 33 – All Types of Talent

Emilio ushered Amos through the doorway leading off of the dim hall. He stepped inside, too, then closed the door.

"What is this place? It looks like some old hotel."

"It is. Or it was. I don't know, but it's a well-kept secret that these folks use for their parties."

"I couldn't retrace my steps out of here if I tried, Emilio. One building led to the next, I think we were underground for a while, then, how many different elevators?"

"Crazy, huh? It's a lot easier to get back out of. You'll see. Oh, speaking of seeing, take a look."

He switched off the light, then cracked open a door opposite the one to the hallway. Amos stepped closer and looked.

"That's a lot of people," Amos said, still studying the room. "Couples, all dressed nice—like, really nice. Tell me they're not all wearing masks."

"Can't tell you that. Sorry."

"It's like a scene from a fashion show or something. Like a bunch of movie stars. It's furnished so luxuriously—chairs all over, sofas. Looks expensive."

"Yeah, it's a good-looking group, and they guard their opulent party room like nobody's business. You should feel flattered that they're considering you as a member. You've met Michael. See him?"

"You're joking. No. I can't tell."

"Not so easy with the masks, huh? Right in the middle. Red tie and a light brown mask."

"Yeah. I recognize him now."

"Good," he said as he bumped Amos to the side and quietly closed the door, then lit the room. "And you're wearing a mask too."

"What? Why?"

"It's just the way they party. I told you they're kind of off-beat. Eccentric. Lots of old money, I think. Anyway, you want to get in with this group."

"I do? I just want to be a full professor, and I think—"

"You think you'd better get tight with these folks. That's right."

Amos scoffed and said, "That's not what I was going to say."

"Probably not. But you'd better. Here," he said, taking a loose cape-like garment off of a hanger, "put this on."

Amos accepted it, turned it over enough to see its construction, then dropped it over his head and let it fall to near his knees.

"Nice. Why, though?"

"You're the special guest. Here, this is even better."

"That's frightening. How about just a narrow eye covering kind like the rest of them?"

"Sorry. Like I said, you're special."

He took the full mask from Emilio and spun it around in his hands. It was fairly solid and unyielding, and it covered his head completely, leaving only two openings for his eyes.

"It's like a gargoyle or something."

"Yeah, get that on. Oh, before you do, take a look inside it."

He did and saw that there were some electronic devices built into it.

"My custom work. You wear these earphones, one for each ear, and see that?"

Amos looked closer while Emilio said, "There's a microphone in there too. Just the lightest whisper will get to me, and mine's rigged up the same way."

"What is this all about? All of those people have them too?"

"Uh-uh, just you and me. You know me, Amos—I'm all about the drama. I think I want to hear whatever you might have to say about this little party."

"You do? Why can't I just speak so everyone can hear me?"

"Uh, about that. You might not want to, and you might not be allowed to. This way, any little snide comments you feel like making, just whisper them out."

"Oh, fine. You're bizarre, Emilio."

"And you're about to have a fantastic time. Like, a surprisingly fantastic time."

"Huh. We'll see. Hey, why both earphones?"

"I'm a philosopher, Amos, not an electronics geek. The signal keeps switching, so you'll need both to not miss anything. Come on. Suit up. Then, go see Michael."

"What are you doing?"

"Getting my own mask on. Then, I'm just the hired help. There are a couple more of us too. You ready?"

"Yeah. Sure."

"Good. Go say hi to Michael, and I'll go stand with the other help."

* * *

Amos walked over to the man Emilio had identified as Michael, then offered a slight wave when the mask was turned toward him. The eyes looked at the hand, then up at Amos's eyes peering through the holes in his mask.

"I'm Amos. You're Michael, right?"

"Yes, that's me. So glad you could attend, Amos. This is more than a career event—it's designed to be quite entertaining—a celebration, so to speak."

"Oh, well, that sounds wonderful. What kind of entertainment should I expect?"

He laughed without any obvious smiling and said, "Well, Amos, I don't believe you'd be prepared for it even if I spoke of it. Which I won't."

Michael maintained a serious expression while again looking around the room, and Amos said, "I'm seriously honored to be considered for any advances at the university. One might say that I'm surprised, pleasantly, as well. I haven't been here very long."

"Oh, long enough, Amos. We can spot talent accurately. All types of talent for all types of things."

"Well, again, I'm very flattered and thankful. What's on the agenda?"

"We like to share conversation for a short while before things get rolling. We find that the anticipation of the main events adds to the excitement. After the entertainment budget is, well, used up, then we'll remove our masks and enjoy the contrast of a civilized meal and more conversation."

"Uh, contrast? Should I be—"

"No, no, no. I tend to get creative with my vocabulary. Please, just have a seat. If anyone speaks with you, don't ask for their names and perhaps enjoy a glass of champagne."

"I can do that. Thanks."

"Here's what else we'd like to see from you, Amos, something that all will be watching and evaluating. Quite simply, we want you to show us that you'd like to be part of our select group. That's it. It's that simple. It only means that you participate in our party, follow any directions that are given, and overall, just enjoy the heck out of the evening. Does that sound acceptable?"

"More than acceptable. Thank you."

"Oh, and Amos, one more thing: if you don't earn passing grades at this event that we all treasure so dearly, it will surely count against you."

"Um, against me?"

"Well, let's just leave it at that. I don't believe a situation of that sort will manifest. Oh no, we expect you to show your unfailing determination to share in these festivities, then, share in the rewards of a rapidly advancing career at our humble school."

"Well, that sounds fair enough. Thanks."

"Just one other thing: when the events begin, please, no speaking from you. As our special guest, we'd like you to remain a witness only until you're asked to participate, which, of course, you should not decline. I truly believe you'll want to participate. And even then, silence is, as they say, golden."

"My lips are sealed. Uh, when the show starts."

"Very good. Now, we have an entertainer that meets our requirements which, I'm only slightly ashamed to admit, are quite perverse. I hope that doesn't trouble you."

Amos turned his mask toward Michael and saw that he was still looking forward and waiting for his response.

"Well, no, that's fine. One might say that perversions are present in all of us anyway. At least, uh, once."

"In you as well, Amos?"

"Uh, maybe. It might depend on how the word is defined."

"Yes. For some of us, they're only yet to be discovered. Our entertainer will be escorted in by my wife, Eva, who is, oh, I might as well just say it: she's a bit on the cruel and domineering side. But it's all showmanship, Amos—no need for alarm."

"Uh, of course. Cruel?"

"She does enjoy the drama. Sometimes, perhaps a little too much."

"I see."

"And our performer has been rehearsing to play her role just as we need for our special brand of festivities. At a specific time, she might feign fear or reluctance to continue, but that's all part of the drama. We do love our drama."

"Uh, yeah, I remember that. Okay, so, some kind of performance?"

"Hmm, some kind, yes. We have alternating events that favor the men, then the women. Are you gracious enough to listen to a brief description of each?"

"Uh, sure. Why not?"

"Well, Amos, because we do take our perversions seriously. Just keep in mind that it's all for fun. Tonight is the gentleman's night. We revel in contrasts and build drama around that. You've noticed, I'm sure, that all of our members are either married or very close couples, male and female?"

Amos turned his mask around to give the room another look, then said, "Uh-huh. Yeah, all couples."

"Yes. On a gentleman's night, our guest entertainer will, sequentially, perform oral sex on the men. And for the drama, while she's doing that, the wife or significant female other is required to kiss the receiving male, tell him she loves him, and is happy that some unimportant slut is servicing him."

Amos stared at him through his eye holes. A few quiet seconds crawled past.

"She's also encouraged to take liberties with the entertainer—generally humiliate her as she wishes."

Amos kept staring, his lips, unseen inside his mask, fumbling soundlessly.

"It's a situation rife with drama for each of them. And it's also made to thoroughly degrade the woman performing the sex act. It's stressed that she's worthless and of no value whatsoever but of course, the receiving male enjoys it immensely. It amplifies the notion that she has no other value."

"I've, uh, never heard of such a thing."

"Well, no, Amos, we don't provide press releases," Michael said, laughing easily.

"And when it's the, uh, women's turn? Their night?"

"Each of them gets a stud to fully satisfy her, and I mean finish the act—in whatever way she desires. And all the while, the husband must be attentive to his wife getting screwed by some young stud, who is also ridiculed as being worthless. Drama, Amos."

"Oh my goodness."

"And Eva, my darling wife, has cooked up an unusual twist for tonight. Let's just leave that as a surprise, hmm?"

"This is . . . not what I expected. I did believe that this would all be more like an interview of sorts."

"Of sorts. Yes, that's correct because we're all very interested in your reactions to all of it, especially dear Eva's fun little game later. Do keep in mind, Amos, that your cooperation and willingness to play along are being evaluated in light of your quickly advancing career at the university. Does that all sound reasonable?"

"Uh, yes, of course. A, uh, surprise twist too. A game, you said?"

"I think it's a bit too much, but Eva is quite, well, passionate about her pleasures."

"Perhaps that's commendable?"

"Hmm, we'll see. Oh, and remember: don't speak. Just nod or shake your head. Just a formality."

"Uh, okay. Alright."

"Have a seat."

"Uh, sure," Amos said, then sat where Michael had directed him.

He watched as the masked man turned his back, walked over to a small group, and left him alone and quiet and sweeping his gaze all around.

"Oh my gosh," he whispered inside his mask.

Chapter 34 – Just a Soft Little Thing

Looking at an unfolded paper in her hand, then forward, Lenore mumbled to herself, "How many hallways and stairways does it take?"

Groaning softly, she pulled her hood forward, pushed her large sunglasses back into place, then straightened the long raincoat that she'd used to cover her new dress.

But it wasn't long enough to hide the very tall, spiky black heels that she wore and though she walked carefully, she still made distinct clicks against the old tile floors.

"It'll be worth the hiking around," she said softly after glancing again at the notes from Emilio, then taking the stairway down as indicated. "I have to do this."

She folded the paper but still held it in her hand as she came to the next floor down, then took a left.

"Mm, I do like hearing what I am."

She giggled and said, "I could say it. But it's so much better when it's for real."

Before her, another long, deserted hallway, dim from almost all of the overhead lights being burned out, led to a closed door that she could see at the very end.

"Yep. Good work, Drake. Just like you said."

She stowed the paper and walked toward the door, then tried the knob. At finding it locked, she scoffed and took out her phone.

"Laura, hi. This seems familiar. Not the place so much."

"Hi, Lenore. I know what you mean. This reminds me of how you called me when you almost took my place at the Frat Chat. Now, look at you, all dressed up and ready for the Frat Chat 2."

"Oh, you *should* look at me. I sure am dressed up very nicely. Well, except for the raincoat, hood, and sunglasses. Oh, and I left that necklace at home too."

"Smart. You'll be leashed soon anyway."

"Oh, that's just silly, Laura."

"Either way, you won't be dressed nicely for long. I'd bet that makeup is just perfect too," she said, then giggled.

"Also not for long?"

"Uh-uh. No, that's getting ruined in such a sexy, degrading way. Oh, Lenore, they're going to have so much fun with you. I hope you didn't eat too much for dinner."

"Oh, I didn't even think of that. You really think?"

"Do I think they're going to force you to swallow, then swallow more, then even more? Oh, yeah. Even if you beg them to stop."

Lenore giggled, keeping it low in the seemingly abandoned building.

"Hmm, even if I beg. Well, I'm actually kind of hungry."

"Huh. They won't care if you are or you aren't."

"Oh God. Well, I won't say no, no matter how many."

"You're such a bad girl. You're ready. That and making up your mind that you'll do exactly as you're told at all times."

"Ooh, the drama. Yeah, I will. What else would you expect from–"

"A soft, vulnerable, about to be used-up, worthless—"

"I'll finish: cocksucking slut. Oh God, I'm losing my mind, Laura."

"It's your own fault, pretty girl. You should have done the Frat Chat. It's like you got close to the biggest thrills of your life, then tried to just switch it off and go back to life with a saint. Uh-uh. Doesn't work that way. Now, it's taking over."

"Hmm. And you're there to enjoy it."

"Uh-huh. Damn right. Every chance I get. We should actually schedule a day for playing hooky from work and taking a hot shower and—"

"Wait. Hold it. Someone's coming."

Lenore turned her head to hear the distinct clicking of heels, not being softened or hushed, and saw a figure approaching.

"That's funny, Lenore."

"I guess it is. But really, there's someone down the hall. Long coat. Very determined walk."

"Black hair?"

"Uh-huh. Gorgeous black hair. Long and really thick."

"Sounds like Eva. Long coat, you said? Anything else?"

"Just the hair, and she's wearing some really high black heels."

"Eva for sure. Hey, she's coming to get you, you dirty entertainment party girl."

"I thought maybe Michael would greet me."

"Mm-hmm. Sounds like she wanted that job. I can already tell she's going to take control of you, even more than Michael did."

"Oh my God. Really?"

"Uh-huh. No doubt. You just make sure you do exactly as you're told. I heard she can be cruel, Lenore."

"Cruel? Now, you're telling me? This doesn't sound—"

"Bad choice of words. But it might be Michael that's the cruel one, I'm not sure."

"What? One's good, and one's bad? Laura, which is which?"

"I don't know. Since Eva's coming for you, you'd better accept right now that she owns you."

"She owns me? Oh, this just keeps getting—"

"Uh-huh. You're just a sexy, willing, real-life doll for her now. Have fun."

"Oh, God, I'm a living doll. I don't know about this, Laura. I think maybe—"

"Remember, Lenore, they're theater people—all about the drama!"

"I remember. But Laura, maybe I should just run while I—"

"Don't you dare! Bye!"

Lenore saw that Laura had ended the call, so she stuffed the phone in her pocket just as the woman took the last several steps toward her.

"Oh God, it's too late," she whispered.

* * *

"Name."

Her black eyes were big like Lenore's and at the same level as she stood close in her own high heels. Thick waves of black hair fell onto her shoulders and back. Red lips, glistening even in the dim hallway, showed a blend of a smile and a sneer.

"Hi. I'm Laura."

"Hmm. I'm Eva."

"Pleased to—"

"Shh."

She grabbed hold of Lenore with both hands and pressed her back into the closed door. She took half a step back, let even the trace of a smile vanish, then gestured quickly when Lenore reached up to remove the sunglasses.

"No, don't. Leave it."

Lenore held her arms at her sides while Eva leaned out to get a better look at her heels. She stared for several seconds, made a light scoff, then lost her smile.

She looked back up at Lenore and said, "This is a very private function. The building itself is very private. I need to know if you saw anyone on your walk here."

"Inside? No, just you."

"You spoke to no one in here, then."

"No."

"Good. Michael said that he has screened you. He said that you were quite cooperative and stated that you understood completely what we expect from you. Tell me that's all true."

"We spoke, yes. He, uh—I think I understand I'm going to be—"

She reached up quickly and gave Lenore's cheek a smack.

"Hey, that's—"

Even more quickly, she grabbed Lenore's chin, then leaned closer, looking from one large black lens to the other.

"Understand this: you are already only what we say. You are nothing but shapely female entertainment. You no longer have any will of your own. Say you understand that."

Unable to speak clearly with her chin in a strong hold, Lenore said, "Uh, yes. Uh-huh, I do."

"It is important that all of this remains private. So, you told no one your location."

"Uh, no. No one."

"Michael has told me that you have no one special in your life. You told him that no one even cares enough to wonder where you are or to ever look for you."

Lenore nodded as well as she could, and Eva didn't let go of her chin.

"That's because you are worthless."

She raised and held up her eyebrows.

"Uh, yes. I am."

"And you are a slut."

Lenore nodded and said, "Yes."

She let go of Lenore's chin.

"Good. You're a worthless slut that no one will ever look for. That's what we need. Open your overcoat."

Lenore kept the hood up and her sunglasses on as she loosened the belt and let the coat hang open on its own.

"Hold it open."

She did, and Eva nodded while focusing on the large mounds of Lenore's breasts, then her tiny waist, then the curve of her hips. She almost smiled when looking below the hem of her short black dress at Lenore's bare legs.

She reached out with both hands, aiming for her breasts, but she took hold of her waist instead.

"Hmm, very slender. That's intriguing."

She reached up higher, her palms against Lenore's sides and just high enough to give a slight lift to her breasts.

"Take a deep breath and hold it."

Lenore inhaled, held it, and watched her through her dark glasses.

Staring at her more prominent breasts, Eva said, “What you offer is all very nice. You may exhale.”

She reached to the side and typed a code into a keypad, a beep sounded, then she turned the knob and opened the door.

“Your wardrobe is lovely, but you will dress as I wish.”

Then, she nudged Lenore through the doorway and reached inside to flip a light switch. The overhead fixture illuminated a small, square room with a plain couch and a rack with a lacy white garment on a hanger. Another package rested on a shelf above the garment.

“Be quick about it, then wait for my return.”

She closed the door with a thump, and Lenore heard the heavy latch mechanism engage. She tried the knob carefully, making no sound, and found that it was locked again.

“Oh my goodness . . .”

* * *

Lenore dressed herself as Eva had required and waited in the small room. A beep from the door was followed by the mechanical unlatching, then the door swung in.

“That highlights your shape very well,” she said, studying Lenore.

“Uh,” Lenore said, observing Eva’s outfit as she tossed her overcoat onto the couch, “wow, so does yours. I feel kind of silly in this mask, though.”

While she was stepping inside, then locking the door behind her, Lenore was taking careful backwards steps toward the other door, a much heavier and more ornate one, and Eva took the few steps needed to stand in front of her.

“Your mask is quite cute. It’s playful.”

“I’d rather have one like yours.”

“Oh, sorry. That’s the one you’ll have to wear. Hey, I’m so sorry you got yourself involved in all of this. Sorry for being so rough out there too. Look, you’re in more danger than you know.”

"What? I know this is kind of an extreme party, but Michael—"

Eva shook her head and said, "Michael! He has bad things planned for you. He acted nice when you spoke with him?"

"Um, kind of. He kind of took control, but he was polite."

"It's all an act with him. Now, he's got you here, and there's no way out. Every door is locked. I wish I could have warned you to stay away."

"But you just slapped me and—"

"The hallway is monitored—I had to pretend to be mean to you. This room is safe, and I can be myself. I'm actually very gentle, and I already feel only affection for you."

She shrugged, offered Lenore a genuine smile, then brushed some of her blond hair back over her shoulder.

"Our only hope—for both of us—is that we both do exactly as I say. Otherwise, maybe neither of us will get out of here."

"What are they going to do to us? What is this all about?"

"Oh, that Michael is more than just a pervert. He's a truly dangerous man, and he has a whole scenario worked out for this."

"Like what? What do we do?"

"He expects me to be in control of you, and he wants you to submit to everything. You must, or we're both finished."

"Everything, like what?"

"First," she said, her voice quick and urgent, "tell me that you'll play along and do as I say. Tell me you will!"

"Okay, calm down. Um, sure, I think I kind of have to anyway."

Eva sighed and smiled, shaking her head, and said, "Oh, good. We can do this, Laura. But you have to go along with *everything* I demand of you."

"I can. But what kinds of—"

"Like this," Eva said, then held Lenore by her shoulders, gave her a light push, and got her back against the door.

"This, um, like pushing me around and—"

"And like this," she said as she leaned closer and pressed her lips into Lenore's.

After ten seconds of kissing her, she let go of her shoulders, laced both arms around her waist, and pulled them together.

From close enough to touch their lips again, she said, "*Everything.* Say it for me. It's our only hope."

Nodding and gazing into her eyes, Lenore whispered, "Everything."

"Oh, good, we have a chance. Your identity is hidden behind your mask, but I want to warn you that one or more guests might know you."

"What? Someone might—"

"Michael is diabolical. It does add some drama, doesn't it?"

"Uh, yes. It sure does. Oh my goodness."

"Forget goodness. What's important is that you have told Michael that you will do as you're told."

"Um, yes—I did at the interview."

"You mean everything, right?"

"Especially now—yes."

Eva gave Lenore's behind a soft squeeze with both hands, blinked her eyes slowly, and said, "I need to know for sure."

"Okay. Just—"

"Say you love me."

"What? I, uh—"

"It's part of Michael's game. You'll have to say it if I tell you to. Laura, we have to play his game or else. Please, show me that you can say it."

Eva was already tipping her head, ready to kiss her again and watching Lenore's lips.

"I . . . I love you."

"Mm," she said, "it's all harmless fun, Laura. Why not say it again?"

"Sure. I love you."

"Mm, and I love you too. And I'm going to kiss you again."

Several seconds passed as she smiled and gazed into Lenore's eyes, and Lenore made no effort to evade or escape.

"Hmm," Eva said, grinning.

She then locked Lenore in a long kiss while holding her behind and keeping their bodies pressed together.

After slowly ending their kiss and letting their wet lips rub gently for a few seconds, she stepped back and said, "Remember that I have to stop being nice because of Michael. Out there, for the party, Michael expects you to be only something soft and obedient for me to command, and you must trust me if we're to survive. Please, tell me you'll trust me, even when I have to seem cruel."

"I will, Eva. I, uh, have to trust you."

"Yes, you do."

Chapter 35 – For Our Amusement

At the sound of a heavy door opening, the room fell silent and Amos, from his seat, had an unobstructed view. Eva took one step into the room and stopped.

She wore only a robe that ended at her knees, entirely black and silky. Her legs were bare and glistened as if they'd had lotion applied, and her black heels were high. Long black hair fell over her shoulders and back, and the front was arranged and tied to display her generous cleavage.

Hiding her face was a feathery mask resembling a predatory bird. It was notched at the bottom to allow a clear view of her chin and her full red lips.

"Ah," Michael said loudly for all to hear, "the exquisite Eva."

"Well, hello, Michael and all of our valued members," she said with a pleasant smile. "Meet the shapely, feminine thing that is donating herself for our fun."

Looking back through the doorway, she tipped her head toward the party room, and Lenore entered and stood beside her.

She wore short, delicate white lingerie that puffed out softly all around the bottom, giving the guests more than a hint of her new lacy panties. Thin straps left her shoulders and back bare, and the front was cut low enough to barely cover the prominent details of her breasts, though those unmistakable details were both shamelessly announcing their presence through the sheer material that hung loosely over them.

Most of her face was concealed by a cute mask, an almost cartoon-like version of a playful, innocent pink mouse. Like Eva's, it fit close to her skin and left only her chin and red lips visible in a smooth cutout at the bottom. It covered only her face, and all of her long blond hair was on display. Bare legs ended in her new black spiky heels.

"She's an eager little mouse girl for us to enjoy for the evening."

There was light applause and soft chatter, all approving.

Eva let them quiet on their own, then said, "She's a very obedient little mouse, too, and wants to fulfill my every wish. Observe."

She held out a sparkling collar and a thin chain leash, and Lenore looked at it in Eva's hand, then turned her head to look at dozens of pairs of masked eyes all focused on her.

"Oh my God," she whispered and rushed back through the doorway.

Eva turned to face them all and said calmly, "Just a moment. Little mouse girls sometimes need to be reminded that they exist only for our entertainment."

She strode through the exit after Lenore and slammed the door.

* * *

"Amos," Emilio whispered inside his mask, "Can you hear me?"

"Yeah, I just now turned on this thing. All of the voices are off—deeper. Distorted, I think."

"Yeah, it's the earphones. Sorry. You still understand them?"

"Yeah. Hey, what was that? She changed her mind?"

"Huh," said Emilio. "Too big a crowd maybe. I barely saw her."

"Long blond hair. Wearing white. Some kind of mask."

"Looks good, though."

"Yeah."

* * *

Eva rested her hands on her hips and watched Lenore struggling with the locked door leading to the hallway. Every attempt at turning the knob shook around her delicate lingerie.

"We are quite trapped, little mouse."

Lenore spun around and started to remove her mask, but Eva quickly said, "Don't. I'll tell you why."

She let her hands drop to her sides and said, "Fine. Why?"

"Come closer. Walk to me."

"I changed my mind about all of this. There are so many people out there! And you said one or more of them might even know who I am?"

"Little mouse. You're not changing your little mouse mind about any of this. I'm at risk here too."

"Hey, I know there are recordings of me, but I just don't care. To anyone that sees them on the Internet, it's just some blonde named Laura that—"

Eva's laughter stopped her.

"What's so funny?"

"Come to me, and I'll explain."

Lenore stared for a few seconds, then walked until she was two steps from her.

"Hmm. Closer."

She scoffed and took another step, close enough to easily touch her.

"Okay. What?"

Eva stepped to her and reached around her waist. Lenore looked down at the arms embracing her for only a second, then back up into her eyes, and she didn't try to get away.

"Remember that we're in this together. I'll explain if you put your arms above my shoulders. You did say 'everything,'" she said with a friendly smile.

Lenore scoffed loudly, then complied, and they were close enough that their breasts were touching. Eva gave her a quick kiss on the lips, then held her close and spoke in her ear.

"Because, little mouse girl Laura, you're not Laura at all."

Lenore tried squirming back from her, but she was held too tightly.

"Oh, no you don't. Stay in my arms, Lenore Cassidy."

No longer squirming, Lenore whispered close to Eva's ear, "So, someone told you a name, but that doesn't—"

In her ear, Eva said, "That damn Michael has researched you well. Shall I recite your address? Your business name? The names of your clients?"

"I don't care—it's not worth it," Lenore said but not trying to escape Eva's hold on her. "Tell everyone. Even if I have to move, I'll—"

"Oh, think of the real Laura, then. I do. Michael said her reputation isn't worth much, but we both care about her health, don't we, Lenore?"

Lenore sighed and relaxed in her arms, and Eva reached up to fuss with her long blond hair, gently smoothing it down.

"There, there. That's better. Do you see that being an obedient little mouse for me is worth keeping you and me and Laura safe?"

Lenore nodded.

"Good. Just be a darling little mouse for me. Everything will be fine as long as I hear again how you truly feel about me. Use my name too."

While Eva held her head close to speak in her ear, Lenore sighed in her arms.

"Eva," she whispered, "I love you."

Eva leaned away enough to look into Lenore's eyes and still held her waist with one hand and her masked cheek with the other.

"I love you, too, Lenore Cassidy, my pretty little mouse girl. You should admit that there's some excitement to this situation we're in. Let yourself enjoy being just a playful mouse in lingerie for me. Are you my sweet, obedient little mouse girl?"

"Yes. Yes, Eva."

"Mm, that's nice. Let's kiss, then, just Eva and her sweet little mouse, then we'll go play together."

With her lips almost touching Lenore's, she said, "I love you."

Without hesitation, Lenore said, "I love you too."

"Mm, my soft, pretty little mouse."

Lenore barely noticed that she was touching gently Eva's thick black hair as they kissed for several minutes, until there was a pounding on the door leading to the party room.

Chapter 36 – A Plaything Only for Fun

The door swung open, and everyone watched in silence as Eva strutted back out, taking graceful steps and swaying her hips.

She smiled to the room and said, "The mousy little thing just needed a quick scolding. She's ready now."

At a subtle head tip from Eva, Lenore again walked out and stood beside her, and Eva again handed her the collar and leash. Lenore accepted it without any complaints, then fastened the collar around her neck, then attached the leash.

Eva accepted the handle loop when Lenore held it out to her and said, "Such an obedient little mouse."

She gave it a hard pull, causing Lenore to gasp as she stepped quickly toward her.

"Lovely," she said, then pulled her closer and kissed her, earning approving murmurs and light laughter.

She ended the kiss, then stepped back, still holding the leash and looking around at the party crowd.

"Don't be fooled by all of the delightful feminine curves she's showing—she's really just an insignificant little mouse. A plaything only for fun."

Strutting calmly, Eva led Lenore to a place among all of the guests, most of the couples sharing wide, upholstered seats, some standing. She moved behind Lenore, fluffed back her hair, then reached around with both hands on her belly.

Speaking near Lenore's ear, she said, loudly enough for all to hear, "You're just a little mouse, aren't you?"

Lenore nodded and said, "Yes."

"Will you be a very slutty mouse for me?"

"Mm-hmm."

"Hmm, we all want to have our fun with a slutty little mouse girl."

She shifted around to Lenore's other ear and raised her hands up to hold both of her breasts.

"Mm, even a pretty mouse like you is worthless. We're going to use you all up, aren't we, mouse girl?"

"Mm-hmm. I'm here to be used."

"I said *all* used up."

Lenore hesitated, and Eva gave her leash a small tug.

"Yes. I'm here to be *all* used up."

"Mm, and I'm going to enjoy using you all up, you soft, slutty little mouse."

Never letting her go, Eva stepped around until they were face to face, and she held Lenore's waist with both hands.

"It's a boys' night. That means you, little mouse girl, are going to give all the boys a treat. Do you like giving treats, dirty mouse?"

Lenore nodded and said, "Yes."

"Mm-hmm. Little mousy girls like to suck cocks?"

The laughter was loud but ended quickly.

"Mm-hmm. Yes."

"Of course. So, tell us what kind of mouse you are."

"I'm a, um, cocksucker mouse."

"Yes, you are. Before you show us what a cocksucker mouse you are, tell us all why you're so eager to do what I tell you."

Lenore tipped her head, and her lips fumbled for a second.

"Repeat what you told me a moment ago, when I scolded you and made you my mouse girl."

"Oh."

The crowd grew completely quiet.

"Because . . . because I love you. Eva."

Over the sounds of hushed laughter, Michael said, "Oh, Eva. It's always something with you."

"Shh, Michael. She means it. Don't you, my slutty little thing?"

Lenore nodded.

"Mm, such a slutty little mouse for whatever fun I want."

She pulled Lenore in for a long kiss, amid laughter and comments and Michael saying, "Huh. I think we all love her."

* * *

"Shit, she's hot."

"She's gorgeous," said Amos. "Some figure."

"She called herself a cocksucker mouse. Who does that?"

Amos said, "A slut."

"Obviously. A leash and collar too."

"It's symbolic," Amos said. "A sign of submitting."

"Huh. Submitting to who?"

Amos laughed.

"Mostly to that woman. Even said she loves her."

"She might."

* * *

Eva gave the leash a hard pull downward, and Lenore groaned and fell to her knees. And since Eva hadn't stepped back, she was able to reach around and pull Lenore's face toward her, and she held her there, head turned and with a masked cheek pressed against the black robe covering her thighs.

Fluffing out again Lenore's hair, Eva said, "Hmm, such a pretty mouse."

She backed away just enough to let Lenore hold her head straight and said, "Mm, I do love a mouse on her knees."

She took enough steps to stand directly behind Lenore, then said, "She's pretty, but she's slutty too."

She knelt behind Lenore, then reached around to hold both of her breasts. Squeezing them and shifting them around, running a finger inside the thin cloth over one, then the other, Eva looked around at the staring guests.

"Since it's the men's turn tonight, our curvy little mouse is going to suck all of the male guests. Isn't that right, mouse girl?"

Lenore nodded but didn't speak.

Eva jerked the leash and said, "Tell us, pretty little thing, what you're going to do."

"I'm going to suck cocks."

"What are you, and what aren't you?"

"I'm a worthless cocksucker mouse. I'm nothing else."

"The rest of your life is just pretending?"

"Mm-hmm. I'm really just a cocksucker."

"Yes, that's all you are, and you belong on your knees," Eva said.

She took the bottom edge of Lenore's lingerie and lifted it high enough to show everything up to the generous bottom curves of her breasts.

"Such skimpy panties this mouse wears," Eva said, scoffing. "And look at that tiny waist. Men, do your best to fill the cocksucker mouse's belly."

She held the garment up and rubbed Lenore's belly with one hand.

"Would you like to fill that tiny belly, worthless little mouse?"

While Lenore was nodding, Eva said, "Of course."

"And you'll be quick about it—I can barely wait for all that is planned for you. Mm, some truly delightful things for a dirty mouse."

Eva stood, straightened her robe, then pushed Lenore down onto her hands and knees.

"Time to put a hard cock in your little mousy mouth."

* * *

"She's going to do them all?"

"Use the right word, professor."

"Suck."

"Uh-huh. Swallow too."

"You knew about this, Emilio?"
"Yep. It's more dramatic that you didn't know. Can't back out."
"Why a mouse?"
"Don't know. That's a surprise."
Amos said, "Michael said the wives are involved."
"I heard that. They love their drama."
"What kind of woman does this?"
"You tell me, Amos."
"She's a cocksucker. That's all."
"Yep."

Chapter 37 – I Think I Want a Turn

Eva's quick pull on the leash got Lenore crawling.

"Good. Kneel right there, dirty mouse."

The thirty-something man, with a lean, angular face and dressed quite well, was seated beside an equally attractive young woman who glared down at Lenore where she knelt between the man's legs.

"You're about to suck a cock," said Eva, "that belongs to another woman. Ask the wife for permission, dirty little mouse."

Lenore looked up at the seated woman and said, "May I please suck your husband's cock?"

The woman sneered at her and replied, "You worthless little mouse. It's all you're good for, isn't it? Sucking cocks?"

"Yes. Nothing else."

"Suck, then, you dirty little cocksucker. You worthless slut."

Lenore only nodded, unfastened everything while the man was playing with her hair, then took it out and held it close. As she was tipping her open mouth to it, the wife leaned toward her.

"Kiss his wife first, you dirty mouse, then suck his cock."

Lenore let out a shaky breath, then turned her head and met the woman's lips, all to laughter and more comments from all around the room.

While they were kissing, Eva said, "What an obedient little darling—a soft, curvy, cocksucking mouse."

The wife backed away from the kiss, then used one hand to push Lenore's head down onto her husband, and Lenore hurried her mouth open.

"That looks stupid," the wife said, sneering. "There's a worthless slut mouse sucking your cock."

"Yes, dear, but it does feel good—it doesn't mean anything that a mouse is sucking me. You know I still love you."

"I know you do, Honey. Taste her filthy mouse kiss on my lips."

She and the husband began a kiss, holding each other and totally ignoring Lenore.

Eva knelt beside Lenore, touched her hair gently, and said, "Good little mousy girl. Suck the hard cock."

Lenore kept bobbing her head on it, and Eva nuzzled around her ear and played with her hair.

Michael lifted Lenore's lingerie with the handle of a black leather whip and said, "I know you and the mouse are in love, Eva, but I just might give her fine ass a little whipping."

He slid the handle between her cheeks, rubbing smoothly along the fabric of Lenore's panties. Lenore panted and moaned softly.

Eva laughed and said, "No need to torment the playful mouse, Michael. She's sucking so nicely—we don't want her to bite!"

"You're very wise, dearest Eva. Her smooth mouse ass is tempting me, but her mousy lips and tongue are slurping so obediently."

"Yes, she's an eager little mouse with a cock in her mouth."

Lenore held still and stroked with both hands while Eva kissed around her ear, and the couple kissed and paid her no attention for a minute.

"Tell me she means nothing to you," the wife said as her husband was about ready, neither one even looking at Lenore.

"How could she? She's filth—just a worthless mouse Eva brought here to suck cocks."

"Exactly. I hate her beautiful hair, so I'm doing it."

She grabbed Lenore's chin and pulled her away from her work long enough to give her an open-mouth kiss, then tell her, "Don't you dare swallow, dirty mouse. You give it all to me."

Lenore nodded and whimpered from the tight grip.

"You slut. You taste like my husband's cock."

She forced Lenore's face back onto her husband, and she continued like before on him.

"The dirty mouse does have nice hair," she said.

"She doesn't deserve any better, dear. What kind of slut would pretend to be a mouse to suck cocks at a party?"

"Hmm, one with no self-respect at all."

They resumed their kiss, and Lenore moaned and gave him long strokes with both hands. He groaned while his wife held him in a constant kiss, sometimes backing away to say things like, "Just like that. Give it to the mouse, Honey. Feed the disgusting mouse."

After Lenore had finished him, she tipped her head back and held her lips closed. The wife grinned and leaned toward her.

"Give it to me," she said and kissed her for several seconds, both of their cheeks working, then sat up and rudely tipped Lenore's head forward, facing her toward the floor.

From directly above her, she dribbled it all out into Lenore's hair, distributing it as widely as she could while everyone, including Eva and the husband laughed and commented on what a disgusting slut Lenore was.

"There. Not such a pretty mouse anymore," she said, then she worked it all in deep, raking it all around and twisting her hair into wet strands. "Dirty cocksucker. Clean my fingers, you filthy thing."

Lenore stayed quiet, on her knees, and looked into the wife's eyes while she sucked one finger at a time.

* * *

"Disgusting," Amos whispered.

"Pink mouse, white lingerie, sucking cocks. You think?"

"Quick, though."

"Yep," said Emilio. "Crawling to the next."

A minute later, Amos whispered, "She's swallowing this time."

"That's two. On to the next."

Several minutes passed.

"She's sucked five," said Amos. "Three wives have spit it on her."

"Something to see, huh?"

"What kind of woman does this?"

"It's like the Frat Chat—women like going crazy sometimes."

Many more minutes passed.

"She's sucked about twenty," said Amos. "Half is in her hair."

"It's a mess. So degrading. I think I want a turn."

"Go ahead. For the drama."

"Yeah. Walk up, whip it out, jam it in the mouse's mouth. Never got sucked off by a mouse before."

* * *

Seconds later, Emilio said, "Damn, that's her true calling in life."

"Just this?"

"Yep."

"Go on before Michael whips her ass. Or worse."

"Oh, that'd be a sight. Look, she's kissing the next wife."

"She likes that too," said Amos.

"Yep."

"Aren't you getting in line?"

"Uh, maybe not," said Emilio.

"What happened to every man for himself?"

"Uh, I'll pass this time. I just . . . can't."

"Leave that out of your book, then."

"Yep."

Chapter 38 – Her Dirty Lips Found It

Eva tugged up on the leash after the wife had spit Lenore's work into her hair, then stood close behind her to address the room.

Reaching around to rub her belly and breasts, Eva said, "While you're digesting all that and the rest is drying in your hair, tell us all the dirty things you did Wednesday."

"I, um, met someone named Drake for a first interview. I told him I'm just a slut and a cocksucker."

"Yes, and now a mousy one. You told him you'd be our plaything for the party?"

"Yes, and we rode an elevator up for me to see Michael."

"You were a slutty girl even in the elevator?"

"Yes. Drake got my breasts out and played with them, then he told me to loosen my pants. He felt me up front and back."

"You never resisted?"

"No. And I told a stranger getting in the car that I was a cocksucker."

"Well, you certainly are. Would you have knelt right there and sucked his cock?"

"Mm-hmm. Yes."

"Like an obedient mouse girl."

"Yes. Then I knelt for Michael and sucked his cock."

"Before that, you admitted what kind of cocksucker you are?"

"Mm-hmm. I told him I'm a disposable cocksucker."

"Oh," Eva said, touching Lenore's breasts more gently, giving them light pinches. "Mm, disposable is the sweetest. You meant that?"

"Yes. And I was touching myself while he convinced me that I was just trash. Mm, it felt good."

"Touching yourself or being trash?"

"Hmm, both, I think."

"Mm, a soft, worthless little girl. So, you're on your knees, sucking him, then you swallowed it all?"

"Uh-uh. I begged to have it sprayed on my face—I knew that was all I deserved. I was rubbing myself like crazy while he was spraying it all over my face."

"And no one knew you were out doing such dirty things?"

"Uh-uh. No one."

"You fixed yourself up pretty and went out to run errands, but you were in a hotel room being a dirty cocksucker?"

"Mm-hmm. Yes."

"Mm, I love dirty little girls like you."

She stepped around in front of Lenore and pulled them close together.

"Mm, kiss me, dirty girl, for everyone to watch. First, whisper to me what else you are."

The room got quiet to listen.

Lenore touched her lips to Eva's ear and whispered, "I'm disposable. I'm a soft, disposable cocksucker."

"That's adorable. One more delightful thing—tell me again."

Lenore put her arms up over Eva's shoulders, then spoke softly, just enough for Eva to hear.

"I love you."

"Mm," Eva moaned as she reached around her waist and looked into her eyes. "You love me, and you're disposable at the same time."

They'd been kissing for a minute, with Michael circling them with his whip, dragging the handle across each of them as he passed.

"Ah, isn't that sweet," he said, getting a few laughs. "Eva. She's a disgusting cocksucker mouse, a filthy slut, and we all want you to have your own fun with her dirty mouse face."

Eva broke the kiss and looked past Lenore toward Michael, who was grinning back at her.

"We all want to watch you enjoy her dirty mouse face, Eva."

"Hmm. I know just where to put that little pink mouse's face."

She kissed Lenore for only a second, then whispered in her ear, "Please, play along! We have no choice!"

She began walking, towing Lenore by the leash, and said for all to hear, "Come with me, dirty mouse girl. It's my turn to enjoy your filthy mouse face."

* * *

"Damn," said Amos, "that's how she runs errands?"

"Bet nobody even knew. Probably said she's just going out for stuff but really getting felt up and sucking a stranger's cock in a hotel."

"She's disgusting."

"Well, professor, she's a slut. Hey, what's going on now?"

"Something about Eva enjoying her face. Even I can guess where this is going."

"Yeah, that slutty pink mouse is about to get busy on Eva."

* * *

Eva took the several steps needed to lead Lenore to a special chair located central to all of the guests. It was padded comfortably, had a tall, narrow back and a very shallow seat, almost like a shelf. She stood where she could seat herself, then pulled Lenore closer with the leash.

Standing face to face, she gave her a quick kiss, then whispered in her ear, "Please, just play along. Please!"

Leaning away from her again, she said for everyone to hear, "Tell me again how you feel about me, little mouse girl."

"I love you. Mm-hmm, I do love you."

"Hmm, so sweet. We've all seen how much you like sucking cocks,"—she touched Lenore's lips, causing a quick giggle—"but let's show everyone just how much you love me too."

"Okay."

Still holding the leash, Eva sat back on the narrow ledge of the seat, then tugged down on the chain connected to Lenore's collar.

"On your knees for me, pretty mouse."

Lenore knelt, then Eva spread her knees wide apart, but her black robe still covered most of her thighs.

"Touch yourself, little mouse girl."

Lenore sighed and reached her left hand between her own thighs and began a gentle rubbing through her panties.

"Good mouse. I have something soft and warm for my pretty little mouse."

She kept her robe tied but carefully parted it from her waist down, shifting the silky cloth over her thighs and revealing that she wore no panties.

She shifted her thighs farther apart and said, "Do you see what I have for you?"

"Mm-hmm. Yes."

"Come closer, little one," she said and caressed a cheek while tugging on the leash, too, and Lenore leaned with one hand on Eva's thigh, then sat back on her heels.

Lenore's mask was touching the insides of Eva's thighs, and Eva stopped her with a gentle touch.

"Look up, little mouse girl, and tell me again."

Lenore looked up, her big eyes bright through the cutouts of her mask, and said, "I love you."

"Everything about me?"

"Mm-hmm. Yes."

"Hmm, that's so nice. Mm, kiss me, eager little mouse."

Lenore tipped her face closer and began long, slow licks from bottom to top, and everyone all around murmured approvingly, some commenting on how a mouse likes much more than just sucking and swallowing.

"Oh, that's so nice," Eva said as her eyes closed and she tousled the dry regions of Lenore's hair. "My very good little mousy girl. Oh, that tongue. Such a nice . . . warm . . . mm, mousy tongue. Mm . . ."

The crowd mostly stayed quiet and watched Eva playing with Lenore's hair while the cute mouse mask kept tipping up with every stroke of her tongue. And the mask was fitted so well that everyone close enough could see her wet tongue extended, traveling upward on Eva, sometimes apart and connected only with a shiny line of saliva.

"You'll suck cocks if I tell you to, but this is what you truly love doing, isn't it, my pretty mouse?"

Looking up, her tongue still touching Eva, Lenore nodded a few times.

"Mm, so nice," she said, then gently pulled her robe closed from both sides, covering Lenore.

Eva looked around, smiling weakly, and said, "Mm, my little mouse girl does love licking me. Such an adventurous little tongue she has. So warm and wet for me."

She held Lenore's head with both hands, focusing her attention on a specific need, and shook lightly for half a minute before sighing, then petting her head through the silky black material.

"Such a good little mouse," Eva said, then she untied her robe.

She opened it completely, letting it hang toward the floor and revealing that she wore nothing beneath it. With both hands, she held Lenore's head gently, then began coaxing her to raise herself higher.

"Come to me, good little girl. Give me sweet kisses."

Lenore stopped touching herself and rose higher on her knees and held Eva's waist, then paused when Eva held her cheeks with both hands.

"Hmm, right there first, little girl."

Lenore's lips were near Eva's breasts, and she looked up into her eyes.

"Sweet kisses for me there, little mouse."

Lenore kissed one, then the other, all while gazing up at her.

"Mm," Eva said, still holding her in place, "little mouse girls like to suck too. Suck for me, little mouse."

With Eva holding and guiding her, Lenore did as she'd been told, one then the other repeatedly, using her lips and tongue, while the audience laughed softy and made approving comments.

After several minutes, as Eva left Lenore to choose on her own and played with her hair, she guided her higher to where their lips could meet.

"Mm, my sweet, disposable little mouse," Eva said, then pulled her in and kissed her to the sounds of light applause and comments.

* * *

Emilio whispered, "That's a sight. She likes licking Eva as much as sucking those guys."

"Never imagined a scene like this."

"Shit, I have. All the time. Looks like she has too."

"She even likes kissing her."

"Yeah, Amos. And saying she loves her."

* * *

Eva slipped her lips to one side, close to Lenore's ear, and whispered, "That was good, but Michael is cruel. We have to do more. Please, can you play along?"

Lenore whispered, "Um, okay. Yes."

"Thank you! You're wonderful!"

After tipping Lenore back and sneering at her for a second, Eva said, for everyone to hear, "You're still a disgusting cocksucker mouse. It's time to hide that filthy mouse face."

"Mm-hmm. Yes."

"Back on your knees, dirty cocksucker mouse."

Lenore dropped quickly, and Eva spun herself around and put one spiky heel up on the chair's low seat. She gave the leash a snap.

"Keep touching yourself."

Lenore reached down with her left hand and resumed her gentle rubbing.

"Good. It's time to put your cocksucking mouse face right where it belongs."

She lifted her robe and held it around her waist, uncovering everything below it, her bare thighs and cheeks close to Lenore. Many men and women gasped and made comments at the sight of Eva's shapely legs and everything else, all smooth and bare.

"I want a long, sweet kiss, you slutty mouse. Hide your dirty mouse lips as deep as you can."

Lenore hesitated. Eva snapped her leash.

"Tell us you love licking my ass, dirty mouse."

"I, um, love licking your ass. I do."

She reached around to hold the front of Eva's thigh, then kissed the backs of both thighs, then both cheeks all over, earning encouraging comments.

When Eva leaned forward, tipping herself closer, Lenore burrowed her uncovered mouth tight up between her cheeks, with her head angled back and big eyes looking up at Eva's black hair.

"Oh, just like that," Eva said, looking around at the couples laughing and making comments.

"Did she get the right spot, Eva?" said Michael.

"Mm-hmm. Her dirty lips found it."

She flapped her silky black robe up and let it drop, covering Lenore where she knelt, still holding Eva's thigh and rubbing herself.

"Mm, the filthy thing has such warm, wet lips, and she's so eager to please. She's a busy mouse girl—so affectionate with her lips and tongue."

"Eva," said Michael, "that is quite a sight. Is she in close enough?"

"Hmm, I'm sure she'd love to be closer."

She reached back with both hands, pulled her cheeks apart, then wiggled her hips, allowing Lenore to wedge her mouse mask in deeper.

Michael laughed and said, "Huh. That dirty mouse is buried deep."

"Hmm, her dirty mouse tongue is in exactly the right place. That feels so good—I can't help myself."

She slipped her robe off of her shoulders until it got trapped near her elbows, leaving her large breasts in clear view. And she reached down between her thighs with one hand and held Lenore's head, under her robe, with the other.

Everyone heard her start moaning.

"Eva, you're splendid," Michael said, and everyone murmured their agreement. "I meant only to humiliate our little mouse girl for a second or two, but you seem to adore what she's doing for you."

Gasping, Eva said, "I do adore it. She loves me, and her sweet little tongue loves me too."

"Such a dirty mouse girl," said Michael, then he held up the whip. "To any wife that didn't yet get to watch the filthy mouse girl suck her husband: the slutty mouse can't hide that shapely, soft target from your wrath."

"Her mousy ass is mine," said a stunning redhead in a short dress and high red heels, and she strutted over and took it from him.

* * *

"Damn," said Amos, "she'll do anything."

"Yep. Kneeling with her face in Eva's ass. Covered up too."

"What kind of woman is that?"

"You already know: worthless."

"Good just for sex."

"Yeah, Amos. You'd screw that mouse right now, I'd bet."

A few quiet seconds passed.

"Amos?"

"Um, I think maybe . . ."

Chapter 39 – Quite a Helpless Thing Now

"Or," Michael said to the redhead holding the whip, "since the slut mouse is practically begging for it, maybe your husband should take a stab at that?"

"Mm," she said, "We'd all like that. A hard stabbing would teach the disgusting mouse a lesson."

Michael was standing behind the chair, trying to kiss Eva, but she barely noticed from touching herself and from Lenore's eager attention.

"First, give that man a clear target," he said.

"That's half the fun," she said, and sat back on her heels by Lenore's side. "Mm, a dirty mouse in lingerie. Lovely."

She lifted up Lenore's sheer garment and pulled it up onto her back, revealing her slender waist, curvy hips, and her new lacy panties with bows tying the sides.

"I think I'll just . . ."

She loosened one bow, and the material began to fall away.

"Oh, she has such a pretty, smooth ass. One more little bow."

She reached around to undo the other one, then pulled the cloth out between Lenore's thighs.

"Mm, you brought us a gorgeous little mouse, Eva," she said while rubbing Lenore's cheeks and thighs and sometimes leaning close to kiss her all over.

Still kissing a cheek, she saw that her husband was in place, unzipped, and obscenely ready.

Eva said, "Everyone, gather close. It's not just the sight of it—ooh, the sounds too."

As everyone stepped closer, surrounding the action, Eva reached back and patted Lenore's head through her robe.

"Be a good little mousy girl. You're about to get what a dirty mouse girl deserves."

The redhead was still hugging Lenore around her hips, rubbing and kissing, and said, "I just can't help myself. She's adorable."

She wedged the rigid whip handle straight up between Lenore's cheeks, getting a soft gasp from her.

"Oh, I know—you're so soft there . . ."

She worked it in tighter, as far as she could, then laughed contentedly as she began twirling it and nudging it up and down.

"Eva, if my husband wasn't here, where would I have to put this rough leather thing?"

Eva panted from approaching her orgasm but said, "Ooh, a soft, dirty mouse would love that."

* * *

"Hey," said Emilio, "it's getting wilder."

"In her ass too? She'll let them do anything."

"She's sexy as hell, Amos. Admit it."

"I'll admit it," Amos said. "She's sexy—for a pink mouse."

* * *

The husband held Lenore by her hip with one hand and his wife's head with the other.

"Hey, we're saving her sweetest treat for later," Eva said.

While his wife had her cheek pressed into Lenore's hip, her wet lips priming him, he said, "Fine by me."

He grinned, pulled it from her mouth, got it started gently, then drove it halfway into Lenore.

And Lenore let out a high-pitched squeal, causing Eva to smile and pat her head.

"Oh, she sounded just like a scared little girl! She's such a vulnerable little mouse girl. Make her squeal again."

The man withdrew partway, then rammed it in farther, causing another shrill squeal from under Eva's robe.

"Mm, that's adorable. Such a soft, obedient little mouse girl."

"I just have to look," said Michael, and he lifted Eva's robe and held it out of the way.

Lenore's mask was mostly above Eva's cheeks, making it obvious where her mouth was, and she was looking up at Michael.

"Such big eyes you have, little mouse. Think about where you're taking it,"—she lurched from a hard push, and Michael paused to smile at another little-girl squeal—"and your little mouse tongue is so busy with that part of Eva. Carry on."

After snapping Eva's robe back over her, he said, "Eva, how's that slutty mouse doing with your ass?"

"Oh, Michael, she's such an eager little thing. She has such a wet, curious tongue. Mm, it's obvious she adores what she's doing."

"Every one of us would trade places with her. But she's a cocksucker, too, and I can't wait much longer for my turn."

"Not yet. My very affectionate mouse girl doesn't want to stop. Mm, she loves exploring with that wet little tongue . . ."

* * *

"Unbelievable, Emilio."

"Disgusting, but I liked that squealing."

"It probably hurt. I think she adjusted."

"Uh-huh. She's digging it. Still licking Eva's ass too."

"Huh. More than licking. Exploring, she said."

"Wow, yeah. Think you'd ever kiss that woman?"

"God, no. Her mouth has been everywhere."

* * *

Michael lifted Eva's robe and said to Lenore, "Do you deserve any respect?"

"Mm-mm."

"Obviously," he said, laughing. "You've got your tongue in Eva's sweet ass."

Eva gestured to the man taking steady deep plunges into Lenore.

"The dirty mouse deserves it in her pretty blond hair."

"Okay," he said. "Happy to."

"Try to find a dry place."

Everyone laughed.

He backed out quickly, causing Lenore to gasp and the listening crowd to chuckle. He stood to one side, and his wife joined him, taking a firm grip.

"You filthy little slut," she said. "Tempting my husband with that slutty mouse ass."

The man groaned as his wife gave him a long, slow stroke, leaving a thick line across Lenore's hair.

"Dirty mouse girl."

She kept stroking and kissing her husband as she finished it all in Lenore's hair, neither of them even watching.

"Mm," she said, still not looking at Lenore, just wiping him around in the blond mane, "we got her good, Honey. Such a disgusting, filthy mouse."

"Mm-hmm."

Eva said, "Good, she deserved that. Time for the cocksucker mouse to suck your cock, Michael."

"Uh-huh. She wants to taste cock again."

Eva leaned herself forward, and everyone saw Lenore still holding out her tongue. Eva turned around and stood near the chair, then reached down for Lenore's chin.

"Up, little mouse—dirty mouse girl with disgusting hair."

Lenore got coaxed up onto her high heels, and Eva turned her around and stayed close behind her.

"We all want to see more of what belongs to us. Stand very still, dirty mouse girl."

Lenore nodded, and Eva took hold of the lingerie at the bottom and lifted it, prompting Lenore to raise her arms straight up. She pulled the garment up and off of her, tossed it aside, then guided her arms back down.

And Lenore stood before all of them wearing nothing but her new, spiky, high-heeled shoes and cartoon mouse face. Everything else was just bare skin above the delicate straps around her ankles.

"There we go," said Eva. "Just a soft, naked little girl for our fun."

"Mm-hmm."

"Your hair is a mess. You do such disgusting things."

"Mm-hmm. Yes."

Then, she leaned closer and said, "My, you are a pretty little thing. So soft and smooth. So,"—she looked around her and grinned at Michael—"trusting. We adore pretty, trusting little girls. Do you like being soft and naked for us to use?"

"Yes," Lenore said, nodding her mask gently.

"We love using up soft little girls."

Lenore stayed quiet as Eva spoke in her other ear.

"So soft and pretty and naked—a thing to be degraded for our fun. Do you have any self-respect?"

Lenore paused, then shook her head and said, "No."

"You're just a soft, worthless thing for us to use?"

"Yes. That's all I am. I'm worthless."

Eva stepped to the side as she pulled back and down on Lenore's sticky blond hair.

"Sit, worthless naked mouse girl."

Lenore sat on the low seat which was barely deep enough for her, and Eva walked around behind the chair.

"Michael," she said, "Her mouse mouth is ready."

"Here you go, little mouse," he said, then slipped it in between her wet lips, a little at a time, then he paused and smiled at her lips holding on tight. "You're a very good little girl when there's a hard cock in your mouth."

In Lenore's ear, Eva said, "Touch yourself, mousy plaything. Rub that very warm and wet place between your thighs."

Lenore moaned a second after getting started, and Eva reached around to fondle her breasts.

"Ah, her mouth is warm and wet too," Michael said. "She's an adorable cocksucker."

He touched her chin, as she looked up at him through the holes in her mouse mask, and said, "Under that silly mask, did you fix your face very pretty for us?"

"Mm . . ." she said while nodding.

"Good girl," he said and began a steady pumping between her tight, wet lips. "Shh, now. Let's just pump that pretty mouse face awhile."

* * *

"God, she looks perfect."

"Yep. Perfect breasts, tiny waist. All stripped down now."

"She's gorgeous."

"Yeah," said Emilio, "but she never stops sucking or licking."

"Huh. So, she's a gorgeous cocksucker. Said it's all she wants to be."

"No other life? No one knows she's like that?"

"No one would want such a disgusting slut. What's with that weird chair they put her in?"

"You heard Eva—they're saving her sweetest part. She's going to get screwed."

"By who?"

"Guest of honor. Who else?"

"You mean—"

"Yeah, professor."

Chapter 40 – All Used-Up

"Oh, just like that," Michael said. "Yes. Keep those mousy lips closed and hold it tight. Good girl. You know from our hotel time together what kind of fun game we want to play."

"Mm-hmm," she said while still rubbing between her thighs.

"Good. Now, nobody in your life knows you're here?"

She shook her head but didn't lose him.

"Nobody knows that you're here, sucking cocks and getting used in so many dirty ways?"

"Uh-uh," she managed to say with her mouth full.

"Even *after* we've had all our fun and used you *all* up, you're so worthless that no one will miss you?"

Michael backed away but kept it close.

"Mm-mm. No one will miss me."

"This is very important, pretty cocksucker: what else are you besides worthless?"

He backed out just enough for her to say, "I'm disposable. I'm a disposable cocksucker."

"And you know the word's meaning?" said Michael.

"Mm, yes. I know."

Eva moaned and said, "It means something to be bagged up like trash, doesn't it?"

"Mm-hmm. It's all I am: pretty and disposable."

"And after we're done with you," Michael said, "you'll just be soft, naked, used-up trash?"

"Mm-hmm. Yes."

"Mm, I love that," Eva said while pausing to hold Lenore's breasts in a tight squeeze. "Tell me again, Michael, what this naked baby mouse is."

"She's just a soft, disposable, cocksucking girl that no one will ever miss."

"No one will miss her. That's such a sweet thing. Mm . . ." she moaned as she pinched both of Lenore's breasts and pulled them up and out.

Still pinching her, Eva leaned close to Lenore's ear and said, "I do love my disposable little mouse girl."

Eva used one hand to play with Lenore's hair, getting it out of the way, and said, "You do want Michael to treat your pretty face like he did in the hotel, don't you?"

Lenore, shaking softly from her own touch, nodded and said, "Mm-hmm. All on my pretty, cocksucking face."

Eva gently touched the mask still hiding Lenore's face, smiled, and said, "Yes. That's about all you're good for. Let's just get you out of that silly mask, then, okay?"

Lenore kept sucking but shook her head and tried to say, "Uh-uh."

Eva laughed and said, "Oh, the drama. You remember that someone here might recognize you?"

"Mm-hmm."

"But you're such a pretty little cocksucking girl. Don't you want everyone to know that? Won't it feel good to finally admit to anyone that knows you that you're really just a dirty cocksucker?"

Lenore was about to reach a climax, and she increased her pace.

"Think of that, little one: everyone in your life could soon learn that you're really just a worthless cocksucking little girl. Everyone will know."

Lenore whimpered, shaking lightly, then nodded.

"Good girl."

* * *

"Good," whispered Emilio, "you'll see who she is."

"You're serious? They'll want me to screw her?"

"Believe it. You want that promotion?"

"Well, yeah, but—"

"And she's hot as hell, right?"

"God, yeah."

"Even she's saying she's disposable, used-up trash. You might as well screw her, professor."

"What kind of woman," said Amos, "says she has a pretty, cocksucking face?"

"One that you're going to screw when they tell you."

"Um . . ."

"Just admit it: you want to. She's making you crazy."

"Fine. Yeah. God, she looks good."

* * *

"We all want to see your pretty face, but let's be sure you don't move when Michael sprays all over it. You wouldn't want to spoil the fun, would you?"

"Uh-uh."

"We'll need you to be a very good, trusting girl for us, and we'll make sure you don't move."

She held several sashes out for Lenore to see.

"This will help. We have to tie you up nice and tight."

She got her mouth free and said, "Um, maybe I—"

"Shh," said Eva, "it's too late to stop this fun."

Leaning close to Lenore's ear, she whispered, "It's our only hope! Please, just play along!"

Lenore stopped struggling, and Eva waved for two of the wives to come help. They both took sashes from her, put Lenore's arms down and back and quickly tied her wrists to the chair's rear legs. They then looped sashes around her calves, just below her knees, and tied the other ends behind the chair, leaving her wide open and sitting on the edge of the narrow seat.

"Oh, that is a sight," Eva said, then she knelt between Lenore's thighs and held her waist. "You're quite a helpless thing now, aren't you?"

"Yes, I am."

"And look at that: a soft little thing, naked except for her heels and inviting a very deep penetration by absolutely anyone. Hmm, such a slut. Now, let's get that silly mouse face off of you so anyone that might know you can watch Michael spray all over your pretty face."

She gave Lenore a kiss for several seconds, then reached up with both hands and removed the comical pink mouse mask.

* * *

"She's cute," Emilio said. "All tied up for—"

"Oh my God."

"Yeah, I know, she's—"

"No, Emilio, this can't be. That's my fiancé!"

"No time for jokes, Amos."

"I swear to God. What the hell?"

"She, uh, your fiancé said and did all of that?"

"God, yeah. I don't believe it."

"Amos, she just agreed to be tied to that chair."

"Yeah. Damn. She's . . ."

"She's what?"

"A worthless, goddamn slut. Just a goddamn slut."

"Yeah, I'd say so. Damn. What else?"

"Like they all said: just a filthy, disgusting cocksucker."

"Well, this sure is dramatic . . ."

* * *

Eva gave her another kiss, then said, "Now, everyone knows who you are."

Holding both of her breasts, she said, "Mm, such a soft little thing. Are you a cocksucker?"

"Yes."

"Just a worthless slut?"

"Mm-hmm. Yes, I'm a worthless slut."

"Mm-hmm. Good girl," Eva said, then moved to one side of the chair and reached a hand between Lenore's thighs, where she began steady rubbing.

"We have a guest of honor that's going to enjoy you. But first, let's get that pretty face ready for some fun. You're just a gorgeous, disposable little thing. You're so perfect, and no one will ever even miss you?"

"Uh-uh. No one."

"Good girl. Hold very still for him to give your pretty face what it deserves, and I'll just touch you where you're so warm and wet for me. It is for me, isn't it?"

"Mm-hmm. Yes."

"Ah, she does love you, Eva. She loves this too."

Michael gave himself long, steady strokes and left sticky strips all over her face. A thick line crossed her nose and dripped down toward her lips. More hit all around her puckered lips, and she held still even as some ran onto her chin. His last big efforts aimed around her eyes, gathering globs in her eyebrows and eyelashes.

"Oh, so soft. Let's just use your face to clean up a bit," he said while wiping it around on her cheeks.

Eva said, "Do you feel beautiful now?"

"Mm-hmm," Lenore said. "Yes."

"No, don't move, little mouse," he said standing close. "Hold your sticky face very still while Eva enjoys how wet you are for her."

"Mm," said Eva, "so very soft and wet for me," then began a playful kiss.

Lenore relaxed, and she let out a soft, high-pitched moan through the kissing.

"There you go," Eva said close to Lenore's ear while still rubbing between her thighs. "Your lips are quite sticky, but let me give you a nice orgasm while we have more fun with you."

She nodded, Michael brushed a few wisps of her hair aside, then produced a clear, thick plastic bag. He worked it down over her just enough to cover her forehead, leaving her big eyes wide open and looking up at him.

Eva, still rubbing her, whispered in her ear, "There's something so exciting about a beautiful little thing like you being hidden away like this. Wouldn't you agree?"

Lenore moaned softly with Eva's skillful fingers busy on her, then nodded.

"Hmm," said Eva, "a little bit more. You're just sweet, used-up trash, aren't you?"

Lenore nodded and moaned from the rubbing as Michael tugged the bag down until only her lips and chin were still visible.

"We love the anticipation," Eva said between kissing her neck and throat, "just knowing that soon, your very pretty but sticky face will be hidden away so completely."

She sped up her rubbing and said, "You're my soft, disposable naked girl?"

Lenore groaned and nodded and gazed into Eva's eyes.

"Hmm, you like hearing what you are. You're soft and helpless, a disposable girl for sucking cocks, and you're almost all used-up."

"Mm. Mm-hmm."

"And it feels so good, doesn't it?"

"Mm . . ."

And with the bag still partway covering Lenore's face, Eva leaned around and said, "You're a disposable, naked little girl that's about have an orgasm?"

"Mm-hmm. Yes," she said, taking quicker breaths.

"Kiss me, soft little girl, while I enjoy how soft and wet you are for me."

Lenore tipped her head, offering her lips, and they both moaned during a long kiss.

* * *

Amos said, "What's with the bag?"

"Don't know. Something for fun, I'd guess. You're mad at her anyway."

"God, yeah. I never knew she's such a slut."

"So, who cares about that bag? She wants it."

"Yeah, she does, the slut."

"And you might as well get that promotion."

"I might as well. Damn slut."

"Sorry about before—wanting to get in line. Didn't see her face with that mask."

"You couldn't see it, Emilio. The slut would have done a good job."

"Oh, yeah. I mean, uh, I guess. Yep."

* * *

Eva backed away from the kiss and said, "Tell us again: you're really only good for sex, nothing else?"

Lenore nodded and said, "Mm-hmm, nothing else."

"That's right, you soft little thing. Can we cover that pretty face a little bit more?"

"Mm-hmm. Okay."

Eva pulled it down to almost cover her lips, then whispered near her ear, "It's all for the drama. Just play along, okay?"

Lenore whispered, "Okay."

Back away from Lenore, Eva spoke loudly again for all to hear.

"So much prettier already. You're really just a disposable cocksucker, aren't you?"

She hesitated, groaning softly, then the entire bag nodded with her, and she said, "Yes. I'm disposable."

"Just a cocksucker," Eva repeated. "And so disposable. I love that you're a disposable girl."

"Mm," Lenore moaned, still being rubbed by Eva.

"And no one knows where you are right now?"

"Uh-uh. No one."

"And no one will ever even look for you?"

"Mm-mm. No."

"And this is all you're good for, you worthless, disposable cocksucker. Won't it feel so much better if you're all used up, little girl?"

"Mm-hmm. Yes."

"Perfect," Eva said, then quickly pulled a thick twist of cloth into Lenore's open mouth, then tied it behind her, causing her to groan and open her eyes wide.

Despite Lenore's mild struggling against her bindings, Eva was able to whisper in her ear, "Michael is the good one not me. Oh, you're in so much trouble now, my helpless little mouse."

Lenore whimpered, causing Eva to grin, but she stayed close to again whisper in her ear.

"You very well might be all used up soon. Your only hope is to not fight what I'm doing to you."

Lenore calmed herself but still whimpered softly.

"That's better. You licked me all over, took it in your tight ass, and sucked a lot of cocks. Now, you're just a helpless, captured little girl praying for my mercy."

She gave Lenore a kiss on her lips, then she and Michael together tugged the bag farther down, and it was long enough that it ended up resting loosely on her chest.

Lenore's excited breaths were puffing it up and then letting it relax, over and over, even as Eva chuckled and kept pulling it down more tightly.

Then, she smoothed it down and looked through at Lenore breathing through her nose while gagged inside the bag.

Eva said, "You've never been a lovelier girl than now, when we're so close to being done with you."

Lenore nodded roughly, gasping into air already becoming more stale.

Eva gave her a quick kiss through the plastic.

"You're so soft now, all hidden away behind the plastic. Such a pretty, disposable little girl."

Eva gave each of her stiff nipples a gentle twist while still rubbing her.

"Yes, just like that, little girl. A soft, used-up, disposable girl."

Lenore groaned and fought against her bindings, but they allowed no room for her to move.

"Struggle if you want, precious girl, but it won't stop the orgasm I'm giving you. Mm, you're still so wet for me."

Lenore moaned and writhed, but she was tied too tightly. Eva kept rubbing, focusing her efforts and smiling at Lenore shifting her hips higher, making herself more accessible to Eva's touch.

"Mm, such a greedy little girl. You're in so much trouble, and you still want so desperately the orgasm I'm giving you. Oh, you're such a wet little girl for my touch."

With her hips locked up as high as she could go, Lenore shook quietly, jiggling her breasts while holding her breath and keeping the bag still.

"Oh, good girl. There you go, pretty cocksucker girl. Mm-hmm. Such sweet, disposable trash, having a pleasant orgasm for us."

Lenore's breasts bounced with her renewed efforts at breathing, but she no longer struggled against her bindings.

"Shh, now," Eva said as she got behind her again.

She reached around and lifted both of Lenore's breasts, jiggling them toward Amos.

"She's a disposable little girl now. All sticky and staying very quiet for us. All hidden away in a bag like any other trash. And no one will ever miss her."

She let go of one of Lenore's breasts and leaned out over her shoulder, then turned her head to face her.

"Such a quiet and pretty little thing for us now. You just needed a very nice orgasm, didn't you?"

Lenore nodded, tipping her plastic bag.

With her lips close to Lenore's, Eva said, "Try to kiss me, little one, to show that you still love me."

Lenore moaned and tipped her head closer, trying to press her lips into Eva's.

"Mm, so sweet for me now."

When Eva pulled her in and pressed their lips together, with only a layer of thick plastic between them, Lenore groaned but showed no sign of struggling with any of her bindings.

Chapter 41 – God, She Feels So Good

Eva stood behind Lenore's chair and held her bagged head while looking around at all of the guests.

"Our pretty little slut has sucked so many cocks to fill her belly. She was happy to get her pretty hair sticky with it. She showed me how much she loves me with her eager, busy little tongue where I forced her pretty face. She even gave us exciting little-girl squeals when she was impaled just the way she wanted it—in a very tight place. And she had a very wet orgasm for me after getting a sticky spray on her face, then agreeing that she's disposable and no one will ever even look for her. Now, she's restrained so securely and bagged up like any other used-up trash, so it's time for our guest of honor to have his turn."

She turned and pointed toward Amos and said, "She's prepared just special for you. She's a very happy little thing right now, especially after sucking so much, and she'd love to have you force yourself deep into her, pump her, and fill her there too."

Amos stood but didn't approach them.

"She might even pretend that she doesn't want it."

* * *

"I'm going to screw that slut," Amos whispered inside his mask.

"That's the plan. Yep."

"She doesn't even care who's screwing her."

"Amos, she's having sex with everyone. You might as well get your share."

"Damn right. God, she's such a slut."

* * *

Eva forced Lenore's head to nod slowly a few times, then added, "But she's right where she belongs, and she knows it. She knows she's always been nothing but a disposable cocksucker. Just a pretty slut that's meant to be used up. Come. Enjoy her."

Amos, not speaking, took his place kneeling between Lenore's thighs where she was tied securely to the chair with a loose plastic bag covering her gagged mouth and big eyes staring out at him.

"Go on. Look how ready she is for you. We can all see how wet she is, the soft little girl."

Amos quickly got it out, then stabbed it partway in, but he stopped when Lenore began a soft moaning.

"Oh, don't pretend you don't want what she's offering. Go on. She loves it and wants it very deep."

He drove it in all the way and watched Eva, from behind the chair, gently bouncing Lenore's bare breasts around.

"Isn't she soft and wet?" said Eva.

Amos nodded and picked up his pace, ramming it into her.

"Oh, no, no, no. Take your time. Go slow with the helpless naked thing."

He slowed himself but kept a steady pace, and he watched Eva leave Lenore's breasts alone, then hold out from side to side a long silk scarf. Lenore's eyes grew wider and watched it too.

"Yes, nice and slow. She's such a sweet, wet little thing."

When she started to loop it around Lenore's neck, Lenore's eyes darted left and right as she began shaking her head, and Amos didn't slow at all, still driving deeply and steadily into her.

Still thrusting into her, Amos took the ends of the sash when offered to him and held them out to the sides.

He paused his efforts to glance down to watch Eva's hands again gently squeezing Lenore's breasts as her chest rose and fell, each breath a struggle. Eva sometimes pushed them from side to side and sometimes pinched her nipples and stretched them forward, grinning at Amos's unwavering stare at them.

When Eva spoke, he looked into her eyes.

"She's gorgeous, but she's a worthless slut, nothing else. You heard her tell all of us that she doesn't truly care about anything else. Just being a slut and sucking cocks."

Amos drove in deep and held it, and Eva smiled and nodded.

"She's just a disposable thing that would suck every cock she can. Look at her slender, soft belly."

Amos tipped his head to look at it.

"And think of how many cocks she sucked. This slutty little girl would never stop sucking and swallowing."

He looked back up when she continued.

"She's very pretty, but she could never be trusted. She would always sneak away, every chance she had, to suck as many cocks as she could. She's nothing but a cocksucking slut."

Through the plastic, he saw Lenore quiet but shaking her head, eyes wide and mouth gagged, and sticky spots and streaks visible all over her face.

And he resumed his slow, steady driving deep into his captured and helpless fiancé.

* * *

"She's worthless," Amos whispered. "A goddamn slut."

"Amos. That scarf. Why did Eva—"

"She's only good for getting screwed and sucking cocks. Would have sucked yours."

"Um, but she didn't."

"What kind of woman is this?"

"Tell me you won't pull on that thing around her neck."

Amos stayed between Lenore's tied legs, pumping her, while Eva fondled her breasts. He still held the sash in both hands.

"Amos. Amos?"

* * *

"She's all bagged up so pretty now," Eva said while still fondling Lenore's breasts. "Mm, she's so adorable right now."

She leaned around, turned Lenore's head, and kissed her as well as she could. Lenore, inside the bag, was breathing more rapidly, puffing out the plastic and submitting to Eva's kiss.

Eva broke the kiss and said to her, "You're just a perfect little girl now. More beautiful than you've ever been because you're so disposable, and no one knows where you are, no one cares, and no one will even look for you."

She gave her a quick kiss, then got behind her again with both hands busy on her breasts.

Looking past her at Amos, she smiled and said, "How does that feel? Doesn't she feel very good this way?"

Amos nodded and grunted, still driving into her.

"It's because she's disposable, bagged up like any other trash. She's trash, and this is what must be done with such cocksucking trash."

She let go of Lenore's breasts and rested her hands on Amos's. When she started nudging them apart, tightening the loop, Amos didn't fight her.

* * *

"Amos, don't! Don't pull that any farther!"

Eva, smiling at Amos, kept his hands moving apart, drawing tighter the loop around the bag covering Lenore.

"Amos? Don't help them with this. Don't do it!"

"She's just a slut, Emilio," he whispered. "All this time—just a slut."

"Amos, no! Whatever she is, you can't do this. Stop!"

Amos didn't stop.

"Amos? Amos!"

* * *

"We do want to keep our trash girl quiet and still, don't we?"

Amos nodded.

"Yes, of course, we do. She wants that too. Just look how excited she is."

He glanced down at her breasts and saw telltale signs of her feeling pleasure even with all that was happening. He scoffed silently at the sight of her eyes stretched wide and staring into his.

"Yes, she wants to be all alone with the hot, sticky treat that she sucked so hard for. She loved having it sprayed all over her pretty face."

When she coaxed his hands farther apart, he kept going on his own, drawing it tighter around Lenore's throat.

"Just tie a pretty bow now," Eva said. "She needs a pretty bow."

Amos nodded, snapped it tighter and tied it, then let the ends drop and lay across her breasts.

Everyone in the room watched the bag puffing and relaxing as Lenore inhaled the same air repeatedly.

"Yes, just like that. Does the wet little thing feel even better now?"

Amos nodded, grunted, and kept pumping her.

"She's warmer? Wetter for you too?"

Amos groaned and nodded.

"Yes, she knows she's good only for this. Slow. Very slow. Just enjoy the soft, worthless little thing."

Amos looked down when Eva again took her breasts in her hands.

"She's a perfect, gorgeous slut for our fun."

One hand slid down to her belly and rubbed all around.

"Hmm, and she so loves to swallow. This little darling sucked so many cocks. Think about how much she would always want in her belly."

Amos grunted and gave her a harder stab.

"Slow now," Eva said. "She wants you to take your time now that she has that pretty bow."

* * *

"Amos, you can't do this. Just stop!"

"She's never felt any better, Emilio. God, she feels so good."

"But Amos, you're about to—"

"Look at her big, soft, perfect breasts shaking as she tries to breathe. God, Emilio, she's never been more beautiful . . ."

* * *

"Doesn't she feel wonderful?" Eva said.

Amos nodded.

"Here's what you must do: go very slow, feel every stroke deep inside her while you enjoy how beautiful she is right now. But don't let yourself finish. Do you understand?"

Amos didn't respond.

"Don't let yourself go until she's very still and quiet for us—just a sweet little doll. You must wait until I tell you she's been quiet and still long enough. That's when she wants it from you the most. Do you understand?"

Amos nodded.

"Hmm, good. So good. Remember that she's enjoying it too. All of this darling girl's life has led her here for this. It's what she wants more than anything."

* * *

"Amos, you've lost your mind! Stop it, you're killing her!"

Amos held Lenore's trim waist, his eyes focused on Eva's hands toying with Lenore's breasts and dragging the loose sashes across them, and he kept pumping her slowly and deeply.

"Amos, dammit, I'll stop you. I'm going to stop you!"

* * *

Lenore was barely moving, eyes closing, her head weakly tipping from side to side.

"Oh, she's just adorable," Eva said as she held her head up with one hand. "With all she's done, this is my favorite time yet, when our disposable girl has become too weak to even pretend to resist."

Eva started kissing her cheek and fondling her breast with her free hand.

"Mm, such very large, perfect breasts too. She's just adorable."

She rubbed Lenore's belly again, laughed, and said, "Mm, she was so eager to swallow so much. Think of that while you're pumping her, how even after she's very quiet and still, she'll be just a soft, quiet little thing, and we'll have more fun with her."

Amos kept going.

"Think about that. She'll be so quiet and still, and everyone here will take their time and keep enjoying her all night long."

Amos was pumping very slowly, staring at her closed eyes still smeared and sticky behind the plastic.

From close behind him, in a dead silent party room, Michael laughed loudly and said, "Eva, dear, you always take things too far. Just stop."

"No, Michael—we're so close this time! You know how much I've always wanted a very quiet little doll to play with!"

A woman laughed and said, "Damn, Eva, you're too much sometimes."

Her husband snickered and said, "You said 'after she's quiet and still, we'll have more fun with her?' God, you're nuts . . ."

Someone else in the crowd laughed and said, "Really, Eva, come on. Hell of a show, but let that poor girl go."

"Oh, dammit," Michael said, "If you weren't so gorgeous, Eva, I'd bag you up too. Because damn, you really are quite insane."

He grabbed the bag with both hands and smirked at the anguish on Eva's face.

"Eva, really, you've gone too far. I think all of us would much rather have this sweet girl reprise her performance another time. You just don't need a quiet little doll. God, none of us do."

He gripped the plastic and ripped it open, then embraced Eva and took her a step away from Lenore.

In the quiet seconds after, everyone commented and offered relieved laughter at the sound of Lenore taking deeper breaths, though she remained mostly unconscious.

And Amos was still pumping her.

Until Emilio grabbed him and pulled him out of her, then dragged him back a few steps.

Whispering inside his helmet, he said, "Amos, you're as crazy as Eva and as disgusting as your fiancé! Look, tell me your address, and I'll get her home."

"Huh?"

"Listen to me! I'm taking her home. None of these punks can stop me. And you, don't come home for an hour. You got that?"

"An hour. Yeah."

"Remember, she doesn't know you were here at all. She has no idea."

"She doesn't?"

"No, you're wearing a mask, right? And for God's sake, zip up!"

Chapter 42 – You Wouldn't Believe Me

An hour later, Amos swept in the front door and almost jumped inside the house. With his hand still strangling the doorknob, he locked his eyes on Lenore, who was seated near the middle of the couch.

She wore her robe like thick, fuzzy packaging to cover the contents completely. The only hint of the substantial flannel pajamas beneath the tightly tied outer shell was below the garment's bottom hem, where the pant legs cloaked her calves, and the slippers and socks had locked away any sight of her too.

The neat ball of clipped and banded blond hair piled on her head was wet and dripped in a few places.

"Lenore."

Her eyes lingered a few more seconds on the muted TV, and the clock on the wall filled the void as well as it could with a steady cadence. Then, she turned weary eyes toward Amos, gave every indication of a scoff save the sound of it, and patted the cushion beside her.

Amos set his keys quietly on the tall wooden table near the door, then eased the door shut. His walk to the couch was slow and deliberate, and he maintained eye contact with her every step of the way before standing in the narrow gap between the coffee table and the couch.

As she let her eyes drift back to the television, she also patted the seat beside her again, and Amos sat. He sat near the middle, too, and both of them left their usual locations at the far ends vacant.

Their shoulders touched, as did their arms. Their legs were pressed together, and both put their feet up against the table's edge—one pair of clean dress shoes and one pair of ratty, worn slippers.

"How . . . how are you, Lenore?"

He felt her shrug, kept his eyes on the TV, too, and let the clock rule the room for a few steady clicks.

"I'm . . . at a loss for words."

"Try me."

"Let's say I just had . . . a dream."

"Okay. A dream."

"Yeah. One so bizarre that it . . . surprised me."

"The things that happened, you mean?"

"Yeah. They were outrageous. The things that I . . . that happened."

"Okay. Things happened. So, it was a nightmare, then?"

"Uh-uh. No, and that was outrageous too."

"What was?"

"That I . . . I loved it."

"You did? Which, uh, which parts?"

"Hmm. Every single detail of it."

"Every, um, every—"

"Everything. Yep."

"How, uh, how did it, um, end?"

"That was the most outrageous part—the ending."

"Oh, yeah, I'd bet. The ending was like a nightmare, then."

"Uh, no. What was outrageous was that . . ."

"Yeah?"

"I loved that too."

"Even, um, the very ending?"

"Yeah. Huh. Loved it."

He turned toward her and saw the tired smile as she kept looking forward.

"You did?"

"Mm-hmm," she said, nodding weakly. "How was your college thing?"

"Oh," he said, joining her to stare at the TV, "it was, uh, something."

"Good, you mean?"

"One might say that one can learn much about one's self when—"

"Amos. Come on."

"Right. I, uh, faced an odd, um, capability. For my, um, behavior."

"That's vague."

"So is your, um, dream."

"Maybe we could talk about it sometime. Not tonight."

"No," he said, then reached for her hand and held it tight, "not tonight. Maybe over breakfast."

"Mm-hmm. Okay. I'll have wine."

"Yes. Me too. And you can tell me every one of those details. Of your, um, dream."

Lenore scoffed weakly and said, "You wouldn't believe me."

Amos scoffed, too, then said, "Huh. I just might."

Enjoy the Story?

Thank you for reading! If you enjoyed the story, please consider telling the entire world on your social media and, best of all, just talking with friends. You'll be helping your fellow readers to meet Amos and Lenore and helping the author greatly too.

For more about Edward Allen Karr and his books, visit:

www.LakesideLetters.com

About the Author

Edward Sechkar is a writer and producer who resides in Ohio, USA. Under the pseudonym of Edward Allen Karr, he has written more than twenty novels across multiple series and genres. The stories range from middle-grade coming of age (A World So Close series) to books that are best enjoyed by mature readers (Risk and the Killers series; Thrills N Kills in the Hills series).

To see all series and books, visit:
www.LakesideLetters.com

www.ingramcontent.com/pod-product-compliance
Lightning Source LLC
Chambersburg PA
CBHW061656190726
48289CB00006B/1903
* 9 7 8 1 9 5 0 8 8 6 7 5 3 *